Death on the Lagan

The Irish Mysteries — Book Three

PADRAIG O'HANNON

ISBN: 1537462776
ISBN-13: 978-1537462776

padraigohannon@gmail.com

Other books by Padraig O'Hannon:

Murder in County Tyrone (The Irish Mysteries, Book One)

Child of a Cruel God (The Irish Mysteries, Book Two)

That a dream should ne'er been dreamt,
lessens not the sting of its death.

CHAPTER ONE

"Suspended? What the hell?"

I couldn't believe my ears.

"You heard me, Costa," Jim Finnegan grumbled, tossing a few personal items into a box. "Suspended pending review, or so they tell me. I don't know what the hell they're going to review. Seems like they've already made up their minds."

"Let me talk to them. By the time I'm done, you'll be in charge of the whole damned place."

"No," he growled, "that's quite all right. You've done more than enough. Thanks to your harebrained scheme, I managed to get my prisoner killed, failed to capture our most-wanted escapee, and stirred up quite a kerfuffle between the UK and the Republic of Ireland in the process. I've seen people get the sack for far less. Bloody hell," he grunted, "I wonder what this is going to do to my pension." His voice trailed away.

For the first time in the four years that I'd known him, the

Police Service veteran seemed human, even vulnerable. I stumbled to find words, but none came out. It was because he was right. My stupid, ill-conceived maneuvering had orchestrated the situation. And to what end? Shanagh Grady, the leader of a shadowy terrorist organization founded by her stepfather, Connla Grady, remained at large. Her daughter, my ill-fated love interest, Angela, was dead, and my remaining friendships felt strained. Three Police Service analysts were killed, and one remained in the hospital. And all because of me.

Sure, there were bright spots. We had prevented nearly a billion dollars worth of diamonds from funding more violence, but even that seemed hollow. Political squabbles erupted over the ownership and dispensation of the funds. Instead of being put to good use, the treasure sat helplessly in a political morass.

"I'm sorry," Finnegan said, before I could speak. "That was below the belt."

"It wasn't," I said, weakly. "It was true."

"I made my own decisions, John, and I have to live with the consequences. I'll have to ask you to turn in your security pass. Miss MacDonald and Miss Boyle will need to do the same at the next opportunity. My superiors have rescinded your access. You can come by tomorrow to collect your belongings."

I nodded, silently.

"As I seem to have an abundance of spare time," he sighed, "are you and your friends available for dinner tonight?"

"We are."

"About seven then?"

I nodded.

* * *

"Costa, John," the humorless security officer droned as I turned in my badge. She paused to read her computer screen before continuing. "Come by in the morning to secure your remaining belongings. Please place your satchel on the table and pass through the scanner."

Upon news of Finnegan's suspension, I had hastily collected a handful of personal items along with our case notes and laptop computers. It took nearly an hour before the examiners were satisfied that I wasn't removing Police Service property or evidence pertaining to the Shanagh Grady case. Tired and frustrated, I stomped to the elevator and made my way to the main entrance.

Before I could leave, an unexpected voice interrupted my journey.

"Sir! I mean… John!"

I spun to see Kelly Hamilton chasing after me, waving. I stopped, setting my satchel down and returning a halfhearted wave.

"I just heard," she said, her expression decidedly forlorn. "I'm sorry. I really enjoyed working with you."

"Me, too," I said. "You're wonderfully talented with computers, Miss Hamilton, and I appreciate all that you did for us. Your work saved many lives, and the Police Service is lucky to have you in their employ. You *are* still employed, aren't you?"

"I am," she said, forcing a smile. "I'm actually up for a commendation and a promotion, none of which would have happened without you. The letter you wrote on my behalf was very kind. I just wanted to thank you."

"My pleasure. I'm glad to hear that you're getting proper recognition for all that you did."

Before I could say anything else, she hugged me tightly. "I better go before I start crying. I promised myself I wouldn't cry."

"I'm not dying, Miss Hamilton."

"I know," she whispered, "but you're officially off-limits to the police service. Doubly so for me. I've been ordered not to have any contact with you or your friends. I don't like it, but I need my job."

I sighed. "Understood. So this is goodbye, then?"

"I'm afraid so," she said, giving me one last hug.

"If circumstances ever change," I said, "please feel free to look me up."

She nodded, fighting tears, before scurrying away. I collected my satchel and made my way to a waiting taxi.

* * *

I tossed my satchel onto the bed of my hotel room and flopped into the nearby chair. I fumed. This was not how things were supposed to unfold. I wanted to go after Shanagh Grady in a unified offensive. Instead, we were fragmented and weakened.

As I pondered my next steps, I shifted my position. As I moved, I became aware of something in my back right pants pocket. Frowning, I reached back and removed a business card. It was Jim Finnegan's Police Service card, but I couldn't recall pocketing one. Confused, I flipped it over to see a handwritten phone number. The writing was distinctly feminine and unfamiliar to me. Kelly Hamilton must have slipped me this card during our brief goodbye.

I grabbed my phone and dialed the number. A monotone, computer-generated voice greeted me:

Saying goodbye sucks, so I won't, and the brass can kiss my arse.

Take a stroll on High Street.

If you can't read the time on the leaning tower, you've gone too far. If you can see Samson and Goliath, you've more to go.

There's a wee shop that repairs cell phones. Ask for the owner, a Bosnian man named Adnan.

Tell him the Poppy sent you.

And don't ask any questions.

* * *

It was a good day to take a walk, brisk but not raining, and I didn't have much else to do but sit around my hotel room and brood. My ace researcher and best friend Jillian MacDonald, or Mack as I called her, was at the hospital for a check-up. Shanagh Grady's strong man Paddy Bannion had delivered quite a beating to Mack in an attempt to extract information. It culminated with a nasty broken arm that was healing, albeit slowly and painfully. From there, she planned to spend the day with Karen Boyle.

Karen, Angela Grady's long time friend, and Mack had become close friends. In recent months, circumstances conspired to cool my fledgling romance with Karen, but signs pointed to a vigorous rekindling. Emergency surgery saved her life, but an infection slowed her recovery. All that behind her, she dove into physical therapy, and rebuilding her strength with zeal.

Karen had spent much of her life in Angela Grady's shadow, especially in terms of romance. Men used her to get to Angela, often treating her as an afterthought along the way. She described an equal number as *Angela's cast-offs*. Arguably, I was part of the latter, and my noticeably broken heart lingered. To her credit, she remained patient with me, allowing the natural grief process to run its course. As I walked, I vowed to move on and give Karen her due attention.

* * *

I made the turn onto High Street at Queen's Square, Albert's Clock looking down at me from atop its leaning tower. The old shipyard's great cranes, nicknamed Samson and Goliath, loomed in the distance.

Why didn't Kelly Hamilton just give me the damned address? I made several passes up and down High Street without finding what I was looking for. I even ventured down Church Lane and Pottinger's Entry, pedestrian-only side streets, with no luck. They didn't meet Kelly's cryptic instructions — I couldn't see the clock — but I was getting tired and frustrated, maybe even a bit desperate.

Needing a break, I found a nearby coffee shop and settled into a small booth, watching people coming and going on High Street. I sipped my coffee, staring off into space. Eventually, my eyes focused on some upper story windows of the building across the street. One contained a small, printed sign advertising office space available to let. Dammit. I had been looking only at ground floor shops, completely ignoring the possibility that my target was in an upper story.

I finished my coffee quickly, resuming my search with renewed vigor. Another twenty minutes of searching led me to a narrow stairway. On the wall near the street, a simple sign pointed the way:

```
Cell Phone Repair, Unlocking
Quick. Guaranteed.
Third Floor
```

I climbed, exiting the aging stairwell on the third floor. The cellular shop was at the far end of the hallway. It appeared to be open for business, although I surmised that it looked little different when closed. I opened the door, and a bell chimed gently announcing my presence.

A young man, looking to be of Eastern European ancestry, glanced up at me indifferently. His focus returned to the disassembled cell phone on the counter in front of him. I walked over, allowing the awkward silence to continue until I could no longer stand it.

"I was told to ask for Adnan," I said, hesitantly.

The man stopped what he was doing and looked up at me with an annoyed expression.

"I can give him a message," the man said, his accent confirming my suspicions of his origin.

"No message," I said. "Do you know when he will be back?"

"No." He, said, returning to his previous activity. "Try later, maybe."

"I need to speak to him now," I insisted.

He exhaled, glaring at me. "Try later."

I wanted to reach over the counter and punch him in the face, but I controlled my temper. "Fine," I grunted. I slammed the door behind me. I made it a few angry steps down the hallway before the distinctive sound of a shotgun being racked stopped me in my path. Dammit. In my anger, I had become unaware of my surroundings. Instinctively, I slowly raised my hands.

"That's far enough," a man said. His accent was similar to that of the young man working at the shop. "Keep your hands where I can see them, and turn around slowly."

I complied, cognizant of every motion. Even breathing seemed risky.

The man, silhouetted in the dark hallway by the light from the window behind him, ordered me through a doorway on the side of the hall opposite to the store's door. I made my way carefully into the darkened room. The man turned the lights on.

He, like the younger man, looked to be of Eastern European origins, although he was taller, at least twenty years older, and had significantly less hair. His face, expressionless, looked rough and bore the trademarks of a difficult, perhaps violent, life. "Talk," he grunted, motioning to me with the barrel of his shotgun.

"I was told to ask for Adnan."

"And who told you to ask for Adnan?"

"The Poppy sent me." I didn't want to play my hand, but staring down the barrel of a twelve gauge shotgun convinced me it was worth the risk.

He remained silent, studying me intently until his phone chirped. He moved back a few feet and quickly glanced at the screen. All the time, his firearm never drifted off target.

"I am Adnan Jasik," he said, gradually lowering the gun.

"John Costa," I said, collecting myself.

"I have something for you."

Fortunately, it wasn't the business end of his shotgun. He handed me a cell phone and a business card. The back contained two codes, handwritten.

"Memorize these, and then destroy the card," he instructed. "If this phone were to fall into the wrong hands and these codes revealed, the Poppy would be in great danger."

I nodded. I had a million questions, but remembered Kelly's explicit instructions and remained silent.

"You've found your way into a dangerous game, my friend. You don't have the slightest idea the breadth and scope of the people you're dealing with. You're rash and careless, Mister Costa. You let your passions rule your actions. The Poppy trusts you, and for that reason alone, I do this thing for you." He motioned to the phone. "But I will not do so again if you continue to be reckless."

I lowered my eyes briefly, acknowledging the accuracy of his assessment.

"Harun will show you out the back way. Turn off your phone

and avoid High Street on your way back to your hotel. There is a decent chance you're being tracked. If anyone happens to ask why you were here, tell them you needed a new battery. Don't turn it back on until you get to your room."

"This way, sir."

The voice behind me startled me.

"You see?" said Adnan. "Again, you were caught unaware, even after I scolded you. I worry that I will read your name in the obituaries. You're an old dog, Mister Costa, hopefully you can learn some new tricks." His expression eased. I couldn't tell whether the smile that crossed his face was genuine or sarcastic. "Always with the beautiful young women I see you. Perhaps they like your money, or maybe it is something else. Maybe the old dog knows a few tricks, after all," he said, laughing. "Harun, see that our guest gets safely back to his hotel."

CHAPTER TWO

Jim Finnegan was far more talkative at dinner than I expected. His conversation occasionally bordered on jovial as he discussed some of his plans, most based on the assumption that he would be sacked shortly. Ideas ranged from reconnecting with long lost relatives to traveling. It all sounded good; he was saying the right things. What I wasn't certain of was whether he meant it or was trying to convince himself.

My thoughts wanted to drift elsewhere, namely to whatever Kelly Hamilton was working on. If I was playing a dangerous game, whatever she was into seemed far worse, and likely deadly if done wrong. Lacking instructions to the contrary, I kept the special phone she arranged for me to have powered on and tucked carefully in my jacket pocket. Several times I excused myself from the table for a restroom break in the hopes that a missive had arrived, but each foray was met with disappointment.

Forcing my mind back into the present, I tried to reengage with the conversation. It worked briefly before another observation derailed my focus.

Mack's recovery had progressed to the point where she felt well enough to work. In recent weeks, and even more so in recent days, she was becoming intently focused on her project, the details of which she hadn't shared. Maybe it was my imagination, but I perceived a cooling in Mack and Karen's friendship. Nothing overt surfaced, just subtleties, and likely related to our stressful situation. Tonight, however, they seemed to be getting on better.

* * *

Many hours and drinks later, I poured Finnegan into a taxi and stumbled back to my room.

"You seemed elsewhere tonight," Karen said, running her fingers through my hair. "I guess I can't blame you with all that's been going on. Let me know if there's anything I can do to help. The doctors were pleased with where I am today," she said, pretending to flex her muscles, "and I want to start pulling my weight and helping where I can."

"Honestly, Karen," I sighed, "with the recent turn of events, I don't know how much we're going to be doing. It may be time to pack up shop and head back to the States."

She frowned. "I thought you wanted to get Shanagh Grady. Ever since Angela died, I've heard nothing but revenge coming out of your mouth, and now you're talking about going home? Giving up? Why the sudden change of heart?"

"Maybe I should leave all this in the hands of the people that actually know what they're doing."

"Looks to me like they're about to get rid of the one person that truly meets that description."

"Yeah. I don't get it."

"Speaking of which, has Mack said anything to you lately? She's been a little distant as of late, and I was wondering if I did anything that upset her."

"No. She's not said anything in particular, but I can ask her if you'd like."

"Don't trouble yourself. It might all be my imagination, anyway."

* * *

I was almost asleep when an unfamiliar chirping demanded my attention. I almost ignored it until I realized its origin was my new phone. Fighting to shake off the cobwebs, I fumbled around trying to grab it from the nightstand. Eventually, I succeeded.

A single message awaited with instructions on where and when to meet. A quick glance at the location and the time told me I couldn't afford any delays. Still groggy, I dressed warmly and headed out.

Perhaps the Bosnian was right about my rashness. I realized I was laboring under the assumption that the message was from Kelly Hamilton. I could easily be walking into a trap. After a fleeting moment of indecision, I hailed a taxi.

* * *

The cab dropped me off at the end of a quiet street lined on one side by brick houses. I paid the driver and started walking in the prescribed direction. I reached the start of two walking paths and, as instructed, took the one on my right. As my luck would have it, clouds had rolled in during the late hours of the evening, bringing with them a misting rain. I donned my hood and quickened my pace, feeling that I was running late.

Maybe my imagination was working overtime or fatigue was setting in, but I had the distinct impression that I was being followed. I tried to look around, even making a contrived stop to tie my shoe, but the night was dark and the path unlit, and I saw nothing.

I crossed a narrow pedestrian bridge, arriving at the designated spot. Nobody was there.

The path split into two directions. One branch continued on, more or less, in my previous direction of travel. The other turned left and into some trees. Feeling that I could not afford indecision, I selected the left branch. I was only a few paces into the woods when a voice startled me.

"Good choice," Kelly Hamilton said.

"Dammit," I growled. "You just aged me ten years."

"Come on," she said, motioning me forward.

We walked a bit in silence before she spoke again. "You made the right choice. Did you know I was waiting for you?"

"No. I just figured I shouldn't be standing out in the open like I was waiting for someone, so I just went with my gut."

"Well, your gut was right. I can't wait to tell Adnan; he owes me ten quid. He bet you'd stand there in the open waiting for me."

"All this was some kind of half-assed test for a bet you made?"

"Hardly."

"And your friend Adnan — that man is a psychopath! What the hell are you involved in, anyway?"

Kelly's voice lost its normal, lyrical quality as she turned serious. "Careful? Yes, but hardly a psychopath. He saved my father's life during the Bosnian war. In turn, we got him out of the country."

"We? The Bosnian war ended over twenty years ago. Were you working for the Police Service at the age of two?"

"I'm a bit older than I look," she said. "It can come in handy at times. People don't take me seriously and let their guard down."

"What was your father doing in Yugoslavia?"

"My father worked for one of our intelligence organizations. I don't know everything he was working on, of course, but what I've learned will be of great interest to you."

"You have my undivided attention, Miss Hamilton."

"As tensions flared in the Balkans, black market weapons started to flood the Balkans. My father was working on this, and traced one of the sources back to our dear old Emerald Isle and Connla Grady."

"Angela's grandfather and architect of the organization Shanagh leads today…" I muttered, my voice trailing away.

"Exactly," she said. "They were sourcing armaments to any and all combatants, using different names and operatives, of course, so their subterfuge wouldn't be discovered. Dad's investigation got too close to someone, and it quickly became too dangerous for him to stay in the Balkans. Adnan kept him safe until a team was able to transport all of them to safety: my father, Adnan, and his family."

"Interesting, but I'm not sure how it translates to all this cloak and dagger stuff."

"You're being watched by at least three different groups, including the Police Service, and likely one or more of them followed you here. They can't come see what you're up to, though, without risking exposure. My father trained me to be a field agent, but my computer prowess proved to be more valuable. I was able to learn things someone in the field would never discover."

"That still doesn't explain why you're talking to me, Kelly? Why are you out here putting your career at risk?"

"Because we have mutual adversaries and might be able to help each other."

"Adversaries? I'm only aware of one."

"There's Shanagh, to be sure, but it doesn't end there. I'm convinced that we still have a traitor within the Police Service. Finnegan's suspension all but confirmed that for me. And then there's Geryon…"

"The hacker that Mack stopped from stealing my identity way back when? I'd all but forgotten him. What's he got to do with anything?"

"Not *he*, John; *them*. Geryon is a group of ultra elite hackers, four maybe five people. We don't know how or why they got involved, but our sources indicate that Shanagh has approached them to propose an alliance. If true, it's really bad news. Geryon is well funded and connected. They're dangerous, and all the more reason for you and your friends to be careful."

"Duly noted, but…"

Kelly interrupted me before I could continue. "I don't think you follow me. There's a good chance that Geryon is responsible for the death of the hacker you knew as Zira. There were precious few people who knew that you contacted Zira. There's a few in the Police Service, but a handful of them are in your immediate circle of friends. Not accusing anyone, mind you. Just want you to keep your eyes open, as the saying goes."

"You know," I said, stopping, "Shanagh said the same thing to me the last time she called me. I assumed she was trying to stir up discord."

"A very real possibility," she said, as we resumed our walk. "I don't envy you the position you're in. You've got a couple of people you can trust, at least: Finnegan and Jillian MacDonald. Beyond that, I can't vouch for much more."

"Present company excluded, I assume."

"I wouldn't; you've no real reason to trust me or Adnan. We haven't earned your trust yet."

"Fair enough."

"We've been here long enough. Keep that phone with you, and we'll contact you as we can. Keep walking on this path; it will loop back to the footbridge. Stay on the bridge for a few minutes before heading back. If anyone asks, you just needed some time to grieve. They'll shut their gobs straight away."

I grunted my acknowledgment, and continued down the path. Kelly's parting words had struck more of a nerve than I wanted to admit. The frenetic pace of events had left me little time to embrace the grief that boiled within. The package bearing Angela's ashes and an envelope containing her final wishes remained unopened in my hotel room. My schedule was an excuse to avoid facing the harsh reality of the situation. Everyone knew it, but mercifully left it unspoken. I lingered on the bridge, watching the River Lagan slip quietly toward the ocean.

My jacket's claimed water resistance had failed sometime during my walk, and I returned to my hotel room soaked and shivering. A warm shower helped, and a quick shot of whiskey sent me quickly back to sleep.

* * *

Sounds of a passionate discussion, likely a disagreement, in the suite's adjoining room shook me awake. Still hazy, I could only pick up bits and pieces of it, but whatever it was, Mack and Karen were clearly not in accord. I stumbled toward the door.

"Do you think you could hold it down a bit," I rasped, pounding on the door to the other half of our suite. My throat hurt, and I started coughing before I could say anything else.

The conversation stopped, and I heard the lock click open. Karen and Mack looked at me, concern painted on their faces. "You look like hell," Mack said.

"I'm just a little tired. You two bantering on woke me up." My words were interrupted by a vigorous bout of sneezing. "Is everything okay over here?"

A brief, awkward silence followed, broken by laughing and assurances from both that all was well.

"I've got some cold medicine," said Mack, motioning for me to wait. "It tastes awful but works wonderfully."

I tried to lodge a brief protest, but Karen hushed me as she escorted me back to bed. "You really don't look good this morning," she said, caressing my hand. "Get some rest and rebuild your strength." She brought her lips near to my ear. "You're going to need it," she whispered. "One more check-up from the doctor, and I'll be cleared for all physical activities. *All*," she said, winking.

I offered a faint smile, but before I could say anything in reply, Mack returned, carrying a bottle and spoon.

"Here you are, Sneezy McSniffles. Take this…"

Her description hardly did the vile concoction justice. It was all I could do to avoid spitting it out. I wanted to let fly with a barrage of cursing, but a desperate search for a glass of water took priority. I glared at Mack as I gulped my drink. She smiled, sticking her tongue out at me. Sleep called before I could offer any additional protest.

* * *

I awoke to find Mack keeping a solitary vigil from a nearby chair. The gentle clicking of her laptop keyboard was the only sound in the room. The cast and sling on her left arm barely slowed her down; her right hand danced deftly across the keyboard. She glanced up, her expression unchanged. "You really need to start taking better care of yourself," she scolded.

I started to say something, but was stopped abruptly by her hand, fingers up and palm facing me.

"That includes traipsing out in the rain in the middle of the night."

"I had a lot on my mind," I mumbled.

Her nose wrinkled. "Grieve in your own way, I suppose, but if it includes lying to me, count me out. You didn't leave like a man with a lot on his mind. You left like a man with a purpose."

"You were spying on me?"

"I was awake anyway, working on something. But yes, I'm also keeping an eye on you. Someone's got to do it."

"Thank you, Mack. I… uh…"

"When the time comes, let yourself grieve, John. I've known you long enough to see through the facade, my friend. Go on a bender, cry for three days straight, beat the hell out of a punching bag, but you've got to let it out."

"You're right," I sighed. "It's just that poor Karen's been in Angela's shadow her whole life. Even in death, she can't seem to break free. I don't want to make it worse."

"Every minute you hold on does exactly that," she said, preparing another dose of the vile medicine.

"I hadn't looked at it that way," I said, nearly gagging from the wicked concoction. "Speaking of Karen, you two seemed to be having a bit of a kerfuffle this morning. What was that all about?"

"Oh, nothing. Mostly girl stuff," Mack said, returning to her chair.

"Now who's fibbing?" I said, eyebrow raised. "I went out to meet an informant this morning. We met somewhere not conducive to eavesdropping, which, sadly, happened to be outside in the rain. Ergo my cold and the soaked clothing drying in the bathroom. But I think you'll find what I learned to be interesting."

"Well?" Her eyes sparkled.

"Provided, of course, you share with me what you're working on, and what the hell is going on between you and Karen."

"Fine," she groaned. "Do you want tea or coffee?"

"Why?"

"Because that cold medicine contains some ingredients to help you sleep, and we have a fair amount to talk about, I think. Oh, damn!"

It was too late, and sleep collected me, fight as I might, before we could continue.

CHAPTER THREE

It was in the early evening hours before the sound of a slamming door stirred me from my slumber. Through the door into the neighboring suite, I caught a glimpse of Mack. Her face looked pained.

"Mack," I grunted, working my way out of bed. I wasn't sure if my failing voice was strong enough for her to hear me, but she had, appearing in the doorway.

"Welcome back," she said, collecting herself.

"I'm hungry, but don't feel good enough to go anywhere. I'm going to call for room service. Care to join me?"

"Sure," she said, flopping into the nearest chair.

"Go ahead and order whatever you want. Shepherd's pie for me, please. I'm going to get a shower while we wait."

* * *

I still didn't feel very well, but a warm shower and dinner helped.

Mack's company, on the other hand, was distant. We exchanged little more than small talk and pleasantries over dinner. Finally, I summoned my strength and asked the obvious question.

"Mack, what the hell is going on?"

She sighed, poured a glass of red wine, and drank most of it in one gulp. "Karen and I aren't getting along right now."

"That's become painfully obvious. What isn't obvious is why…"

"It all started when I felt well enough to start working again," she said, propping her feet up. "I probably should have talked to you before now, but it all kinda snowballed before I realized it." She bit her lip, briefly.

"Go on, Mack," I said, taking my last bite of dinner.

"Maybe it's my fault. You know, when I get on something and can't find a satisfactory explanation, I just won't let it go. Maybe she's right."

"Maybe she's right about *what*, Mack? You still haven't told me the crux of the problem yet."

"There are some details that are bothering me, and I just can't seem to let them go. I wish I could, but I can't."

"Mack!"

"Oh, I shouldn't have said anything…"

"Mack!!"

"Fine. Suit yourself. Karen feels that I'm stopping you from moving on, that as long as I'm working on the case, you're never going to let go of Angela. Maybe she's right. Maybe we should just go home and stay far away from this mess. I'm sure between your money and my technical abilities, we could stay off the grid fairly easily for a few years."

"I suppose so," I said, studying her intently. "Is that what you want, though?"

"No," she sighed, "but I also want you to be happy. If that means I need to quietly fade out of your life, I'll do it. I don't want to be a third wheel."

I sat in stunned silence for several moments before being able to speak. "A thought like that has never crossed my mind, Mack. Is this something Karen told you?"

"Not in so many words, just what I inferred reading between the lines."

"Well, I hope you didn't infer anything from me. You're my friend, Mack, and I love you. Hell, you're my best friend, probably the best friend I've ever had. I can't imagine my life without you in it." I took her hand to reassure, but I could tell from her expression that she was still troubled. "What is it?"

"Does our deal from earlier still stand? You know, the one where we trade information?"

"Of course it does. Want me to go first?"

"No. I will. You know, when Shanagh's thugs kidnapped me, her henchman, Paddy Bannion, took great pleasure in making me uncomfortable. The real rough stuff didn't happen, though, until we left the boat where they initially held me. I really couldn't put all of it together until my head cleared and the painkillers got out of my system. But now its bugging me because the timeline doesn't work out."

"Go on," I said, intently focused on her words.

"He kept trying to get me to reveal what we had done with their hacker, Zira. As time passed, they got more desperate for answers, and the ferocity of his beatings increased, all the way up to a broken arm. I didn't crack because I couldn't. I simply didn't know. We've labored all this time under the assumption that Shanagh had Zira killed because he betrayed her."

"True…"

"According to what you've told me, though, Zira was dead by the time Paddy Bannion gave me this little gift," she said, tapping the cast on her left arm. "If Shanagh had him killed, why did they continue to ask about him?"

"Maybe Paddy took pleasure in beating the stuffing out of you."

"Oh, he did, no doubt, but that isn't why. I overheard more than I let on. They didn't know Zira was dead, because they didn't order the hit. Someone else must've arranged for his untimely demise."

"Zira, before he died, hinted that there was another faction of Connla's organization involved."

"I don't think so," she said, wrinkling her nose. "I overheard communication with at least six people that I assumed were regional leaders. There wasn't an ounce of dissent to be found. You've not spent much time around Shanagh Grady, John. She's truly terrifying. Paddy Bannion was one of the toughest, hardest bastards I've ever had the displeasure to meet, and she scared the hell out of him. It was obvious in observing their interactions."

"So what are you getting at, Mack?"

"That there's another powerful organization somewhere in the picture."

"Like Geryon?"

The mention of the name startled her. "Perhaps, but how…"

"Mack, not a word of this to anyone. And I mean *anyone*."

"I promise."

"I know because my informant told me that there is a good

chance that Geryon is responsible for Zira's death. There's rumor of a proposed truce between Geryon and Shanagh, too."

Mack shook her head. "This is bad. Really bad."

The sound of the suite's door opening stopped our conversation.

"That isn't all that's on my mind," she whispered quickly, before the door opened.

Dammit. I wanted to hear the rest.

* * *

Karen was pleasant, even bordering on apologetic, as she tried to be sociable. Mack seemed to be receptive to the tacit peace offering, so a quiet, harmonious evening looked to be a possibility. The truce lasted about an hour, long enough for me to drift somewhere between sleep and wakefulness.

I didn't witness what started the dispute, but raised voices quickly vanquished any hopes of a long, restful slumber. I stumbled out of bed, hoping to put an end to the rapidly escalating confrontation. Words flew, something about text messages and meddling, and by the time I reached the door connecting our suites, a full-on row threatened.

The door was unlocked, so I barged in without thinking or knocking. The normally diminutive and zen-like Karen was showing a previously unknown side of her personality. She unleashed a barrage of verbal fury at Mack worthy of every saying and legend surrounding Irish women and their temper. Mack, her red hair seeming nearly aflame, wasn't backing down. An escalation to fisticuffs and certain ejection from our hotel seemed inevitable. Risking life and limb, I separated the combatants. A few tense moments of angry staring preceded an uneasy truce.

Lacking the energy and clarity to play the role of Solomon, I escorted Karen out of the room and down to the lobby. Some pleading and a few hundred quid slipped surreptitiously to the manager secured a room one floor below our suite.

Returning to our suite, I plunked the key card on the table. "One of you is moving to this room," I growled. "If you can't come to an agreement on your own, I'll pick. I'm too tired and don't feel well enough to deal with this tonight."

Silence.

"Fine," I grunted, pulling a coin out of my pocket. "I'm going to let the Queen decide. Heads, Karen moves; tails, Mack moves. And don't even think about arguing, or you'll both be looking for another hotel. And just so you know," I said, gritting my teeth, "this is a normal coin. Elizabeth on the front, *New Pence* stamped on the back." I flipped the coin over a few times so they could see it, and then sent it flipping.

* * *

Karen barely said two words the entire time I helped her collect her belongings and move. As I turned to leave her room after delivering the final suitcase, her hand caught mine.

"Sorry," she whispered. "I don't know what came over me."

"Try to get some rest," I said, kissing her forehead. "We've all been under a lot of pressure and tempers are frayed."

"Maybe revenge isn't a game I'm cut out to play," she sighed. "Perhaps it would be better if I went home and got back to work on my charity, and left finding Shanagh to the authorities."

"I'll support you on whatever you decide," I said, squeezing her hand, "but don't make a decision when you're tired and frustrated. At least sleep on it."

"I promise," she said, hugging me.

* * *

Mack hadn't moved from the chair in my suite where she served her banishment while I moved Karen's belongings. Her expression seemed distant as she glanced up at me.

"Do you want me to leave?"

"No," I said, pouring a glass of whiskey, "I'm too wired to sleep. That's a side of Karen I've never seen before. Not sure I'm too eager to see it again."

"First for me too," Mack said, getting out of her chair and staring out the window. "We've had little differences of opinion in the past, but nothing anywhere close to this."

"I'm not entirely sure she's thinking straight," I sighed. "She was talking about working on her charity."

Mack shook her head, and continued to stare out the window. Karen's beloved charity was running on borrowed time. Donations had fallen to nothing following the murder of her father and accusations of impropriety. Even though Mack had disproved the claims of mismanaged funds, the stigma lingered, chasing donors away. Six months ago, I would've bet that, through sheer will and determination, Karen would pull it up by its bootstraps. When we parted company this evening, Karen's eyes shone only of dull capitulation.

"She's still taking about six medications," I said, sipping my whiskey, "any possibility of an interaction causing some of this?"

"That was the first thing I thought of," Mack said, as she poured whiskey into her glass. "Even mentioning it started an argument, so I let it drop. "

"But?" I said, in response to her raised eyebrow.

"I snooped anyway, and nothing she's taking has this type of interaction. There's a first time for everything, I suppose, but it isn't likely."

"Then what the hell is it?" I ran my hands through my hair, massaging my temples in an attempt to stave off the headache that had been lurking most of the evening.

"Are you sure you want to know?"

"Mack!"

"It's only a theory…"

"Mack!!"

She finished the whiskey that remained in her glass in one, quick shot. "Be right back," she said, as she headed into the adjoining room to retrieve her computer.

"I graze on these damn things when I get nervous," she said, nodding at the bag of Taytos in her left hand. "You've even got me calling them crisps."

"As Finnegan would say, there's hope for you yet, Mack!"

She smiled, but her demeanor betrayed more serious thoughts. She opened the screen of her laptop. "When I was on the ship, Paddy Bannion would lock me in a room, handcuffed to a pipe, when he needed to step out. One of the times he dragged me into their makeshift office to bark questions at me, I managed to snag a paper clip. From that point on, I could escape the handcuffs whenever I felt it was safe to do so. I tried to make my way to freedom when the ship wasn't at sea, but there were too many guards. I started poking around for whatever clues I could find."

"And?"

"They did a pretty good job of hiding their tracks, but I found one thing: a work order. From the bits that survived, I was able to piece together the name of the company: Ulster Maritime Group, Ltd."

"Any connection to Shanagh Grady?"

"First thing I looked for, of course. Doubly so when I looked at their profile. They do just enough business to keep licensed and be profitable, but no more. No record of fines, citations, labor problems; nothing."

"That smells for the world like Connla Grady's work: a network of small, superficially legitimate businesses networked into a full-fledged crime syndicate."

"I thought so too, but it's owned by a Greek fellow, Kristos something-or-other."

I sighed. "So a dead end…"

"Only to those that aren't as awesome as I am," she said, winking. "I did some more digging and found that Kristos married an Irish woman. They started their business with a loan from a finance company loosely connected to Connla Grady. The same company that loaned money to Karen's parents, ostensibly to help with her mother's condition."

"Oh my," I said, refilling my glass.

"That's not all that's interesting," she said, returning to her chair. "You haven't heard the name of the woman he married yet."

"An undiscovered branch of the Grady clan?"

"Her name is Dianne O'Leary."

"O'Leary? Please tell me Dianne O'Leary isn't related to Karen's mom, Alicia O'Leary."

"I could tell you that, but I'd be lying. Dianne O'Leary is Alicia O'Leary's younger sister, Karen's aunt. I think Karen must've gotten wind of what I'm working on, and it touched a nerve or something."

"I think it's safe to say that there's a lot about Karen's mother we don't know. I have my suspicions, of course. I think she was involved with Connla O'Grady, probably part of his organization, maybe a love interest, who knows. Connla's letter to Angela hinted that his planned successor was unable to fulfill the role. It was a ring bearing the O'Leary name that granted us access to his wealth. I think Alicia was in line to assume control until early-onset Alzheimer's claimed her mind."

"Have you said anything to Karen about this?"

"Not a word. We could investigate Alicia, maybe even discover crimes and obtain a conviction, but to what end? She doesn't know where she is, who she is, or even recognizer her daughter. She's already suffering a fate more cruel than the Prison Service could ever deliver."

Mack sighed. "Perhaps you're right. Sometimes, though, apples don't fall too far from the tree…"

"Jillian MacDonald! Are you saying that you suspect Karen of something? I recall being verbally eviscerated for merely suggesting the possibility…"

"I'm not sure what I'm saying. Maybe you shouldn't take my advice when it comes to women; I liked Angela, too, and we saw how that worked out."

CHAPTER FOUR

"Costa, what the hell are you calling me for, especially this early?" growled Jim Finnegan. "I'm set to get the sack any day now, if you believe the papers."

"We need some inside information, and I don't want Mack to have to break any laws to get it. I'd call Kelly Hamilton, but she told me she'd get fired if she had anything to do with me."

"So you're calling the poor bastard that is already on the chopping block?"

"Something like that. I need some information on the O'Leary family."

"Alicia O'Leary? We're not going to pursue anything, given her regrettable situation."

"No, not Alicia. Her younger sister, Dianne. The one that married the Greek man."

"I think you've got your facts all bollixed up, Johnny. Alicia

O'Leary's sister died in a traffic collision. If I recall correctly, it was a year or two before Alicia's diagnosis."

"Jim, that doesn't make sense. Dianne O'Leary is listed in the public records for the Ulster Maritime Group, Ltd. Mack showed me the filings online."

"I don't doubt that there is someone named Dianne O'Leary involved with the Ulster Maritime Group, whatever the hell they have to do with anything, but it certainly isn't Alicia's sister. O'Leary *is* a fairly common name around here…"

"Ulster Maritime Group received a business startup loan from one of Connla's finance companies, the same one that Karen's parents borrowed from to fund her long term health care. Not only that, Jim, but Mack discovered all this because of a work order she discovered on the ship where Shanagh held her hostage. Now, tell me again about how we have the wrong Dianne O'Leary!"

He paused, sighing loudly before continuing. "Okay, I admit it is interesting, but I really can't do much of anything to help you. I don't have my files, and my remote access is suspended indefinitely. But, I'm sure that if you and Miss MacDonald venture out in the direction of a library, you can read all about the unfortunate demise of Dianne O'Leary. Now, I've got a tee time arranged."

"Tee time? I didn't know you played golf."

"I haven't in years, but I suddenly have a preponderance of spare time, so I'm giving it another go. Then off to a music lesson."

"Music?"

"My cousin, Shannon McLeod, is in town visiting family. You remember her, don't you? I'm learning the flute."

After Angela Grady's confession, Finnegan had taken it upon himself to play matchmaker between me and his cousin from Galway. He was spot-on in his assessment. The talented, kind, and stunningly beautiful Shannon McLeod would have been a perfect match, save for ill-fated timing. Instead, the shadow of Angela made our relationship sputter, finally settling down to a cordial, but somewhat distant, friendship. Jim had never given up hope, reminding me at nearly every opportunity.

"Well, if Shannon is your instructor, you'll do well in spite of yourself. Please relay my best regards."

Jim grunted something unintelligible before hanging up the phone, but I was sure the word *eejit* figured in, somewhere.

* * *

"No thanks, John," Karen said, declining my offer of breakfast. "I'm just going to stay here until my doctor's appointment this afternoon. I've got a lot on my mind."

"I understand," I said. "My phone will be on if you need anything or change your mind."

"Maybe we can get together this evening. I've got some apologizing to do, if I haven't already burned that bridge."

"I don't think any bridges are in ruins. Call whenever you're ready."

* * *

"Feed a cold, starve a fever, Mack! Today, I'm going to treat myself to a proper breakfast for a change. Karen has me eating all sorts of healthy food. The damned stuff tastes like tree bark and gravel, and I'm hungry again in two hours. The plate of grass clippings that pretends to be lunch doesn't stick with me, either. Besides, you're dragging me to the library. The condemned should get to pick their last meal!"

"I've never understood your aversions to libraries," she said, scanning the menu.

"Chalk it up to untreated childhood trauma. I must emit a

pheromone that is utterly repugnant to librarians. Two steps past the threshold and they descend on me like white blood cells to an invading virus, always giving me that look of utter disdain."

"It is all in your imagination, John."

"You don't see it because you speak their language…"

All Mack could do was roll her eyes in response.

* * *

My breakfast, delicious as it was, sat in my stomach like a lead weight, and no amount of excuse making would sway Mack from our destination. Dammit.

The library had the same smell and preternatural silence as every other one I'd visited, and I immediately felt uncomfortable. Mack, however, was in her element, striding confidently to a counter staffed by several librarians. I stayed in the background while she did her thing. The librarian, a golden haired woman who I guessed to be around forty, emerged from behind the counter, directing us to where we could find what we were looking for. Her demeanor toward me was unexpected, and left me momentarily disoriented. Friendly, almost flirtatious, she flitted about until she was certain we had everything we needed. She even made sure that I had her business card, mentioning it on several occasions.

Mack appeared indifferent to the entire situation until the librarian finally returned to her station. Then she looked up, giggled quietly, and returned to what she was doing.

"Here," she whispered.

The article was as Jim said it would be. Dianne O'Leary, sister of Alicia O'Leary, was killed trying to cross the street. An out of control truck careened into her at high speed. Death was instantaneous.

"Can we go now?" I whispered.

"No," she scolded. "We need to figure out who the other Dianne O'Leary is."

Mack returned to the counter. I could provide nothing of value, so I retreated to a bench outside the library's main entrance. The churning of the undigested bits of breakfast made it impossible for me to enjoy what had turned into a pleasant day. The call that arrived moments later didn't help either.

"Good day, Solicitor." The unmistakable voice of Shanagh Grady invariably set off an odd amalgam of anger and fear. "I trust you are enjoying yourself at the library."

In spite of being perpetually a step behind Shanagh, I still found myself surprised that she seemed to know my whereabouts at nearly every moment. "Mack is inside researching geology, so we know which rocks hide the most disgusting vermin. That'll save us the trouble of turning up ones that only hide spiders and snakes."

"There are no snakes in Ireland, Johnny, at least there weren't until you showed up."

"I'd love to spend the day trading insults with you, Shanagh, but unless you're planning on turning yourself in, we don't have anything to talk about."

"I'll be the judge of that," she snapped. "We still have a fair bit of unfinished business. I plan to keep my promise to you. The red-headed tart dies while you watch."

"It didn't work out so well for you the last time you tried that, did it? I think Paddy Bannion would agree with me, were he alive to offer an opinion."

"I got to know Jillian MacDonald quite well while she was enjoying my hospitality. Well, I got quite familiar with her screams, and how she pleaded for her life. She told us all sorts of interesting things about you in an effort to belay her execution. Nevertheless, there are still things I know that she doesn't. Things that make me wonder what, exactly, she sees in you, and how she'd react if she knew the truth."

"She's free to ask me anything. I've no secrets from Mack."

"I can't help but wonder what she's thinking when she sees you ignoring my daughter's last wishes day after day, week after week. Is she asking herself if you'll treat her remains with the same cruel indifference as you have Angela's. The whole thing disgusts me, to be sure. Nothing done; her letters sitting there unopened and unread, collecting dust and all."

Dammit. How did she know that?

"I suppose about now you're wondering how I know what I know. I make it a point to keep close tabs on my employees. Nothing has changed, boy-o. You're still working for me, you just don't have your next major assignment yet. But I've got a little something for you in the interim."

"And what might that be?"

"Your mother wanted to name you Sean, but your father had another name in mind. John emerged as a compromise. Might not be a bad idea for you to discover who you really are, Solicitor. It might improve your decision making prowess."

* * *

Mack emerged from the library several hours later carrying a stack of photocopies and handwritten notes. "You look like you've seen a ghost," she said, frowning.

"Not really. Just a call from Shanagh Grady."

"I have an idea: next time, just hang up on her."

"I get the distinct impression that someone would die as a result."

"It was only an idea. I didn't say it was a good one." She stuck her tongue out at me.

"Mack, she knows stuff about us that she shouldn't. She knew exactly where we were; she knew that I've not dealt with Angela's last wishes yet. There's only a handful of people that know that; five or six, excluding us."

"There's always the hotel staff, and I can check the room for listening devices."

"Not a bad idea." I paused to study her expression. "You know what I'm thinking, don't you?"

"Yeah, and six months ago, I would have slapped you for it."

"And now?"

"Now I'm not so sure, John."

I could tell that Mack was fighting back tears. "Karen wants the chance to apologize later. Let's hear what she has to say. There's always the possibility that she's being forced into leaking information, especially if her family is somehow involved. I can't help but find it interesting that Shanagh chose to break weeks of silence right as we started digging into the O'Leary family."

"Agreed," said Mack, collecting herself. "I doubt that it was coincidental. It could mean that we're drifting off into an area Shanagh doesn't want us researching. And if so, you know what that means, right?"

"Yes. That means we dig even deeper."

"Correct!"

* * *

The bell sounded, indicating the arrival of our elevator. "You go on up, Mack. I have an errand that I forgot to run earlier. Shanagh had me all rattled, and it completely slipped my mind."

"What is it? I'll go with you if you want."

"Appreciated, but no need, Mack. I'm just going to pop over to the pharmacy and look for some cold medicine that doesn't cause me to gag at the mere thought of it."

She smiled and shook her head as the elevator doors closed. I waited until the indicator showed that the car had climbed past the next floor up, then found a seat in the lobby. From my pocket, I retrieved my *special* phone and retrieved the sole message waiting for me.

`Enjoy a tour of fair Belfast on the top of a double-decker bus.`

`More instructions to follow.`

It was only a short walk to the ticket office and a waiting bus. Dutifully, I climbed to the upper deck, selecting a seat near the front. I was in the covered portion of the second level, but I still felt exposed and vulnerable until the bus started moving. My phone chirped again as the bus departed the Titanic quarter.

`Get off at the Gaol. Wait outside.`

Nervously, I endured several more stops until the guide finally announced our arrival at the Crumlin Road Gaol. I exited as instructed. Several tourists did likewise, heading into the old prison for a tour. I lingered outside, scanning for any sign of a contact person, but finding nothing.

A group of several young men approached, but turned at a nearby intersection, and headed toward a residential area. With nothing happening, I pulled out my tour brochure, hoping to look enough like a tourist to avoid drawing attention. A few minutes passed where I studied the disintegrating courthouse across the road from the jail. I must've been more focused than I realized, because a man's voice startled me.

"Don't look at me, Mister Costa," he said. "Get on the next tour bus, and sit in the last seat in the top. Ride until you get further instructions."

I folded my brochure, and turned my attention to the road, scanning for the arrival of the next bus. As instructed, I made my way to the top, selecting the last seat in the uncovered upper deck. The intense feeling of vulnerability returned.

The tour returned to the starting point, and I still hadn't received any instructions. I was about ready to give up and get some lunch when my phone chirped.

`Visit the Titanic Museum.`

* * *

The museum tour routed me through a variety of exhibits. Patiently, I played the part of a tourist, waiting for someone to contact me. I followed the course, gradually ascending floors. Finally, I arrived at the floor where a small queue had formed waiting to ride a small cable car that snaked through the interior of the museum. A man joined the line behind me, chatting non-stop on his cell phone.

Moments before it was my turn to ride a car, he whispered, "let's ride together."

I nodded, climbing into the car and securing my seatbelt as instructed.

The car started its path through a series of exhibits, highlighting the construction and internals of the ship, but my attention was locked on my fellow passenger.

"Here," he said, slickly passing me an envelope which I quickly stuffed into my jacket's interior pocket. "Shanagh's got access to most, if not all, of the cameras around your hotel, and probably most within. Not much we can do about it without tipping our hand, so get yourself a hoodie and stay covered, even in the lift, when you want to slip out unnoticed."

"Got it," I said.

"Expect a lot of pressure from her. Our sources tell us that she's established at least a basic agreement with Geryon, which is probably why she's able to get into the cameras so easily."

"I need access to some police files. Can you help?"

"Not likely. The Poppy has been moved to another assignment. If she goes after anything related to Shanagh Grady or Geryon, she'll be in deep trouble."

"If things change, I'm looking for information on the Ulster Maritime Group and Dianne O'Leary."

"Noted. Our ride is almost done. Good luck to you, Sir."

Before the car dropped us at the next stop, he resumed his cell phone conversation, ignoring me entirely as we exited.

CHAPTER FIVE

Karen's apology was long on words, but short on details. It felt rehearsed and perhaps forced. A few well-timed glances from Mack confirmed my suspicions: she found it less than sincere. To her credit, though, she listened and empathized, maintaining a civil decorum throughout the evening.

Karen pulled me aside, asking to talk privately. "Is it all right if I stay in my room for another few nights?"

"Of course, if that's what you want."

"I don't think we really got anywhere tonight, other than avoiding another row."

"That's something, isn't it?"

"I suppose" she sighed, sitting down. "There's more."

She motioned for me to sit, and I did.

"There's something I need from you that I've not gotten

recently. Maybe you're not able to right now, maybe you never will be, but that doesn't stop me from hoping. Johnny, I need to know if there's any future for us. Ever since you caught a glimpse of Angela, your mind and your heart have been elsewhere. I know it hurts, she was my friend, too, but what's done is done. She's gone; I can't make it any more plain or simple. I don't expect you to forget or get over things overnight, but you've not even started; you've made no effort at all." Her eyes settled on the still unopened package from the mortuary.

"I'm sorry," I said. "You're right, of course: I can't change what has happened. I guess I didn't realize how mentally ill-prepared I am to deal with it."

"The first step on any journey is often the most difficult. Open the package, we'll do it together."

I stared at it, silently.

"I'll fetch a knife and we'll cut the tape on the package."

"No, Karen. I'm not quite ready yet."

"Just read her wishes, nothing else. You don't have to do anything else." She stared at me, hopefully.

I shook my head. She tried several more times, unsuccessfully, before turning her attention to a stack of envelopes held together with a simple rubber band. They were the unsent letters Angela wrote me from prison. Like the package containing her ashes, I couldn't bring myself to read them.

She sighed. "Fair enough. Then read one of her letters. You haven't even removed the rubber band. Start with just one. Nothing else. We'll read it together if that will help."

I declined, politely. As before, she pressed. It was gentle and well-intended, but steadily growing more insistent. Finally, I reached the point where I could tolerate no more. A tear rolled down my cheek. "I'm sorry. I hear what you're saying, and it is probably wise advice, but

I just can't. I don't exactly know why, but I can't make myself do it."

"I understand," she said, wistfully. She rose, and kissed me gently on the forehead. "You have a good night, Johnny."

* * *

A gentle knock on my suite door was followed by Mack's voice. "You okay over here?"

"Yeah," I sighed, "how much of that did you hear?"

"I was being nosy, so I heard most of it. Sorry. I should mind my own business."

"No worries, Mack. Am I in the wrong here?"

"I don't think so. Grief doesn't follow a schedule. It isn't like you're sitting around drinking yourself into a coma on a nightly basis. You *do* need to move on, but it'll happen when it's meant to happen."

"I suppose you're right."

"As usual," she added, winking. "I managed to make it through most of my research from the library. A few interesting bits here and there, but nothing concrete."

"Is Finnegan right? Are we looking at a different Dianne O'Leary?"

"Uncertain," Mack answered. "I'm going to have to dig deeper."

"What does your intuition tell you?"

"That there's something fishy going on."

* * *

I was tired, but couldn't quiet my mind. Several attempts at sleeping resulting in wide-eyed staring at the ceiling. Finally, I gave up trying, and turned my focus to the papers passed to me earlier by my contact. I had opened the envelope before Karen's arrival, but hadn't found an opportunity to do more than flop them carelessly on my desk.

The hodge-podge of documents made little sense upon initial examination. One document was an organizational chart, another resembled a portion of a spreadsheet. Others looked to have been hastily scanned or even photographed with a cell phone; many were hard to read.

As I perused the documents, I found additional organizational charts. Closer examination revealed their ages, allowing me to arrange them in chronological order. Their common thread was obvious: Jim Finnegan. His name appeared in each chart.

During his time as a police officer, Jim had not stayed solely within one department. As I studied his career from afar, another name started to become obvious: *William Hayes.*

The oldest chart, dating back to the days of the predecessor to the Police Service of Northern Ireland, the Royal Ulster Constabulary, covered the time period of the Strabane bombing. Hayes was Finnegan's superior officer, ranking two levels above. This pattern held throughout all the charts. Wherever Finnegan went, there was Hayes, always two steps up in the food chain.

I flipped through the remaining pages, hoping to find more on William Hayes. I was destined for disappointment. His name appeared on only one page, a barely legible document that looked to be a hurried photograph of a poor quality photocopy. The page was skewed, and the entire lower half was a mass of solid blank ink.

It didn't take me long to realize that the only legible portion of the document contained everything that I needed to know:

William Hayes (born 16 December 1954, Portadown, Armagh)

74-0102* 97-0048*

The image showed part of a Constabulary Indexed Reference document. They were rarely seen, and I only knew one person who could help me: Tom Preston, the semi-retired Police Service anti-terrorism expert.

Dammit.

* * *

The late night caused me to sleep well past my normal hour. I showered and dressed quickly, breakfast suddenly at the top of my agenda. I emerged to find the suite door open.

"Good morning, sleeping beauty," Mack said, rolling her eyes.

"Breakfast?" I grunted.

"I've already eaten. Some of us were up early, working. But, I could use some more coffee, now that you mention it."

I wasn't feeling adventurous, so we made our way to the hotel's restaurant, stopping by Karen's room to see if she cared to join us. We knocked several times, but got no answer. I was momentarily worried, until Mack reminded me that today was Karen's final cardiology appointment.

* * *

"I'm stuck between a rock and a hard place, Mack" I said, taking a bite of my black pudding. "My informant told me not to trust anyone, but I'm not sure they can get me what I need. On the other hand, I'm reasonably sure that Tom Preston would be able to help, but is he willing and can I trust him?"

"He helped before, although I don't think you two like each other very much," Mack said, sipping her third cup of coffee.

"We don't," I sighed, "and I'm not entirely sure his help was altogether altruistic. After all, it was his information that ultimately led to you discovering the truth about Angela. I have no idea how he might react when I ask him about a fellow police officer."

"Good point, especially since cops tend to look out for one another."

"I don't think I have much choice, Mack. Let's stop by and see how Karen's appointment went, then I'm going to find Preston."

* * *

The door to Karen's room was partially open, and the housekeeper's cart sat outside. I poked my head in. "Karen, are you back yet?"

An unfamiliar voice replied. "Sorry, sir, but the occupant of this room checked out."

"When?" I asked, frowning and shocked.

"I don't know, sir. I was given instructions to clean it, and get it ready for the next guest. You can speak to the front desk. Perhaps they can tell you more."

We made our way down to the front desk, only to learn that Karen had checked out early that morning. The young man working there was unwilling to tell us anything else. We both tried to call her cell phone, but we were directed immediately to voice mail.

"What are you going to do?" asked Mack.

I shrugged. "I'm going to do nothing."

"Nothing?" said Mack, frowning. "Who are you, and what have you done with John Costa?"

"I'm going to give her time and space, exactly as she counseled me to do for Angela."

The words sounded good, but Mack knew the truth. Hell, she could probably hear my stomach churning from across the room.

* * *

Mack caught me pacing, staring at my phone, looking out the window, and then repeating the ritual. "What are these?" she asked, holding up several of the documents from my informant.

"Oh — I've been meaning to ask you about these. They look like a spreadsheet or a ledger of some sort. I wondered if any of it makes any sense to you."

"Where did you get them?"

Mack's expression troubled me. "From an informant," I replied, hesitantly.

Without speaking a word, she placed the documents on the table, and quickly returned to her half of our suite. Moments later, she returned, laptop in hand. The silence that ensued was interrupted only by the clicking of her keyboard. It seemed to grow more intense by the moment.

"You might want to be sitting down when I tell you this," she said, her voice shaking.

"What is it, Mack? You look like you've seen a ghost."

"Is there any chance that Karen saw these?"

"I'm not sure. I had just opened them when she arrived. They were sitting on the table, so I suppose it's possible."

"Think, John; it's important."

"I really can't say. You're scaring me, Mack…"

"Did Karen see these?" She held up the pages resembling a ledger.

"They were on the top when I opened the envelope and unfolded the contents, so if she saw anything, she saw those pages." I was going to say more, but stopped when I noticed a tear rolling down Mack's cheek. "Tell me."

"If Karen saw these, and if they are real, it would explain why she checked out of her room and isn't answering her phone." Mack's voice was barely above a whisper, and included a noticeable quiver. "Give me a minute," she said. "God, please make me be wrong."

She returned to ferocious typing, faster than I ever thought possible with one hand. It felt like an eternity before she stopped. She looked up at me with distant eyes.

"You're not wrong, are you?" I whispered.

"I'm not," she answered, wiping away tears that threatened to become a torrent at any moment. "And I'm an idiot."

"You're anything but an idiot, Mack."

"I sure feel like one. Remember, how after Karen's father died in the car bomb in Thailand, allegations surfaced of financial improprieties within their charity?"

"Of course I do. You proved that the records were hacked, and prevented Karen from facing any legal issues. Too bad that in the eyes of the public, the damage was already done."

"Correct. Shanagh's hacker, Zira, was responsible for that. I had backups of the originals, or so I thought."

"I'm not sure I follow you, Mack."

"John," she said, fighting tears, "the files I restored were corrupt."

"And that means?"

"Someone hacked my private backups, files I had stored on personal devices that never were connected to a network. The only way to change these files would be to have access to the devices themselves, and to have exceptional computer skills. So we've got two problems. One is, there is one hell of a hacker out there."

"Zira?"

"I don't think so. He was better than I gave him credit for, but I seriously doubt this was within his capabilities."

"And the other problem?"

"According to these," she said, holding up the documents, "starting about two and a half years ago, about a million dollars vanished from the charity. In the time since then, another two have vanished."

"I'm really on the verge of getting lost here, Mack. So Zira hacked the charity to make it look like there was wrongdoing, you restored files that were hacked to make it look like there wasn't, and in reality, millions were missing?"

"Yeah. You've got it. What else did your informant give you?"

I handed her the remaining pages. She set aside most of them quickly, but three caught her attention. Her eyes flitted back and forth between multiple documents before she sighed deeply. "Here it is," she said, spreading out the documents. "It all makes sense now: deposits, withdrawals, transfers, some creative accounting, and the money ended up here."

Her finger pointed to an account number on the page. It would have been meaningless, except someone had circled it with an arrow pointing to the words:

`Probable Geryon Swiss account.`

CHAPTER SIX

"We've got to find Karen," I growled.

"Don't jump to conclusions," Mack pleaded. "I know what it looks like, but there is still the possibility…"

"Then why did she run?" I interrupted.

"Perhaps it was unrelated," Mack said, hesitantly.

"We stumble on records showing nearly three years of charity funds being systematically redirected to an account believed to be used by Geryon, and suddenly it's an emergency that I read Angela's letters and deal with her ashes? There are three, maybe four, people with the access necessary to purloin funds like that. One of them is dead, and one of them is you, Mack. Unless all this is an elaborate confession on your part, I don't think that is provocation for Karen's flight."

"No," Mack sighed, "no confession. I suppose I should do some checking on the charity's financial officer, just to be certain."

"Probably wouldn't hurt," I said, staring off into space, "but you're not going to find anything. We have our answer; we just don't want to admit it. God, I feel like an idiot." I pounded my fist into the desk forcefully enough to send an empty glass crashing to the floor.

"Keep a hold of your temper, John," Mack counseled. "You're going to burst a blood vessel or something. We don't know all of the facts yet. Maybe she's being blackmailed or something and she ran to protect us."

I unclenched my jaw, suddenly noticing the rush of heat in my face. "Maybe so, Mack, but this is just the latest in a series of odd and unpleasant coincidences that always center on the lovely and unfortunate Miss Boyle."

"If this is true…"

"Karen is looking at a lifetime of troubles."

* * *

Mack was deep into whatever she was working on, so I donned my hoodie and, finding a door near a loading zone at the back of the hotel, slipped out, quietly.

It had taken hours of pleading and a sizable sum of money to convince private detective Charlie Hannon to give me the address of Tom Preston. Even when he finally relented, he would only provide the general neighborhood. The rest was up to me. Finally, after scouring the general area and accumulating a substantial taxi bill in the process, I found what I was looking for.

At my request, the driver dropped me off a block away and around the corner from the building where the retired Police Service counter-terrorism expert lived. The once vacant storefront on the ground floor was occupied by an appliance parts and repair shop. I found the doorway and the stairs leading up to the second floor. Steeling myself against the high risk of rebuke, I opened the door and ascended.

My knocking was not answered, but a subtle creak in the

flooring told me someone was inside. I knocked again, then one final time with gusto. The door opened, and I found myself staring at the barrel of a 9mm handgun.

"Slowly now. Lose the hood," Preston ordered.

I complied, not realizing how effective the simple disguise had been.

"Eejit," he grunted, lowering his weapon. "I thought I was rid of you three years ago," he said, closing the door behind me.

"Believe me," I said, "if I thought there was another way, I'd keep you out of this."

"You're like one of those damned American fools, singing rebel songs in a bar in Boston, the whole time not really understanding what you're saying or doing. Ireland's problems should be left to the Irish."

"When I left here three years ago, I was perfectly happy to do exactly that. Shanagh Grady took it upon herself to make these problems find me. I'll not sit back idly while she kills my friends one by one."

"No," he sighed, "I suppose you won't. Tea?"

"Please," I answered, as he escorted me into his office.

The room looked much the same as it had three years prior, although the impressive array of computer equipment appeared more modern to my untrained eye.

"Now then," he said, handing me a warm cup of tea, "what can I do to be rid of you?"

I passed him a flash drive that contained scans of the organizational charts and the Constabulary Indexed Reference file. He plugged the device into one of his computers. The files appeared on his monitors moments later. He studied them silently, his expression unchanged. "If you're expecting me to rat out one of my own, you've come to the wrong man."

"My sources told me that there was another significant leak within the Police Service. I'm only trying to find the truth. I'd think that, by now, you would believe me when I say that. Angela Grady was sent to prison because of me."

His glare softened. "Interesting…" I remained silent as he typed. "There doesn't seem to be any record of William Hayes' reference file. Perhaps the two case files referenced on this document will help."

I sipped my tea nervously, looking for any change in expression as he typed. I noticed nothing.

"This case from 1974," he said, using his mouse to draw an imaginary circle around the 74-0102* entry, "looks to be related to reports of a loyalist attack in a small town in eastern County Tyrone. The lead investigator was James Augustine Finnegan." Preston raised his eyebrow. "Definitely one of his first cases. Hayes was the investigator of record; Jim's supervisor, so to speak. There doesn't look to be anything here, except the case was never solved." He started to say something else, then caught himself. "Maybe I was hasty on my assessment. It seems that Finnegan developed a promising lead and a witness who all but vanished. Odd, this…"

"What is it?"

"Hayes declined to pursue the matter, claiming the witness was shown to be unreliable. The thing that makes it squiffy is that there is no associated documentation showing mental instability, drug use, or any of the other normally disqualifying qualities. Perhaps someone within the Constabulary saw it fit to give Hayes a look, only there is no surviving record of it, other than your scanned document."

He resumed typing, stopping abruptly to stare at me.

"What is it, Preston?"

"The document from early in 1997, 97-0048, hints that Finnegan had established a contact within what we now know to be Shanagh Grady's organization. He had an informant warning him of a major upcoming bombing somewhere in the west."

"Strabane," I muttered.

"Seems likely," Preston replied. "The reference is not specific, but it seems Hayes assigned a special investigator to look into the case."

"Finnegan's brother died in the Strabane bombing. Indications are that he was the actual target of the bomb. The property damage and civilian casualties were merely a bonus."

"There's nothing in here to cause me to conclude that Hayes' special investigator was Gregory Finnegan, but it is certainly within the realm of possibility. By 1997, Hayes had been promoted several times and *was* in charge of the division in which Gregory served."

"If Hayes is working for Shanagh..."

"Now, Costa, don't go jumping to that conclusion. Your informant told you there was a leak, but all of these files are related to *both* Jim Finnegan and William Hayes. You've only considered one possibility. From all indications, Hayes is a loyal and dedicated member of the Police Service."

"Then why did my informant specifically include an Indexed Reference document, and why can't you find the original?"

"I don't know the answer to your first question. The second one is far more troubling to me. What we don't know is if there is a matching Indexed Reference document for Finnegan."

"Is there any way to find out..."

"No. The internal investigation against Finnegan will have everything locked down. Speaking of which, you might find it interesting to discover that Jim's biggest advocate, and likely the reason he hasn't been sacked already, is none other than William Hayes."

* * *

One look at Mack told me all I needed to know.

"I just want to know why," she said, tears rolling down her face.

It was obvious that she had cried considerably while I was meeting Tom Preston. I couldn't offer much more than a silent embrace.

Collecting herself, she shared her findings. The conclusions were undeniable: Karen was systemically moving funds from the charity into an account linked to Geryon. "It gets worse," she whispered. A map of my neighborhood in the United States appeared on the screen of her computer. "You remember when the server in your bar was murdered, right?"

"Pamela Crenshaw. Of course I remember. "Someone made a halfhearted effort to frame you for the killing. There were calls traced to your cell phone, and long red hairs were found at the crime scene. The cellular records were altered to make it look like the calls went to you."

"Yes, so we thought."

"Wait, Mack. You're saying that the calls actually went to your phone?"

"I'm saying exactly that."

"The police searched your phone and found nothing."

"Of course. My phones all run a customized version of the operating system. By design, it doesn't log calls, texts, or data in the normal methods and places. But that isn't to say that I don't keep activity logs. When we discovered that the cellular records were compromised, and the guns didn't match, I let it go. But with the recent revelations, I decided to take another look. The calls went to my phone, and they went at a time when only one person, other than me, could possibly have access to it. Only Karen Boyle could have accessed the phone."

"And the hairs?"

"Zira compromised your security system. We all assumed that someone gained access to your house and collected the strands from my hairbrush. While it might have happened, it would have been a trivial matter for Karen to do so. I just want to know why…"

I held her as she cried.

* * *

A text message from Karen arrived late in the afternoon. "Want to join me?" I said, showing Mack the screen.

"No. I don't think so. I'm too upset right now to think rationally."

"I'm not sure I'm going to be much better…"

* * *

Karen Boyle sat alone on a bench at the Botanical Gardens. She glanced at me with lifeless eyes before returning her gaze to the ground. "I didn't think you'd come," she whispered.

"To be honest, I'm not entirely sure why I did. We know about the charity; we know about the phone calls. We know what you did. I guess we want to know why."

"Please believe me; I had the best of intentions, John."

"The road to ruin is paved with good intentions, Miss Boyle. People died. Mack could have gone to prison. I don't see any good intentions."

"It all started after Shanagh's trial and Angela's sentencing. You and Mack were debating Jim Finnegan about Connla Grady's mythical fortune. I, like Mack, was convinced that it existed."

"And you wanted it for yourself," I interrupted.

"No. I wanted it for my charity. That money was borne of evil, but perhaps I could do something good with it."

"But there were a thousand other ways! We could have formed more corporate partnerships; I could have given more."

"I know, but those things take time, and people are starving *now*. And," she said, hanging her head, "*I* wanted to be the one; not you, not my father. I'm always the damned second fiddle. So I made a deal with the devil."

"Geryon?"

"Yes. I knew of Geryon from the story of how you met Mack. I embezzled funds to entice Geryon to help find the treasure. We wanted to find it before anyone else even knew it really existed. We'd split it, and they could help channel my half of the funds to the charity through avenues that looked legitimate. Unfortunately, it proved impossible to find. Then Shanagh escaped and bollixed the entire lot. I knew you'd find it, so my only hope was to eavesdrop on enough information and beat you to the finish line. It might have worked, too, until my medical issues put me on the sidelines. I was flat on my back in the hospital while you claimed the prize."

I could offer no response beyond staring into space and shaking my head.

"I had no idea what I was getting into or what Geryon really was. Nobody was supposed to get hurt, and certainly not killed."

"The waitress that was murdered, Pamela Crenshaw, was working for Geryon, wasn't she?"

Karen nodded. "Her job was to eavesdrop on you and Mack while you were at the pub. Shanagh's people got wise to her, though, and killed her. Geryon responded by blowing up Shanagh's henchmen. I tried to stop it, I really did, but it all spiraled out of control."

"And now?"

"And now," she sighed, "I'm as good as dead. With Shanagh and Geryon uniting forces, I'm a liability. Shanagh hates me, has since long before this, you know. It wasn't a coincidence that she had my father killed first. It was as much of a message to me as it was to you. I can't go home. Once the authorities learn of this, I'm facing capital murder charges. So, like I said, as good as dead."

"Possibly, but you've got a better chance if you turn yourself in than with Shanagh and Geryon. A good lawyer might be able to save your life in turn for evidence or testimony. I can give you some names."

She sat on the bench with her head in her hands. After a lengthy silence, she spoke. "After all I've done, you would still do that for me?"

"Yes, but that is all I'm prepared to do."

"Let me get a few things from my room, and then I'll go with you to surrender."

* * *

Her hotel was only a short walk from the Botanical Gardens. We rode the lift in silence, exiting into a narrow hallway. Several turns took us to her room.

She inserted her card into the lock and opened the door. I followed. A few steps into the room, a man emerged from the darkness and grabbed Karen. I tried to react to her muffled screams, but a sudden, intense pain shot through my neck and shoulder. The room spun briefly, and then went dark.

CHAPTER SEVEN

When consciousness returned, I found myself staring up at the ceiling of the darkened hotel room. My neck and shoulder hurt, and my head pounded with each beat of my heart. It took a while for my eyes to find their ability to focus, and even longer for me to summon the will to move. I fought my way to my side, then reluctantly into a crawling position. A brief attempt to stand was met by intense dizziness, and I quickly retreated to all fours.

After regrouping, a second attempt got me into a seated position on the side of the bed. The clock read 3:30 AM, proof that I had been unconscious for many hours. I fumbled to find my cell phone. A string of text messages from Mack asked about my health and whereabouts. They became more frequent and urgent as time passed.

I fumbled around for a moment, but was finally able to successfully dial Jim Finnegan.

"Costa, you damned eejit. Where the hell are you?"

"I'm in Karen's hotel room. When I got here, someone grabbed

Karen. Before I could do anything else, somebody behind me knocked me silly."

"Now listen to me, Johnny, and you listen good. You get back to your hotel room, and whatever you do, you keep your damned mouth shut. There's been some developments, and I'm doing my best to work on things behind the scenes. Do you follow me?"

"Yes," I rasped.

Dammit. I didn't like the sound of things.

* * *

Developments proved to be a gross understatement, as I entered my room to find half a dozen police officers awaiting. Mack, looking troubled, rose from her chair and ran over to embrace me.

"You had me worried sick!"

"And you called in half the damned Police Service to hunt for me?"

"We are," an unfamiliar voice interjected, "quite interested in your whereabouts this evening, as well as those of Miss MacDonald. She claims to have spent the entire evening in her room, but she has nobody to corroborate her story."

"Exactly who the hell are you?" I growled to the man.

"William Hayes," came the answer, and with it the likely reason Finnegan insisted that I keep my mouth shut. And so I did, nodding and offering nothing else.

Hayes continued. "Karen Boyle was found about two hours ago, dead, hanging by her neck from a footbridge across the Lagan. A worker, staying late at a nearby office complex recalls a man and a woman, matching your general descriptions, rushing to a vehicle in the nearby car park and driving away. Nothing was made of it at the time, but when the body was discovered a bit later, it was reported. I find it very interesting, indeed, that neither of you can account for your whereabouts. Furthermore, the hotel staff have reported that you and Miss Boyle had a row a few short days ago, and that she moved out."

I sighed, a sick feeling building in my stomach, and tossed my jacket onto a nearby chair while emptying the contents of my pockets onto my desk. I grabbed the pen from my shirt pocket and tucked it into a jar containing several other pens.

"Now, I'll ask again," roared Hayes, "where were you two tonight? I will be forced to take you both into custody on suspicion of murder if you can't produce something to dissuade me!"

"You'll do nothing of the sort!" A familiar voice surprised all of us. Morton Molloy, the silver-haired solicitor I hired to defend Angela Grady, entered the fray with confidence.

An immediate and angry confrontation broke out between my solicitor and Hayes and raged for several minutes before calmer heads prevailed. "We've come to an accord," said Molloy, his voice barely above a whisper. "You both will surrender your passports, and agree to check in with the Police Service before traveling outside of Belfast. In turn, you will be spared a trip to Police headquarters and a night in jail. You also agree to produce a statement when the shock of losing a close friend has passed. Deal?"

I looked a Mack who nodded to me. "Deal," I said. "Now get these people out of my room," I growled, my eyes never leaving William Hayes.

* * *

"How did you know, Morton? Did Finnegan call you?"

"Actually, Tom Preston rang me, then I rang Finnegan. I hope you have something that can keep the Police Service at bay. Hayes seems to have it in for you, my friend."

"Of course he does, and that's why I wouldn't tell him anything.

I think there's a chance that he's in league with Shanagh Grady, and I'm working on proving it. The fact that Preston called you tells me there's some fire to go with the smoke. If Hayes has somehow gotten wind of it, nothing better to shut me up than locking me away."

"Or an unfortunate accident," said Mack. "What the hell happened to your neck?"

"Someone knocked me out while I was with Karen."

"Let me get a picture of that before you put any ice on it," Molloy interjected. "Mack, I need something for scale. A bank note would be fine."

They spent the next few minutes examining and discussing my wound. They even summoned the hotel's night manager to sign a statement attesting to the veracity of the pictures and measurements. Finally, I was allowed to take a pain killer and apply some ice. "What Hayes doesn't realize," I said, relaxing in a comfortable chair, "is that I have the whole sordid bit recorded."

"Your pen!" said Mack, positively beaming. "You listened to me!"

"Of course I did, Jillian MacDonald," I said, pretending to frown. "It's actually quite a clever thing. Records hours of audio and video, quite well, actually. Just," I said, sighing, "like you said."

"Of course," she said, retrieving the pen. "You always seem surprised when I'm right, in spite of the fact that it happens so often." She stuck her tongue out at me as she copied the contents to her computer. A second copy was provided to Molloy. "Are you up to watching it?"

"Yeah," I said, "but shouldn't we have a witness? Someone could claim we altered the video."

* * *

Tom Preston was unexpectedly cordial, in spite of our early morning call. "You have something to watch?"

"Yes," I said, and we're going to provide you with a copy. "I refused to talk to Hayes or show him this video."

"Probably wise," he said, offering no additional information.

The video started before I arrived at the Botanical Gardens. Much to the pleasure of Molloy, I captured images of a storefront that showed the date and time. Karen's confession followed. Mack remained stoic, but I could tell her heart was broken.

The section that followed was worse. The camera captured a man grab Karen, exactly as I had reported. After being struck, I landed in a direction that obscured the camera's view, but not its audio recording. The sounds of a brief scuffle ensued followed by silence.

"I think I broke her neck," a man with a heavy accent said. "Damn. I think the plan was for her to suffer a bit."

"Let's take her to the bridge anyway, like nothing happened," another man replied. "Dead is dead, what does it matter? Go get the laundry cart; I'll keep an eye on things here."

The sound of a door opening and closing followed. Then the camera started to show an image again. The man dragged me into the main portion of Karen's hotel room. To make it easier, he rolled me over onto my back, and in so doing, exposed his face to the pen's secret camera.

The door opened again, and the second man hovered over me. "How about I finish this one, too. Two for the price of one, so to speak."

"No," said the first man, emphatically. "The boss lady wants him alive. Why, after all the trouble he's caused her, I don't know."

"Poor bastard," the second man said, staring down at me. "Be easier for him if I took care of things now."

"Maybe, but then I'd have to kill you, and frankly, mate, I'm not in the mood to deal with three bodies all by myself. Get the woman loaded and let's get out of here, exactly as planned."

The room went dark, briefly interrupted by light from the hallway as the men exited. Mack fast-forwarded through hours of utterly boring video, until the camera captured my slow and painful return to consciousness. It wasn't nearly as painful as the aching in my heart. From the expression on her face, I could tell that Mack was in the same miserable place.

* * *

"Not that I had any doubts," said Molloy, "but this recording cements your innocence."

"Agreed," added Preston. "It also helps us establish time of death, if what the killer said is true. Plus, we have recordings and images of the real killers. I'd bet money that they've enjoyed the hospitality of Her Majesty's Prison Service in the past. It should be relatively easy to find them. I'll work on that. I'll work on the audio track, too. Perhaps there are more secrets lurking within that weren't audible to us."

"Morton," I said, "I want the recording held back as long as possible. I want Hayes to think he's got the upper hand. If he's bad, he'll relay the situation to Shanagh, and we can use it in our favor."

"Fair enough," said Molloy. "Try to get some rest. You look like absolute hell."

* * *

Rest was not in my plans. News of Karen's murder hit the early morning newscasts and papers, and with it, our phones started ringing with messages of disbelief and condolences. We dealt with it politely for a few hours before shutting off our phones.

"I'm sorry, Mack. I guess I let my guard down."

She glanced up at me from what she was working on. "I'm sorry, too. I trusted her, and it put you in danger."

"That thought never occurred to me, Mack. I need to get something to eat. Care to join me?"

"Sure," she said, "but only if you promise to indulge me with something."

"What is it?"

"I'm not quite sure how to deal with all that's swirling around in my head, so I decided to do some work. We can't access the crime scene, but that isn't what I'm interested in."

"Go on…"

"Look," she said, pointing to the screen. "The entrance to the footbridge is surrounded by a tall hedge row. It is hard to tell exactly how tall, but it looks to be at least eight feet. And the angles are wrong."

"What do you mean?"

"Hayes claims to have a witness that described us driving away, but the layout of these buildings and the orientation of the hedgerow make it impossible to see the car park from the majority of the office complex windows. I need to see it in person, though, to know for certain."

"But what's the point, Mack?"

"Maybe we can figure out who the supposed witness is. Bring a roll of cash with you. We might need to buy some information."

"Sure, but I still don't see what good it will do us."

"Insurance, John. Insurance."

"I still don't get it, but let me shave and get ready."

"No. It will be better if you go as you are. You've been in the news a few times in recent months. The fact that you look like a bum makes it harder for people to recognize you. We don't need attention right now."

"Gee, thanks, Mack."

CHAPTER EIGHT

After lunch, which we enjoyed in a secluded alcove in the hotel's restaurant, we headed south. A short drive later took us near the crime scene. The walkway to the footbridge was blocked with crime scene tape, and guarded by a member of the Police Service. Fortunately, access to the car park remained open.

"That's good," I said, pointing to a sign indicating that office space was available to let. "We should be able to get a partial tour of the building just by pretending to be interested, even though I look like a bum."

Mack laughed, quietly. "Look at the entrance to the walkway. Even more obstructed than the computer maps indicated."

She was right. The hedgerow itself was only about four feet tall, but the line of trees and bushes behind was significantly taller. Unkempt undergrowth made visibility through the brush nearly impossible. "I count nine windows at the most that could have a view of the entrance to the walkway and still see the car park. If our witness is legitimate, we know where to look."

* * *

It didn't take long for Mack to convince the building manager to give us a tour.

"Excuse his rough appearance," she said, touching his arm lightly. "It is part of the whole genius thing, I guess. I used to fight it, but now that all the money is rolling in, I just go along with it." The man nodded, melting noticeably under the heat of Mack's charm.

"I'm interested, in particular," I said, "in my ability to access the facility after hours. Inspiration doesn't always follow the regimens of a traditional work day."

The manager explained the building's after-hours access procedures in detail, as well as an enthusiastic advertisement for their security system, complete with cameras. Mack took all of it in, asking questions she likely knew the answer to already. Eventually, she reached the manager's knowledge limit. He politely asked us to wait while he fetched the head of security.

"How do you want to play this?"

"What do you mean, Mack?"

"I can either pump him for enough information so that I can hack in later, or you can get out your roll of money."

"Let's try the money, first."

The manager returned with a sharply dressed man who he introduced as the chief of security. Mack engaged the man in technobabble until the poor manager announced, "please come get me when you're done with the discussion of technical details."

That was the opportunity I needed. "I always hear this and that about security systems, and every day I'm reading about another one getting compromised. A hundred quid says you can't tell me if anyone was in the building after midnight last night."

The security chief paused. Mack whispered something to him, and they resumed their conversation.

"Two hundred quid!" I paused as the security chief considered my offer. "Like I thought. Let's look somewhere else," I said, motioning for Mack to follow me. "Given the goings on outside, obviously, this isn't the type of neighborhood we want to be in."

We were almost out the door before the pressure became too much for him. "Fine," he said. "Two hundred quid?"

"Two hundred."

He escorted us into a small office. A few moments later, what we wanted popped up on a screen. "There," he said, "Ed from K & T Enterprises was here from 10PM until about 4AM."

"Not bad," I said, pretending to be impressed as I handed him the money. "Ed must be quite the night owl," I remarked.

"Actually, that is something else the system can tell us." He paused, and I understood what his silence was telling me. I peeled another hundred pounds and handed it to him. "In the four years of records since the system was first installed, this is the only time he's ever come in late."

Another hundred quid bought me Ed's full name and address, and a hundred more convinced him to forget the entire conversation.

* * *

"His shoes, Mack," I said, answering her unspoken question as we walked to the car park. "You're going to ask me how I knew that money would work."

"Now that you mention it…"

"His suit was nice, definitely purchased off the rack, but his shoes were a dead giveaway. Artificial, overly shiny, and obviously uncomfortable. Conclusion? They pay him poorly, but make him dress like he's well off; all designed to give us a false sense of confidence."

"Well, look at you!" she said, winking. "Do you have any more brilliant deductions?"

"I wouldn't be the least bit surprised to find that Ed either has significant debts or that he's gone missing in the last twelve hours or so."

She nodded, "I'm not going to take you up on either one of those bets. Something's still bothering me, though," she said as we climbed into our car.

"And that is?"

"Assuming for a moment their goal is to frame us for Karen's murder, why not trick us both into going to Karen's hotel, then leave us holding bloody knives or something? And why hang her body in public?"

"To send a message," I interrupted. "That much seems clear."

"I get it, but send a message to *who*, though? It isn't like Shanagh has been subtle or mysterious in sharing her murderous intent with us. I could see, perhaps, a message to Geryon, but if they've formed an alliance that theory doesn't hold water, either."

I rubbed my chin. "You've got a really good point, Mack."

"And why is William Hayes threatening to arrest us? Even without the recording, he's got questionable evidence at best."

"He's sizing us up, at least that's the impression I got this morning. But for what, I'm not exactly sure."

"From the sound of him this morning, matching *his and her* nooses comes to mind."

"Could be, or perhaps he's trying to see how easily we'll scare. Nothing quite like the threat of a murder charge, as they say, to get someone to back off."

"In our case, though, we've been looking in seventeen different directions. Which are we supposed to back off of?"

"Another good point, Mack."

* * *

Ed Cooley lived in a simple, modest flat not too far from the airport. Mack and I posed as John Baxter and Mackenzie Ramey, reporter and editor from a Cork-based internet news agency. Much to my surprise, he invited us in for tea.

"Thank you, Mister Cooley," I said, as he passed me a cup. "We're writing a story on the unpleasant discovery at the footbridge last night. We received an anonymous tip that someone working late might have seen something. We were only able to copy down a handful of names from the directory before security chased us away. Do you have any idea who might have been there working late?"

He nodded. "Oh yes, a most unpleasant event," he said, adjusting his thick glasses, and running his fingers through his gray hair. "Nothing like that has ever happened in our area before. It is usually quite a friendly spot, really." He yawned.

"A few others mentioned the same thing to me," I said, hoping he would remember the original question. "If you're tired, we can do this another time. No bother at all."

"Oh, no. I'm tired because I was the person working late. I was almost ready to turn in for the night when I got a call from our auditors asking that I look into an irregularity on our books first thing in the morning. I pride myself in accurate, fastidious books, Mister Baxter. I knew I couldn't sleep with such an accusation hanging over me, so I spent the better part of the night looking for the error. Naturally, I found nothing out of order."

"And your office has a view of the car park, then?"

"I got up to stretch my legs and rest my eyes a bit. These thick glasses are fine for bookkeeping, but I need a break now and then."

"I find as I age, I'm getting a bit nearsighted. Maybe I'll need something like your glasses soon."

"Oh, no. I'm farsighted. I only need these for seeing things nearby. Like I said, though, I was taking a break when I saw two people run out of the walkway and into the car park. They got into a car and zipped off. I didn't think much of it until the Police Service showed up and started asking questions."

"And did you get a good look at these people? I'll leave your name out of the article, of course, if you're worried about possible reprisals."

"I saw them quite well. Like I told the investigator, a tall, bald man and a slender, dark haired woman."

I made small talk to legitimize our interview, but I had the information I wanted. It was all I could do to hide the fact that my blood was boiling.

* * *

"Okay!" cried Mack, "I get that you're mad, but your driving is going to get us both killed. Take it easy!"

I took a deep breath and eased off the accelerator pedal. "Sorry, Mack. I'm so mad I could spit nails right now."

"Talk to me."

"Ed Cooley's description matches my informants perfectly. Dammit. I can't believe it. I've been set up!"

"How so?"

"They gave me this phone," I said, producing the special phone Adnan Jasik had provided. "The damn thing is probably tracking me, even though they told me it wouldn't. They told me to wear a hoodie, so I wouldn't be seen, and I end up unable to prove my whereabouts. They gave me the information on William Hayes, and now the crooked bastard is on me like a junkyard dog."

"And the information on Karen's charity, and she ends up getting murdered," Mack added, wistfully.

"I'm a damned idiot."

"I don't think so," said Mack, trying to make me feel better. "First things first. When we get back to the hotel, I'll check the phone, and you can stick your head in a bucket of ice or whatever else will bring your blood pressure back down to triple digits."

* * *

I had barely gotten situated when my phone rang. The day wasn't going to get any better.

"Good afternoon, Solicitor."

"Shanagh."

"My, you have such unfortunate luck with Irish girls, don't you?"

"If I'm as deadly as you say, why don't you come give me a kiss?"

She laughed. "No, Solicitor, you're not my type. I'm looking for a man with a future, not one staring at a murder conviction. What was it the judge said to me? How it was unfortunate that the United Kingdom had abolished the death penalty, because true justice would see me to the gallows. That's how I feel about you, Johnny. Too bad they won't stick a rope around your neck, or that little red tart of yours, either. But don't worry. I'll be here to dispense the final justice. Nothing has changed. In the mean time, though, you're still a useful member of our little family."

"I bet it still galls you, Shanagh. I can hear it in your voice."

"What is that, Solicitor?"

"How Connla planned to leave his entire empire to Alicia O'Leary instead of you. Murdering Karen didn't make it go away, did it?"

Within a few syllables of her reply, I knew I'd struck a nerve. "The whore tried to take what was rightfully mine. And her daughter? Well, that apple didn't fall far from the tree. But it all worked out in the end. I wonder if Karen understood as she hung there over the Lagan, her life draining away. I've heard it is truly a horrible way to die…"

I gathered my resolve and forced a laugh. "You're pathetic. The idiots you hired couldn't even carry out the simplest instructions."

"What do you mean?"

"I was still conscious when they killed Karen. They broke her neck right there in the hotel room, and then they laughed about how you'd never know the difference."

"I don't believe you, Solicitor."

"Suit yourself, but that's what happened. How many of your employees have failed you? That's usually a reflection of a poor boss, but in your case, I'd call it downright incompetence. No wonder Connla wanted Alicia O'Leary to lead his organization. Hell, he even wanted to give control to Angela, even though she was too young and inexperienced."

"Enough, John Costa! I gave you something to research, and I know you haven't done it yet. Do I need to send you another reminder of our arrangement?"

"No, Shanagh. I'll look into it first thing in the morning."

"You do that. I think you'll find it… illuminating…"

CHAPTER NINE

"The phone is clean," Mack announced. "No tracking, proper security measures; quite well done, really." I wanted to throw the damn thing against the wall, and she knew it. "I'm not giving this back to you if you're going to smash it," she said, frowning.

"I'm more mad at myself than anything else."

"You're too hard on yourself, John," she said, handing me the phone. "There's a message waiting for you."

Reluctantly, I read it.

```
Must meet.
Not involved.
Will call soon.
```

"Are you going to take their call and meet with them?"

"I don't know, Mack."

"They *have* given you intriguing bits of knowledge, that which we have been able to sort out," Mack said, reclining in her chair. "We know who's responsible for Karen's death, and neither of them are people you recognized."

"True, but who's to say the killers aren't working for my informants? Just because I didn't recognize them doesn't mean anything."

"They referred to their boss as a female, though."

"Mack, one of my informants is a woman."

She sighed, running her hands through her hair and massaging her temples. "That might not mean anything, either. I think you should meet with them, but take me with you this time."

"It might be dangerous, Mack, or they may want me to come alone."

"Getting up in the morning is dangerous, oh worried one, and maybe you should try playing by your own set of rules instead of someone else's."

* * *

My attempts at an afternoon nap felt less than successful. Between the copious amounts of coffee I had consumed and a busy mind, sleep was a fleeting visitor. Finally, I gave up.

"Mack, what the hell happened to your cast?"

"Today was the day for it to come off."

"You took it off yourself?"

"No. I went to the doctor, had everything checked, and it was ready. Damn, it feels good to have that cursed thing off!"

"You were there and back again? I didn't hear you leave."

"You wouldn't have heard an atomic bomb go off, oh

somnambulant one. I think you slept longer than you realized." She tilted her head toward the clock.

The growling in my stomach confirmed that my short, unsatisfactory nap had extended into the early evening hours. Before I could speak, the special phone rang. I answered, and heard a familiar voice on the end of the line.

"I'm taking a hell of a risk even making this call. Can you meet me tonight, same spot as before?"

"Why should I?"

"Look," she whispered, her voice betraying urgency, "do what you want, but we weren't involved. Will you be there?"

I glanced at Mack who nodded to me.

"We'll be there," I said. "You get us both, or you get nothing."

"Wait for my message, and be careful."

* * *

Not surprisingly, the phone did not chirp until well after midnight. We donned our hooded jackets. Mack left through a side entrance a few minutes before me. I hailed a cab and picked her up a few blocks away. The cab driver thought I was nuts when I asked him to take a circuitous route to my destination, but cash quickly tempered his objections. A bit more cash erased his memory of our trip altogether.

Silently, I retraced my previous steps, crossing the river and following the path left into the wooded portion of the trail. Even though the night was more clear and bright than my earlier visit, visibility was poor once we were under the canopy formed by the trees. We slowed our pace, looking and listening carefully.

As we rounded a curve, a voice to our left whispered, "Over here!"

I strained to see, unable to make out a shape, let alone a path to take. A flashlight, its light covered with a red gel, illuminated briefly showing us the direction to go. As I moved closer, I noticed that a narrow, nearly imperceptible, path extended into the woods.

A hand reached out to me. "Follow me," Kelly Hamilton whispered, as she extinguished her light.

I took Mack's hand, and pushed deeper into the trees. Eventually, we reached a tall, overgrown hedge. A gate creaked open, and closed behind us after we passed through it.

Kelly turned the light on again, revealing that we were in a small, old cemetery. The surrounding hedges made a suitable barricade, and its distance from the walking path assured privacy, or so I hoped.

"This isn't the least bit spooky," I quipped, removing my hood. "How the hell did you find this place?"

"I used to play in these woods as a kid," Kelly replied. "The paths and some of the lands are maintained by the government, but we're off onto private property now. This sad old place is so overgrown, you can't even find it from satellite images."

"Well, someone knows about it," Mack said, pointing to a cigarette butt.

"I'm sure a few local kids do. We always kept it a tightly guarded secret. Thank you for meeting with me."

"I wasn't going to, but Mack talked me into it."

"I'm glad she did," said Kelly. "We had nothing to do with Karen's murder."

"But it *was* you and Adnan that the witness saw, wasn't it?"

"Yes. We located two men thought to be working for Shanagh Grady, and followed them to the footbridge. We had no idea what they were really doing until it was too late. Here," she said, handing me a flash drive. "This is what we know about them."

"I had a visit from William Hayes. If my solicitor hadn't shown up, the bastard might have taken us to jail."

"Yes, I know. Hayes moved me to other cases as soon as Finnegan was suspended. Earlier this week, he transferred me to a different unit entirely. He tried to call it a promotion, but I know what it really is. He's getting me out of his hair, as the saying goes. He tried to cut off a lot of my access, too. Good thing he doesn't really understand how the systems work; he only managed to slow me down."

"Hayes strikes me as a dirty cop."

"Oh, he's dirty as sin, but nobody can ever prove anything. And the bastard manages to get himself in the right place at the right time to get transferred or promoted."

"Is Finnegan wise to him? Is that what got him suspended?"

"On the surface, Hayes supports Finnegan, but the truth of the matter is, the exact opposite is true. Our most senior leadership is on a kick to find and expose any corruption within our ranks. If Finnegan falls, Hayes would stand to benefit."

"How so?"

"I was nosing around in our personnel database the other day, one of those areas of the system where I'm not supposed to be. He applied for another position. If he can make Finnegan appear incompetent, it'll be another feather in his cap, as the saying goes. If he can show that Finnegan is corrupt, the job will be his, almost certainly. And here's the part that's really interesting: the job would put him in charge of guarding Connla's treasure, among other things."

"I thought…"

"No. The political types are still squabbling over the dispensation and equitable sharing of the funds, while 750 million quid worth of rocks sits in a vault."

"A vault that might soon be guarded by one of Shanagh's own. Brilliant."

"That's our theory, at least. It's going to be tough to prove, if not outright impossible, though. Hayes is good at covering his tracks, doubly so with Geryon involved."

"Still about money," I sighed.

"It's a reasonable conclusion. We have an entire task force dedicated to disrupting funding for such organizations. In the last few years we've made extensive progress, especially with funds flowing electronically. Cat and mouse, as the saying goes. They come up with a new technology or method to hide from us, we discover it and implement new counter measures, and then the process repeats itself."

"So something negotiable and tangible," I interjected, "like diamonds, would be ideal."

"Currency and precious metals, too," Kelly added.

"Is Shanagh trying to stoke up the fires that lead to the troubles? Public sentiment, for the most part, seems to be against her."

"Possible, but we think her main interests are in South America. If we're right, she's already got suppliers, shipping, and contacts all sorted. What she doesn't have is the necessary up-front cash."

"And that's the real reason she was so keen to collect Connla Grady's treasure, and perhaps why…"

Before I could continue, the voice of Adnan Jasik interrupted me. "Get the hell down, everyone! Turn off that damned torch!"

Kelly quickly extinguished the dim, red light. I was unaware that I was still holding Mack's good hand, but it turned out to be a fortuitous situation. Lights, likely from flashlights, appeared in the distance. Quickly, I pulled her down, taking cover behind one of the larger monuments in the center of the cemetery.

The lights moved closer, more of their narrow, strong beams penetrating the outer ring of shrubs. The light cast garish shadows from the numerous Celtic crosses adorning the markers. Suddenly, I heard a sound to my left. The lights followed the sound, leaving us in darkness. After a few moments of silence, I could hear the sound of people running.

We waited for a moment, and then Kelly grabbed my hand. "Follow me, you two," she whispered.

I was still clutching Mack's hand, so we quickly got to our feet, heading in the opposite direction from the commotion.

"I'll get you safely to the bridge," she whispered.

"What if he needs our help?" I replied.

"He won't."

We retraced out steps out of the cemetery and through the woods, Kelly Hamilton using only the faint, red light to illuminate our path. My jacket protected my arms from the branches that lashed out as we passed. Finally, we reached the road, and shortly thereafter, the bridge. "If you happen to run into anyone, make like lovers out for a stroll," Kelly whispered.

I nodded, pulling Mack close. The sound of gunshots in the distance quickly drew Kelly's attention.

"Go," I urged, "We'll be fine."

She sprinted away.

* * *

After crossing the bridge, Mack noticed the approaching police officers before I did. I nearly jumped out of my skin when she started giggling and nibbling at my earlobe. I had just enough time to compose myself before their flashlights illuminated us.

The police officers eyed us up and down before saying anything. "And just what brings you two out at such a late hour?"

Mack answered by giggling. I looked at her, then sheepishly at the officers. Their expression remained unchanged.

"There was a report of gunshots." They rattled off their names and assigned station before instructing us that we were being searched for weapons, and to remove our jackets.

We complied, silently. Our garments were returned a short time later.

"What brings you here from Cork, Mister Baxter?"

The officer had discovered our bogus business cards in my jacket pocket. It was the closest form of identification either of us was carrying. I made no effort to correct his error.

"We were sent to report on the recent legislative impasses," I replied, "but then that woman was found hanging from the bridge, and since we were in town anyway, it seemed reasonable to stick around for a bit and file a few reports."

"And if I were to ring up your employer, they would be able to vouch for all of this?"

"Naturally," I answered, "although…"

"Yes?"

"It would be better for us if you didn't mention that you discovered us together, late at night, in a secluded area. Our employer has strict rules about fraternization."

"We have certain rules that govern behaviors in public places as well, Mister Baxter, but we have more important things to do right now. Next time, get a damned room."

"Got it."

"Did either of you hear or see anything suspicious?"

Mack giggled, and I shook my head.

* * *

We didn't speak until returning to the hotel room.

"Jesus!" gasped Mack. "I'm glad they bought my bimbo act, because if they'd ask me to speak, we'd be sitting in a jail cell right now. There's no way I can pass for someone from Cork."

"You could have said you weren't born there, just work there," I said, "and I found your bimbo act to be quite believable."

Her eyes flared.

"Merely credit to your ability as an actor," I stammered, fearing for my life.

"Nice try," she said, smirking. "I must admit, it takes some nerve to lie convincingly to the police. I didn't think you had it in you."

"It wasn't really a lie, Mack."

"Oh, yes it was!"

"No. I merely opted not to correct the poor man's mistaken assumptions. He never really asked for my name, if you recall. I think you forget at times that I really am a lawyer. All kidding aside, though, I didn't want it getting back to Hayes that we were out and about in the vicinity of a shooting."

"Probably a wise choice. Who do you think it was?"

"Hell, I don't know. Take a guess! Rogue cops working for Hayes? Shanagh's thugs? Local drug gang? Maybe the whole damn thing was staged so we'd trust our informants. I'm too tired to think straight right now. Care to join me for a whiskey?"

"Sure. One thing we heard tonight makes sense to me."

"And that is?" I asked, filling Mack's glass, then mine.

"If Shanagh needs funds, it would explain why she's hasn't made a serious attempt on your life yet. She wants your money."

"You're right, Mack. After she escaped, she told me she was going to kill my friends one at a time *and* ruin me." I took a deep drink from my glass. "She's done a pretty good job, so far."

CHAPTER TEN

"Mack, I honestly don't know how you do it! Two glasses of whiskey, and I was done. You stayed up the whole night!"

She looked up at me, smiling coyly. "When you're good, you're good," she answered. "The real secret is caffeine and an incessant streak of curiosity."

"Speaking of caffeine…"

"Room service delivered another pot of it not too long ago," she said, motioning toward a nearby table. "Help yourself."

I poured a cup, and turned on the local news. There was no mention of anything that resembled the events of the prior evening. "Looks like our little night of fun wasn't exciting enough to warrant coverage."

"Probably for the best," Mack said, her mind clearly elsewhere. "Take a look at this."

I peered over her shoulder at the computer screen. The article, which appeared in a local news source, was about eighteen months old.

`Local Business Branches Out`

The article went on to describe several international contracts recently secured by the Ulster Maritime Group.

"Of interest," said Mack, tapping her screen with her finger, "is this bit about South America. They secured a contract for dock operations and shipping rights, specifically for the delivery of humanitarian aid."

Her screen changed, switching to the map of a shoreline.

"The port in question isn't one of the larger ones," she narrated, zooming in. "It does, however, have deep waters and decent land transportation. Not to mention good access to here." She paused, her finger circling the turbulent South American nation alluded to by Kelly Hamilton.

"Humanitarian aid, my ass! Shanagh's version involves guns and bombs. Dammit. She's got it all lined up: shipping, docks, land transport, and likely secure routes across the border. She just needs the money… What is it, Mack?" The look on her face told me there was more.

"Here's an article on the Greek man who owns the shipping company; how they've built their business slowly and carefully. Nothing but jargon really; he's saying all the right, expected things."

I couldn't help but stare at the man's picture. "This man married Alicia O'Leary's sister, Karen's Aunt? He's younger than me! Either that, or he's discovered the fountain of youth."

"Or Dianne O'Leary was quite the cougar before she died," quipped Mack.

"This is making my head hurt, Mack. I'm sorry, I'm terribly confused."

"Well, this isn't going to make it any better," she said, handing me a picture.

The image, blurry as it was, stunned me. "Is this Karen?"

"No. I thought that for a moment, too. That's Dianne O'Leary. The resemblance is striking, isn't it?"

"To say the least. But I'm still confused. Finnegan was adamant that the O'Leary name was merely a coincidence. If he'd ever seen this picture, it would remove all doubt."

"I doubt that he, or much of anyone else, has seen this picture."

"Okay, Mack," I said, sipping another cup of coffee, "spill it."

"I hope you're not too upset with me…"

"Mack!"

"Honestly, John, I just did it to advance the case."

"Mack!!"

"Okay! Your informants sent several messages and documents while you were sleeping. I heard the phone chirp, and, well…"

"Shame on you! Remind me to make you stand in the corner later!"

"Promises, promises!"

"Wait a minute… I had a password on that phone."

"Angela's birthday, rearranged in the way it is usually written over here. Not exactly difficult to guess. You should be less predictable in your choices. I hope you're not using a password like that anywhere else."

"I'm not, Mack. I'm sorry," I sighed, "I really need to let go, don't I?"

She rested her hand gently on my shoulder. "Like I've said before, you're not on a schedule."

"I know she wasn't a good person; I know she used me, but I miss her. I liked being with her; her energy, or whatever it was. It felt good." I caught myself before allowing any tears to escape. "Maybe I can't get closure because of my own inflated ego."

"What do you mean?"

"Mack, when I was a criminal defense lawyer, I represented people, horrible people, who I knew, deep in my heart, were guilty. They lied through their teeth, and I got them acquitted. My gut would churn, but I did it anyway. For some reason, with Angela Grady, it was different. I knew some, hell, most, of the things she was telling us were lies, and I still couldn't convince myself she was a monster. Still can't. Could be my ego won't allow me to admit that my sixth sense has a blind spot when it came to her."

"Or you were marked by consummate experts. She *did* admit that they researched you. You need to allow yourself to be human, John."

"Perhaps," I sighed. "Well, enough feeling sorry for myself. Are you *sure* the woman in the picture isn't Karen?"

"I'm sure for several reasons. First, I can absolutely vouch for Karen Boyle's whereabouts when this picture was taken. Secondly, the woman in this picture is at least six inches taller." I must've looked puzzled, because Mack launched into a lengthy explanation of photogrammetry, and how she determined the mystery woman's height.

"Uncle! You've made your point, Mack," I said, glassy-eyed. "Has the photo been altered?"

I regretted my question immediately, because an equally lengthy and complicated dissertation followed on the authenticity of the image. "Everything within the image is internally consistent. I could be wrong, for the first time, but I think it is genuine," she concluded. Another image appeared on her computer screen. "This is Karen's aunt, Dianne O'Leary, the one that was killed in the car accident."

"I see the family resemblance, but they don't…" The image of Karen's aunt vanished and was replaced with another picture. "This picture is a much better match. Who is it?"

"Karen's mother," said Mack. "It was taken when she was roughly the same age as our mystery woman."

"The resemblance is too good to be a coincidence."

"Unfortunately, unless Alicia O'Leary discovered the fountain of youth, and has been faking early-onset Alzheimer's disease, it doesn't really tell us anything."

"But we can look for births around the right time period."

"Already did. There's no record that Alicia O'Leary had any other children."

"And Alicia's sister?"

"Same. She was single, and died childless."

I sighed. "Mack, when do you think our mystery woman was born?"

"I concentrated my search on the mid to late 1970's. When I didn't find anything, I expanded it a bit."

"Did you check records in the Republic of Ireland?"

"No, just in Northern Ireland. I can check there if you'd like. I don't have as many sources there, especially now that Finnegan is out of the picture. Not that I can't do it, mind you. It might take a bit longer."

"Jillian MacDonald! Are you wilting under the weight of the challenge?"

"Hardly, but it is a bit like looking for a needle in a haystack."

"If it helps, start with County Westmeath and branch out from there."

"Okay, but I'm not sure what it will get us. Both the O'Leary family and the Boyles have been in Ulster for hundreds of years."

"I know it, Mack. Just bear with me. I'm playing a hunch.

Mack quietly retreated to her side of the suite, closing the door behind her. She wanted to work in peace and quiet, and I would respect her wishes. I, on the other hand, had no plans for a quiet afternoon. Poking the bear was the order of business.

* * *

The port of Belfast was bustling. Container and tanker ships were docked for loading, and a large oil-drilling rig from the North Atlantic was in for repairs. There were plenty of places in and around the docks I wasn't supposed to be, and in spite of the array of security cameras and signs, I went anyway.

I worked my way slowly out one of the fingers of land that extended into the harbor. Each time I saw cars parked near a warehouse or office trailer, I got out and pitched the same story: I was John Costa representing the Boyles' charity, and I was looking for the Ulster Maritime Group in hopes of arranging a humanitarian shipment of food to South America.

Mostly, my enquiries were met with shrugs and confusion. A few times, I was chased away brusquely, but most encounters were friendly, although fruitless.

My travels took me as far out on the small peninsula as I could before the road was blocked by a Harbour Police vehicle. Acting like I knew what I was doing, I turned into the nearest parking lot, and strode purposefully toward a small office building attached to one of the larger warehouses. Glancing out of the side of my eye, I could see that I had garnered the attention of the Harbour Police. One of them watched me as I walked, making a call on his radio. Unfazed, I continued to the door, offering my business card to the security officer.

After a brief wait, a man came out to speak with me.

"Mister Costa," he said, extending his hand, "I'm Brett Johnston, the shift manager. How can I help?"

I handed him my card. "I'm looking for the Ulster Maritime Group, but nobody around here seems to know where their operation is."

"Did you try their headquarters?"

"The corporate headquarters is nowhere near the water, strangely enough, and I expect they'll tell me what I want to hear. I'm looking to deliver a significant amount of humanitarian aid to South America, and I want to make sure the company I get to facilitate the operation is truly capable of it. The only way to know that for certain is to see things in operation."

"If I may ask, why Ulster Maritime, in particular? There are at least half a dozen companies that can handle what you're asking."

I showed him the article. "I'm not really experienced in this area, Mister Johnston. This article mentioned they did charitable work, so I set out to find them."

"You're the poor fellow that was mixed up with the Grady gals, aren't you?"

Dammit. I was hoping he wouldn't make the connection. "Yes, that was me."

"Ah! I've got it now. Wasn't there something in the news about a murder recently? My, but you've had a tough go of it lately, lad!"

"Yes," I sighed. "The woman that was murdered ran the charity I represent. There were false accusations of impropriety, so donations have all but dried up. I'm arranging one final shipment of food and medical supplies in her memory. I think she would like that."

"Do you have a spare minute?"

"Certainly."

"You'll need to talk to people at our main office, but I can give you a quick tour and show you my company's capabilities."

* * *

The tour proved to be mostly a sales pitch, but it was interesting nevertheless. Once out of the earshot of the other offices, Brett Johnston was far less reserved in his comments on Ulster Maritime.

"They're little more than a holding company, Mister Costa," he bristled. "They have some fancy term for it, *Services Aggregator*, or something like that, but it means the same thing. They farm their services out, mark everything up, and that's how they make their money."

"Doesn't exactly sound like a sustainable model unless they can get the services at a discounted rate."

"They hire a fair bit of off-union labor, and some of it is questionable, if you know what I mean."

"Then how do they stay in business?"

"Not entirely certain, to be honest with you. Rumor has it, though, that they have some special deals with customs."

"So what you're telling me is that if I contract with them to move my goods, the actual work could be performed by almost any of the firms in the port."

"More or less, although I'm told they do have a small warehouse and operations center on the north side of the harbor. I have no call to be over there, so I could be completely wrong."

* * *

The information from Brett Johnston seemed consistent with the Ulster Maritime Group being part of Shanagh's organization, and only strengthened my desire to find their base of operation. As I walked to my car, I made a quick plan to search the northern side of the harbor. With numerous businesses and buildings, it could easily take several days to complete.

The parking lot had emptied significantly while I was talking with Brett Johnston. Apparently, the shifts had changed, and the arriving shift was smaller. Most of the cars were parked near the office entrance. My car waited alone at the far end of the lot.

As I approached my car, I sensed that something was out of place. As I neared, I realized what it was. A small bit of my seat belt was caught in the door. Barely noticeable, it would have been easy to miss. My pace slowed as I replayed my exit from the vehicle. Convinced that I could not possibly have left the door in such a state, I returned my keys to my pocket and turned around to run back to the office.

Before I could take more than a few steps, a Harbour Police van came tearing around the corner. The back hatch opened and an officer screamed to me, "Costa! Get in!"

I dove into the back, grabbing for anything I could to keep from sliding out of the vehicle as it accelerated. We barely made it out of the parking lot before our vehicle was rocked from the explosion that destroyed my car.

CHAPTER ELEVEN

"How did you know?" I'm sure my voice was shaking, but I didn't have the time to care about my pride.

"We're friends of Jim Finnegan," one of the officers answered. "We've been trying to keep an eye on you for the past few weeks. It hasn't always been easy. Today we got lucky. Barry here," he said, nodding toward an officer dressed in the uniform of the Harbour Police, "happened to notice someone near your car while you weren't watching it."

"Thank you," I said, shaking the officer's hand.

"This place is going to get crazy in about five minutes. Did you see anything or anyone out of the ordinary? Anyone lurking about?"

"No. Just a member of the Harbour Police parked at the end of the road. I assumed it was to prevent traffic into an area where I wasn't supposed to be."

"When was this?"

"About an hour and a half ago, give or take. I noticed him on my way into the offices, but not on the way out."

"Interesting…" said the Harbour Police officer, looking at the screen of his tablet computer. "There was no call for this road to be blocked, and none of our on-duty officers were supposed to be in the area at the time. I'll have to take a look at the recordings from the security cameras for this zone."

"They were parked over there," I said, pointing to the area in question. "Everything looked official, at least to me, but I was more interested in avoiding them than I was in anything else."

We drove down a narrow passage between two warehouses. "Look," said one of the officers, "for any number of reasons, it would be better if we weren't here when the circus begins. Finnegan will be in touch with you, likely this evening. We'll do our best to keep an eye on you, but try to be safe and stay out of trouble."

The vehicle stopped and the men exited, leaving me alone with the Harbour Police officer. He pressed the accelerator and we sped back to the scene of the explosion.

* * *

Within moments, the parking lot went from being abandoned to teeming with activity. The bomb squad arrived first. Fire trucks and an ambulance lurked in the periphery while the Police Service moved in.

A tracked robot approached what was left of my car. It lingered a while, moving around the vehicle and changing the positions of its cameras to afford its operator a better look. Once satisfied, armored men approached slowly, moving deliberately through an inspection. When they were satisfied that all combustible material had been consumed, a fire truck soaked the smoldering carcass with foam.

A cursory examination from a medic was followed by a relentless and repetitive series of questions from the Police Service. I offered only minimal information in response. Finally, a detective arrived. I did not recognize the man, but he seemed to know quite a bit about me. His line of questioning quickly became accusatory and confrontational. My refusal to offer anything beyond the simplest, superficial answers infuriated him. As tempers flared and progress stalled, an argument broke out between the responding medics and the Police Service. They wanted to take me to the hospital for an examination, the Police Service wanted to ask more questions. I broke the stalemate by insisting on medical attention.

The detective fumed as they wheeled me to the waiting ambulance. I kept my eyes on him the entire time, my wry smile likely adding to his skyrocketing blood pressure. As the doors closed, I widened my smile and flipped him off. The ambulance roared away before I could enjoy his reaction.

* * *

"Sir!" the attendant cried, "you're not to use your cellular phone."

"I don't care. Charge me extra for the ride, write me a ticket, do whatever, but I'm making a call. I need to warn my assistant."

"Sir," he said, trying to calm me, "I know you're upset that your car caught on fire, but you can make as many calls as you need once you're at the hospital. Not now, though. Your phone might interfere with our equipment."

"A vehicle fire? Is that what you think happened?"

"That's what we were told. Isn't that what happened?"

"No. Someone packed some explosives in my vehicle. Now, are we going to have a problem if I make a call?"

He shook his head.

* * *

"Mack, listen carefully."

"What the hell is going on? You sound shaken."

"Someone put a bomb in my car."

"Oh my God, John! Are you okay?"

"Yeah. I got lucky and noticed it in time to get away. They're taking me to the hospital as a precaution, but I'm all in one piece."

I could hear the sound of the television in the background. "The news is saying a car caught on fire at the harbor, and the gas tank exploded."

"Interesting spin. Probably for the best, though. Look, the reason I called…"

"Yes?"

"Two things. See if you can get in touch with Jim. We need to move to someplace less vulnerable than the hotel. And Mack, for God's sake, keep your eyes open and get the hell out of there if anything looks or feels out of the ordinary."

"Of course."

"Secondly, see if you can find anything on a Police Service detective named Michael Lonergan. I don't think I've seen him before, but something about his name is familiar. He seemed much more interested in what I was doing around the harbor than who might have wanted me dead. He got confrontational quickly, too, which is why I opted for a trip to the hospital instead of sticking around."

"I'll see what I can find. Hang on, I think someone is knocking at the door to my side of the suite."

"Be careful, Mack."

"Of course."

Had I not been strapped to the ambulance gurney, I would have been pacing. The wait seemed eternal. Finally, she returned to the phone.

"There are two of them," she whispered, "dressed up as police officers. Their shoes are wrong, though. I don't think they're real police!"

I heard the sound of a door gently closing.

"John! I think they're the two men you captured on your video recorder. They killed Karen Boyle!"

"Call 999 Mack, right now, and get the hell out of there if you can!"

"Nowhere to go. I'm going to have to try to barricade myself in your side of the suite. I'm getting off the line to call for help."

In a panic, I screamed to the medic, "where the hell are you taking me?"

"Mater," he replied, "it is the closest."

"No! Take me to Belfast City Hospital. I insist."

"Sir, we're not a taxi service."

"Five hundred quid for each of you if you do it."

There was a brief moment of indecision before the driver made a hard left turn and accelerated. They didn't seem to notice or care that I had extricated myself from the gurney and was watching their progress.

As we neared the hotel, I noticed a police car parked outside.

"Drop me off here," I said, "then pull up to the hotel like someone called for you. And pray that you don't have anyone to transport."

A brief protest was quelled with the promise of another two hundred quid each.

* * *

The police officers were in the lobby talking to the manager. It only took a glance for me to conclude that something was wrong. I interrupted without regard for what they might have been talking about. "Follow me! It's an emergency," I cried.

They returned only puzzled expressions.

"My friend is in trouble," I implored. "Please follow!"

They nodded as I led them to the stairs.

"We received a call, but all the operator was able to make out was the name of the hotel," one of the officers said as we climbed the stairs.

"She was on the phone with me when two men pretending to be police knocked on our door."

"Why do you say pretending?"

"She said they were wearing the wrong shoes. Hurry, please!"

I realized that my adrenaline was carrying me up two stairs with each stride. The officers, younger and likely in better shape, were struggling to keep up. As we approached my floor, I slowed down, making sure that my steps were as quiet as possible.

"We're in the suite at the far end of the hall to the left as we exit the stairwell," I whispered. My room is the last one on the right; my assistant's is the next to last one. I told her to barricade herself in my room."

The police officers nodded. "Wait here," one of them instructed as they opened the door from the stairwell into the hallway.

"Hey! Stop!" one of the officers shouted, before taking off running. Ignoring my instructions to wait, I popped out of the doorway to see a man, dressed in police garb, disappear around a corner. One of the real officers was in pursuit.

The door to Mack's room was open. It took only a glance to realize that it had been forcibly opened.

"Go back to the stairwell and wait, Sir," the officer instructed. "I've got it from here."

He called for backup on his radio, and I retreated as he edged toward Mack's door. I only made it halfway to the stairwell door before the sound of gunshots rang out from the direction of my room. Instinctively, I pressed up against the nearest wall. The officer did the same, lingering just outside Mack's door. He drew his weapon and peeked into the room. Then he entered, disappearing from my view.

Moments later, I heard two more gunshots, and retreated to the safety of the stairwell.

I paused briefly, my heart racing, before realizing that I had no idea what the outcome of the shooting might be. If the real police officers had walked into a trap, the killer might come looking for me. I climbed the stairs, just over halfway to the next floor, and out of sight from the doorway.

There I waited, seemingly for an eternity. Then I heard footsteps approaching, and the stairwell door opened below me.

CHAPTER TWELVE

"Mister Costa?"

The police officer was all but a stranger, but I was damn glad to hear his voice.

"I have someone here who is eager to see you."

I descended the stairs and through the door into the hallway where I was immediately engulfed in a hug from Mack.

"Take it easy, Mack! You're either going to break my ribs or break your arm again. Not sure which."

"I don't care," she said, "both are better than what might have happened if you hadn't shown up when you did."

"Fortunate timing," I said. "What the hell happened? I heard shots."

"They tried my door first, then yours. I heard some voices in the hallway and thought maybe they'd been scared off, but then one of them broke the door into my side of the suite. I did what you said, though, and barricaded myself in your side. They must've been looking for something. It took quite a while before they even bothered checking the suite door. When they found it locked one of them tried to break it down. That didn't go so well, mostly because of all the stuff I piled in front of it. That is when the shooting started."

"You've had quite a day, Mister Costa," the officer said, interrupting us. "I'm going to need you and Miss MacDonald to stick around for a while."

"Of course," I said, nodding.

"I expect that we'll need to keep this area sealed off for a while since it is now a crime scene. Maybe the hotel can make arrangements to get you another room in the interim."

"When you're done with us, I'll check on that."

"That might be a while." The unpleasant and unwelcome voice of William Hayes startled me. "Mister Costa and I already know each other," he said, dismissing the officer.

I responded with silence, and a look of disdain.

"Seal off the area," he ordered. "Nobody goes in or out until I say so. And if these two try anything, put the cuffs on them, and take them in."

* * *

The hotel staff brought up a few chairs so we could sit while we waited for further developments. Hayes had disappeared into our suite leaving several officers in the hallway to watch us.

"Mack," I whispered, "I think the bastard is still trying to figure out what we know and what we have. Our computers, the documents the informant shared…" A sick feeling washed over me. "What if he impounds them?"

Mack, on the other hand, seemed unconcerned. "I scanned them days ago. It isn't like they were originals or anything. However, since they seem to be important to you, I have them in my purse's secret compartment."

"Your purse has a secret space?"

"It does now," she said, rolling her eyes. "A quick bit of improvisation with a sharp knife and some super glue. Hopefully, it will be sufficiently sneaky. Otherwise, our goose is cooked."

"And the computers?"

"Backed up, and in the process of erasing themselves as we speak. It looks like they're running a screen saver, but in reality it is a self-destruct utility I created."

"Can't forensic labs recover data from drives?"

"Yes, but we have several things working in our favor. First, my utility has been running for a while now, and the longer we wait, the less recoverable things will be. Secondly, all our data is encrypted. And lastly, I upgraded all our systems to solid state drives. There's no recoverable slack space on an SSD."

"I have no idea what that means."

"Well, if you'd let me finish, Sir Interrupts-a-lot, I'll explain it."

"If you'd get to the point, perhaps I wouldn't need to interrupt."

She sighed before launching into an explanation that promised to glaze my eyes over very quickly. "When traditional hard drives store data, they use technology akin to a tape recorder. The process is quite good, but due to the nature of magnetic flux, there are areas outside the normal boundaries of the recording track that also get the magnetic pattern of the data. This is called slack space, and labs are very good at recovering data from it. A solid state drive is like a gigantic flash drive; there's no magnetism involved, so no slack space."

"And, therefore, no way to recover files?"

"No way to recover files from slack space. There are other methods, but I know how to defeat them, and that's what my little utility is doing as we speak. The longer we wait, the better."

"I suppose they could make some noise about spoiling the evidence, but I expect Solicitor Molloy would crush any such notions fairly quickly."

Mack was about to say something when we were interrupted by the voice of William Hayes summoning us into the hotel room. Mack's side of the suite was thoroughly ransacked. Every drawer, even the smallest, had been emptied and thoroughly searched.

"They were looking for something," said Hayes, condescendingly. "Any idea what it might be?"

"Money, valuables, drugs; who knows?" My tone was intentionally dismissive, and I could tell it riled Hayes to the core.

"I've had just about enough of you and your attitude, Costa! In case you didn't realize, we were forced to shoot an armed intruder, and we're in pursuit of another. So how about we stop with the damned games?"

"How about you get off my damned back? You came in here and all but accused us of killing Karen Boyle. Now, someone breaks in here and tries to kill Mack, and you're acting like we threatened the damned Queen or something. What exactly did I do to you, anyway?"

"For starters, you managed to get one of our best detectives suspended right when we need him the most. He was trying to do things the right way, you know. Another day, and I could've worked it out, but you had to go talking him into that foolish trip to Athlone. The only reason the man's not totally on the brew now is because I'm putting my neck on the line vouching for him. Even that might not be enough."

His response wasn't entirely a surprise. He continued before I could reply.

"We've had some of our best analysts killed, no thanks to you. Your little stunt today could've gotten more people killed. It was sheer providence that the damned parking lot wasn't full! Not to mention we've got Police Service officers trying to keep you and Miss MacDonald safe. I'm tired of delivering bad news to the poor families of people who tried to help you."

"You sound like a damned politician trying to find a way to blame the victim."

"Why the hell do you think I sent Finnegan to talk to you four years ago when all this started? Why do you think I allowed him to share case details that would otherwise be confidential? It was to prevent you from getting involved; to prevent us from reaching where we are currently."

"And that is?"

"The time for your involvement to end. You and Miss MacDonald are safe. Go home; let the rest of this to us. But before you go, try to do the right thing. You're all about that, aren't you? Trying to do the right thing?"

"Exactly what do you have in mind?"

"Fall on your sword."

"Excuse me?"

"Testify before the board reviewing Finnegan's situation. Tell them how you coerced him, how you pushed him into bad decisions. Maybe you'll save the poor man's job."

"And then what?

"Get on a plane, and fly home."

"I can't do that."

"Why not?"

"Because you have our passports, jackass."

His jaw clenched. "Impound all the computers," he barked, "on suspicion that they contain evidence vital to an ongoing investigation. And take these idiots in for questioning."

* * *

The farce that followed lasted nearly two hours, and ended in a tense standoff. William Hayes was relentless in his questioning, and we were intractable in our responses. Finally, with our request for counsel, the stalemate ended.

Our suite was still part of an active investigation and would remain off-limits for several days. Under the watchful eye of the Police Service, we were allowed to retrieve our belongings. Our computer equipment had been seized, but otherwise, everything looked to be in order. We wasted no time tossing everything we owned into our luggage and every available bag.

"What now?" said Mack.

"I know a nice bed and breakfast in Antrim. Not quite as roomy or convenient, but it is quiet, safe, and they have great connectivity."

"That sounds wonderful, but are you sure they'll have rooms for us?"

"I am."

"Well! Aren't you the confident one?"

"A while back, I anticipated that we might need something like this. One of Charlie Hannon's cousins rented the rooms for me, at a premium rate, of course. The owner is getting an extra share not to care that the rooms aren't occupied, and his cousin is getting a cut because, well, he's related to Charlie. It runs in the family."

"Clever! Remind me to never underestimate you."

"I can't imagine you doing that, Mack." I sighed. "I confess to being a little bit worn out. I'm looking forward to a nice, comfortable bed."

"Me too, but can we make one stop on the way?"

"Sure. What do you need?"

"I need to buy a laptop so I can get back to work."

"Good point. I imagine it is going to take a while to recover all our stuff."

"Less than you think," she said, smiling coyly. "Do you like my earrings?" She pulled back her long, red hair to reveal large, flower-shaped earrings."

"They're quite nice, I guess, although I'm not sure exactly what they have to do with anything…"

"Do they make me ravishing and utterly irresistible?" She ran her hands through her hair, fluffing it.

"Ummm… I suppose so…"

"Oh, you're no fun!" she said, winking at me. She removed one of the earrings. "I had these made specially for me by a friend who works as a magician. Each one contains a secret compartment big enough to hold a microSD memory card. Today, I'm wearing a full 256 gigabytes of unbridled sex appeal."

"And our backups!"

"Yep, along with everything I need to take an off-the-shelf computer and make it useful in about 45 minutes. Now… what's that word you were looking for to describe me?"

"I'm pretty sure it was *awesome*, Mack, but I could be wrong..."

"Oh?"

"It might have been *amazing*, come to think of it."

* * *

My first message of the day was from Kelly Hamilton with instructions for an evening meeting. A similar text from Jim Finnegan arrived shortly thereafter.

"Finnegan wants us to meet tonight, Mack," I said, staring across the breakfast table at my exhausted compatriot. "Are you going to be able to last that long?"

"With coffee, all things are possible," she mumbled.

"You don't really believe in sleep, do you?"

"I can sleep when I'm dead. Besides, I had important work to do."

"I'm sure it could have waited, Mack. You've got to take care of yourself."

"Probably, but once I got started it was tough to stop," she said, sipping her coffee. "Especially since things started to get interesting."

"Do tell..."

"Your hunch was right, for a change."

"Which one?"

"About County Westmeath and so forth. It took some skillful digging, but I found that Alicia O'Leary is receiving her long-term care in Mullingar, of all places."

"Connla O'Grady's hometown. Hard to think of that as a coincidence, Mack."

"It gets better. The facility is private, and incredibly exclusive. Expensive, too." She wrote a number on a paper napkin and showed it to me.

"Wow!"

"That's the annual cost of this place."

"Did the O'Leary family have money? Neither Karen nor her father had the wherewithal to afford something like that, unless, of course, there was more monkey business with their charity than we ever imagined."

"No. Until you entered the scene, the charity was modest in size and scope, and, from all indications, completely legitimate."

"Gee, thanks Mack!"

"No! I didn't mean it like that!" She pretended to be upset. "But we both know someone who *could* afford Alicia O'Leary's long-term medical bills."

"And that is?"

"None other than Connla O'Grady," she said, pretending to pat herself on the back. "It took me all night, but I was able to trace an endowment through about five hops and into Connla's network."

"Connla saw to her long term care… The old bastard loved her, didn't he?"

"In more ways than you imagine…"

"Oh?"

"The relationship between Connla and the care facility pre-dated Alicia O'Leary's diagnosis by years. Either he knew before her family and her doctors, or…"

"He was using the facility for a different reason."

"Bingo, John! The funding arrangement started late in 1969. That puts it right around the time our mystery woman would have been born. It's just a hunch, but I called in a few favors. I should know more in a few days."

"Know what?"

"If there were orphaned children in and around Mullingar from that time period. I think the woman we know as Dianne O'Leary is the love child of Connla O'Grady and Alicia O'Leary."

"Damn… It's thin, Mack, but it would explain a few things. It also gives me an idea: I'm going to make a few calls, too. Maybe there's something in Ryan Boyle's personal possessions that will help."

CHAPTER THIRTEEN

"You want *what?*"

Jerry Keynes' reaction was exactly what I expected. The master information broker and long-time friend typically cited the impossibility of any given task prior to agreeing on a price. Once a fee was decided, previously insurmountable challenges suddenly became manageable.

"You heard me. I want you to find and collect anything from Ryan Boyle's personal items that are relevant to the 1969-1970 era. Anything, really, but I'm especially interested in pictures, journals, and business records."

"I'm not even sure where things are in the probate process or who has rightful claim to his estate, and I'm not about to hire people to break in and steal things!"

"Well, you wouldn't need to steal them. Photocopies or pictures would work…"

"Jack…"

Jerry was the only person on the planet that called me Jack. I didn't see any point in trying to change his habit now. "You've given me an idea…"

"I hope it involves coming home and not being stupid…"

"No, nothing so bold and daring. Perhaps you can use the unsettled nature of Ryan's estate in our favor. Tell them you've found a possible heir, an Irish woman named Dianne O'Leary. See if that gets you access to anything. If that fails, try good, old-fashioned cash."

"*Your* good, old-fashioned cash, Jack…"

"Of course."

Dammit. I had a strange feeling that things were going to get expensive.

* * *

Our meeting with Finnegan and Kelly Hamilton was in Lisburn, and the trip there was silent. Mack, deep in thought, barely said two words the entire way there.

Jim greeted us as we entered the front room of a small cottage. A silver haired woman, who I did not recognize, sat in a corner rocking chair. She seemed oblivious to our presence as she quietly knitted.

"Were you followed?"

"Unlikely," I said. "I borrowed a car from one of Charlie Hannon's many nephews; the one I rented is still parked where we're staying. Are we still expecting another?"

"She'll be here," answered Finnegan, confidently. "So… what's it going to be, you two?"

"What do you mean?"

"This is the first time Shanagh has gone after you directly, John.

Are you looking to lay low for a while? Or maybe you've had enough. I can arrange for you to disappear; I know people... Transferring your assets to a new identity would take a while, but it can happen."

With the assistance of a cane, the elderly woman rose from her chair. "He can do it, quite well at that!"

It was only when I studied her closely did I recognize Kelly Hamilton's brilliant disguise. "Pretty good," I muttered, my eyebrow lifted in appreciation.

"I'm under fairly heavy scrutiny," Kelly said, "so this was my only way to get here. But before I share what I've got, I want to hear your answer."

"My answer? To what?"

"To Jim's question."

"About running away? Not interested."

"Good," she said, returning to her chair and resuming her knitting. "That was what we were hoping to hear."

"Shanagh's going to have to do more than that to get rid of me," I said. "I won't rest until she's put away, once and for all."

"Same here," added Mack.

"I'm sure that William Hayes didn't share with you any of the preliminary findings into the explosion that destroyed your car," said Kelly.

"No. He was more interested in what was on our computers."

Mack laughed, gently.

"He's quite infuriated with what you left for him," Kelly said, "but he knows better than to press the issue. I'll spare you the gory details, but we don't think the bomb was the work of any of Shanagh

Grady's people, at least not anyone we know about. The technology and explosives used were different from her normal *modus operandi*, as the saying goes."

"For a while we thought the Ulster Maritime Group was a red herring," Jim added. "Now, we're not so sure."

"I admit," I said, running my hands through my hair, "that it is easy to conclude that they're involved. I *was* asking about them when someone planted the bomb in my car."

"There were also some members of the Harbour Police observing you," said Finnegan, "and according to my sources, nobody can find any records of them being there, let alone closing the access road."

"So they herded me in for the slaughter."

"Something like that," Finnegan said. "Problem is, we don't know if they're corrupt Harbour Police or impostors. Both theories are still on the table at the moment."

"So why not Shanagh?" I said, standing and stretching. "It is well within her *modus operandi* to employ bogus or corrupt police."

"True," said Kelly, "but ever since that bomb left a crater where your car used to be, chatter to and from suspected Geryon email addresses and networks has gone up two hundred percent."

I did not share the revelation, but Mack immediately perked up. A side conversation erupted, spoken almost exclusively in the language of technology. Finnegan smiled at my confused expression, which remained until Mack turned her attention to me.

"Sounds like Shanagh and Geryon might not be seeing eye to eye," Mack said.

"Our conclusion as well," added Finnegan. "Whatever caused them to align, it might be short-lived. At least we can hope!"

"It is a case of odd bedfellows," said Kelly, answering my next question before I could ask it. "Geryon isn't usually interested in rampant, perpetual violence. Not that they're afraid to be brutal or anything, but it is usually more targeted. And almost always financial. They love to rob the wealthy, extort large corporations, and maybe an assassination here and there if someone doesn't pay up. Arms deals, revolutions, and the like, haven't been their cup of tea so far."

"And we need it to stay that way," Finnegan said, "which is where you come in, if you're up to it."

I returned to my chair, uncertain of what he had in mind. "Go on…"

"It could get very dangerous very quickly."

"Our time here hasn't exactly been safe, Jim," I said, glancing at Mack.

"Fair play," he said, offering only a hint of a smile. "If our hunch is correct, however, we might be looking at a unique opportunity to drive a wedge into the alliance between Shanagh and Geryon."

"We've got too many players right now," said Kelly, still knitting, "and we don't know how all of them fit together. If we can take Geryon out of the mix, it might simplify our job a bit."

"And how do you propose to do that?" asked Mack. "If they're into it for financial gain, they're not going to go away just because we ask them nicely."

"Agreed," said Finnegan, "but we might be able to convince them that their new partner is a liability."

"If they haven't already figured out that Shanagh is utterly insane, they are either stupid or they simply don't care."

"This is where you come in, John," said Jim, pouring a glass of whiskey. "You're the only person who can possibly pull this off."

Finnegan handed me the glass. "Why do I have a feeling that you want me to wear a giant bullseye?"

"That's only part of it," Finnegan said.

"Now I understand why you gave me the whiskey. Should I drink it now, or after I hear what you have to say?"

"Consider doing both," said Kelly, still knitting patiently.

"The first request is something you're well suited to do," said Finnegan, a disconcerting smile crossing his face.

"And that is?"

"Annoy Shanagh until she makes a mistake. How do you say it? Poke the bear?"

"He *is* good at that," said Mack, offering a wry smile to my silent protest.

Finnegan continued. "Chide her for failing to kill you with the bomb. Tell her she's a failure."

I raised my eyebrow. "You might be on to something. She got rather upset when I brought up Alicia O'Leary and Connla. If Mack's hunch pans out, Shanagh's likely to have a damned coronary on the spot."

"If you blame the bomb on her," Kelly added, "it will help disguise what we really know about the situation."

"Which gets us to the second part of our idea," said Finnegan. "How would you feel about offering a reward? It would have to be your own money, of course. And, naturally, an amount sizable enough to capture the imagination of the public."

"Naturally…"

"Of course, you'd want to get a barrister to draft some language around the reward criteria, including a maximum payout, and so forth."

"Of course..."

"And there would be the costs of a call center, staff, and investigators. The Police Service isn't staffed sufficiently to investigate every wanker that calls in with pure rubbish looking for an easy payday. You'd have to filter the tips."

"We would..." I took a deep sip from my whiskey.

"And you'd undoubtedly want to make the appeal in person; maybe film it and run it as an advertisement for a few days."

"Undoubtedly..." Another drink.

"Don't forget the third part," said Kelly, returning her knitting to a nearby table. "The part where you reach out to Geryon."

"This just gets better and better," I said. "And people accuse me of having ludicrous ideas..."

* * *

"Mack, how do I let myself get talked into these crazy schemes?" I said, easing my car onto the southbound dual carriageway. "First, it was Finnegan's insane idea, and now this."

"We've been over and over it," said Mack, quietly basking in the glow of victory. "We can wait a couple of weeks for my sources to investigate, or we can visit Mullingar and find out for ourselves. Tracking down an illegitimate child, especially in conservative parts of the world, isn't easy. Doubly so if a concerted effort was undertaken to conceal the truth. Records are often lost or destroyed, so an in-person approach may be our only option. Besides, it isn't exactly a long drive..."

"You're not the one doing the driving! Please tell me that we have rooms waiting for us."

"Cozy and comfortable," she said, settling back into her seat. "With any luck, we'll be done and on our way before lunchtime."

"Then why did you make a three day reservation?"

"Because I wanted to err in the direction of caution."

I nodded, resigned to my fate. "One thing I don't understand..."

"Yes?"

"Why aren't they pressing the issue on Hayes? Why target Shanagh and Geryon when Hayes seems to be the best and most convenient target? He's dirty, Mack, as dirty as they get. Surely, between all of us, we could find enough to neutralize him. Every time I brought him up, they steered the conversation in another direction."

"Good point..."

"And another thing... Kelly said that Hayes knows better than to press the issue."

"I assumed she was referring to risking legal action from our solicitor."

"I thought the same, but the more I think about it, the more it bothers me."

"Talk to me, John." Mack shifted in her seat, turning to the right and giving me her full attention.

"We're in the wrong on this one, Mack. Hayes aside, we withheld evidence in an active investigation. He could make things uncomfortable for us, and would be well within the law to do so. If it made it into the news, he could even manipulate public opinion in his favor. Ultimately, we'd end up with a slap on the wrist, but more importantly, we'd be neutralized."

"Checkmate..."

"At least as far as we're concerned, it is."

Mack fluffed her long, red hair. "Then why remain silent?" Her eyes drifted away, momentarily. "Yes…" A narrow smile formed.

"To borrow a term from the cold war: *Mutually Assured Destruction.* Hayes can't move against us, or Finnegan for that matter, because we have something on him. Dammit. We have something! We just don't know what it is yet."

"That also means that Hayes has something on Finnegan," said Mack, the smile vanishing from her face. "And thus the stalemate."

"So it would seem."

CHAPTER FOURTEEN

"Rooms, Mack! Plural…"

'You heard them," Mack said, unfazed. "They simply don't have anything else."

"But you said…"

"Must've been a glitch in their system. I asked for two rooms, we got one; it happens, and we'll survive. They're bringing up a rollaway bed."

Dammit. After a long day, I wasn't cherishing the notion of sleeping on what would undoubtedly be an uncomfortable slab of rock masquerading as a mattress.

The attendant, apologizing repeatedly, unfolded the bed, made it, and provided two pillows. I tipped him, generously, and started to assess the condition of the foam mattress.

"I'll take the rollaway," said Mack. "This whole debacle was my doing."

"No, Mack. It wasn't your fault. You take the bed, I'll sleep on this."

She stared at me, silently, before rolling her eyes and shaking her head.

* * *

"We have five names on the list," Mack said, between bites of breakfast. "According to my sources, the top three are the most likely to have information, so we'll start there."

"This could be a fairly sensitive subject to broach with people. How are we going to bring it up?"

"I think we just tell the truth, or at least whatever part of it we're comfortable sharing. We do it gently and carefully, though."

"In other words, I should let you do all the talking."

"Yeah, pretty much."

* * *

It took us most of the morning to track down the first name on Mack's list, only to discover that the woman, once employed at a local hospital, had passed away several months prior. A quick trip to the local library removed any lingering doubts about her death. Well into her nineties, she had been in failing health for at least six months.

I wanted to make the library visit as quick as possible, but Mack had other ideas. "I want to talk to the librarian," she whispered. "It'll only take a minute."

Within moments of their meeting, they were gabbing like old friends, and disappeared into an office. I was left sitting alone, under the scornful eye of an older woman. I had forgotten to silence my phone, and an unexpected chirp threatened to trigger an unleashing of unthinkable wrath. Wide-eyed and furious, she pointed to the *Silence All Phones* sign a few feet from me. Sheepishly, I retrieved my phone, and set it to silent operation.

The message from Jerry Keynes simply read:

`Making progress. Should have something for you in a few days.`

At least *something* was going well. Finally, I couldn't take it any more and stood up.

"Can I help you?" The woman's whisper was like fingernails on a chalkboard.

Lacking any clever retort, I blurted out the first thing that came to mind: "Music." She peered over her glasses at me. "Traditional music," I muttered, hesitantly.

Without saying a word, she motioned for me to follow her. "Did you know," she whispered, "that a meeting held in Mullingar in 1951 was vital in the preservation and growth of Irish traditional music. The annual festival where people come to compete, perform, take classes, or just enjoy the music started right here. I attended the first one as a fifteen year old."

She stopped, pointing to a narrow row of shelves before continuing. "It was a dying art when I was young. There were maybe ten books on all the shelves back then, and now look at it!" Her face formed the closest thing to a smile I'd seen since setting foot in the building. "What do you play?"

"Fiddle, but I've hardly had much opportunity to play recently."

"Oh! Then follow me."

She led me to a stairwell, and we descended several flights of stairs. "We have some recordings preserved here that you might be interested in hearing," she said, holding the door for me.

As instructed, I sat in a small cubicle and donned the headphones provided. They looked like something from the eighties, but were surprisingly comfortable. The recording, made sometime in the early fifties on a portable open-reel tape deck, lacked fidelity. The music, the product of a local fiddle player, was utterly magical. For the first time in recent memory, my mind found some solace.

I had no idea how much time had elapsed when I finished the last of the recordings. Oblivious to my surroundings, I turned, nearly jumping from surprise to see Mack waiting for me. Her amused expression stopped me.

"What?" I said.

"Nothing," she said, suppressing a giggle. "It's probably a good thing that you're the only one down here."

"Mack!"

"For the past forty-five minutes or so, you've been humming along, and tapping your fingers to music that only you can hear. I think the video I took of you will be absolutely hilarious on social media."

"Mack! Don't you dare!!"

"Oh, you're no fun! The good news is that I've been able to revise our list, thanks to my friend, the librarian."

"You guys seemed to be fast friends."

"She helped me when we were investigating the O'Grady family three years ago. We've stayed in touch ever since. Speaking of which, you seem to have made a friend yourself."

"More out of fear..."

"Well, she wanted to make sure you got this." Mack handed me a note. "We're invited to a traditional Irish music session tonight."

"Mack, I don't have time to play…"

"Nonsense. It will do you good. Besides, your new best friend told me that some of the people playing there might remember Connla O'Grady."

"Okay, okay… I'll go. I'm so out of practice, I'll probably make an idiot out of myself."

"No. The video will do that long before the session," she said, sticking her tongue out at me.

"Mack!!"

* * *

The afternoon was consumed chasing down the next two names on Mack's list. Both people proved to be friendly and eager to help, but unable to do so. Frustrated, tired, and hungry, we returned to our room. The day didn't get any better when we learned that the hotel still didn't have a second room available. Dinner and a couple of pints didn't make the prospect of another night on the rollaway bed look any better.

"You *have* to go," Mack groaned in response to my plans to retire early rather than attending the music session. "We might be able to get some useful information."

"You go, Mack. I'm tired, not to mention not wanting to look like a bloody idiot again."

"Again?"

"The video."

"Silly! I didn't take any video. I just did that to make you blush."

"Well, that makes me feel better, I guess. But nah. You go."

She frowned. "I won't be able to make any connections without you there. I'll just be a stupid American girl full of annoying questions. Besides, you've got an ace in the hole that I don't have."

"What's that?"

"Your new friend from the library."

"What does she have to do with anything?"

"You'll see. Now get yourself up and around. We need to go."

* * *

The pub was quiet, except for the handful of musicians loosely congregating in an alcove near the front. I looked around for a familiar face, but saw nobody.

"Mister Costa!" A familiar voice interrupted our progress toward the bar. "So glad you could make it."

The wicked librarian's sinister demeanor was replaced with a relaxed friendliness that caught me off guard.

"I have a few things to show you. We have about fifteen minutes before we start playing."

"Do you play?"

"Yes. Fiddle, just like you. I'm sorry I had to leave before you were finished with the recordings at the library. You seemed to be enjoying them."

"They were remarkable," I said. "Who was it?"

She led me to a wall filled with pictures. "This fellow right here," she said, pointing to an image. "And that's me standing right next to him."

I studied the picture. "Your father, by chance?"

She nodded.

"Hell of a player. Why aren't those recordings available for everyone to hear?"

"He was a modest man, Mister Costa. He didn't want the recordings made at all, but I eventually talked him into it, but only after promising that they'd never leave the family."

"I'm honored that you shared them with me."

"Recognize this fellow?" She pointed to a different picture.

"Connla O'Grady!"

"One of his rare appearances, thank goodness. What an awful musician, and I'm not the only one who'll tell you that!"

"This is you, isn't it?" I pointed to another picture.

"You have a good eye. I was in my early thirties when that was taken. Quite a looker, I was!" She laughed, "That fellow to my right had such a fancy for me. This is the only picture of us together…" The smile drifted from her face as she ran her wrinkled finger over the picture. "He'd get a stupid smile on his face, and get all tongue-tied whenever we were together. Head over heels, he was, but I was too busy with this idiot to notice." Her hand tapped the image of a tall, smiling man in the background. "We were all but set to be married when the bastard went off to Dublin on business and never returned."

"I'm sorry. Whatever happened with this fellow?" I pointed to the man on her immediate right.

"He gave up on me, and moved on. I can't really blame him, I guess. He hadn't heard a single word from me in well over a year. Before I knew it, he was gone — off to America, I expect; it was always a dream of his — and I had no way to find him. It wasn't like it is today, of course. We didn't have electronic mail, social media, and all that. Not that I'm sure it would have mattered; I was so self-absorbed in those days." She paused, staring into space. "Maybe I should have read Yeats more as a young woman, instead of looking in the mirror. But this isn't why I brought you over here," she said, the energy returning to her voice. "This is."

The picture captured my immediate and undivided attention. "That's Connla again, isn't it? But who is this with him?"

"I'll tell you who it isn't," she said. "It isn't his wife. This was taken about a month before she died, one of the times when she was on holiday in the north. Connla brought this woman around here a few times over the years, said she was his cousin or some rubbish like that. They didn't carry on like relatives, if you follow me. And she wasn't the only woman he brought around here, either. His wife, poor Meryl, God rest her, was barely in the grave and Connla was cavorting about! Nobody said anything, of course. You didn't want to get on the wrong side of Connla."

"Understandable. Dang it. I wish this was a better picture."

"Some of the other musicians might remember more about her. Come on, I'll introduce you."

* * *

By the time we returned to the alcove, Mack had already met everyone and was engaged in several lively discussions.

"Your wife is a special lady," the accordion player said, shaking my hand. "Glad you two could make it."

I almost corrected his mistake, but realized it might be better for conversation to let the assumption continue.

"Indeed," added an elderly flute player. "I haven't laughed so much in years."

"She's quite special," I said, glancing over at Mack. She returned a smile and a gentle shrug.

"Here," said the librarian, handing me an aging fiddle case. "You can play this."

"What are you going to play?"

"I've got my own instrument. That one belonged to my father. I keep it maintained, but it needs to be played."

The music started, and I found myself struggling to keep up. A few sets and a few beers later, however, I started to find myself. Mack hovered on the periphery, keeping the musicians well hydrated with the beverage of choice. When they paused for a break, she would use the opportunity to have a brief conversation. I did the same.

This continued until we reached the time when the musicians were ready to leave.

"One last set," the accordion player decreed. "John, pick us a tune, will you?"

"Miss McLeod's reel."

The tune started, and for the next few, precious minutes, I was truly happy.

CHAPTER FIFTEEN

"My wife, Mack?" I said as we walked back to our hotel, fighting the urge to laugh.

"The accordion player came to the conclusion on his own. It just seemed more conducive to our conversation to allow it to go uncorrected."

"Probably not a bad idea, given that we're sharing a room."

"Yeah, about that…"

"Yes?"

"I got an email from them earlier; they still don't have anything available."

I groaned at the prospect of another night or two on the rollaway bed.

"You take the bed tonight, John."

"No, Mack. I've had enough *general anesthetic* tonight that I don't think it will matter where I sleep. People kept buying me pints, and I sorta lost count."

"I hope you're sober enough to remember the various conversations you had through the evening."

"Probably not…" I waited until she rolled her eyes before continuing. "That's why I had my recorder running the entire evening."

* * *

"Hung over, are we?" Mack said, a smile forming at the corner of her mouth.

"Not really," I said, "just a little tired. Nothing that coffee can't chase away."

"Now, aren't you glad you went?" she said, nibbling on a scone.

"I am. As usual, you were right." I took a deep drink from my cup of coffee.

"What's bothering you?"

"Mack, I guess I'm having trouble coming to grips with the notion that a loveless old bastard like Connla O'Grady was having an affair. I could see it, perhaps, after his wife died, but by all accounts, things were underway long beforehand."

"Anything is possible, I guess. My suspicions are, however, that any trysts were likely more related to business than love, up to, and including, his wife."

"You might be right about that. Hell, the old bastard married his business partner's sister. Not sure where all this is taking us, though."

Mack nodded, sipping her coffee. "Lots of tentacles to this beast, John. We're just tracking down another one."

* * *

By the afternoon, we were down to the last person on Mack's list, and our hopes were draining. Finally, after some gentle negotiation, a meeting was arranged.

"Please come in," Linda MacRory said, inviting us into her modest flat. "I'm sorry about the mess, but I don't get many visitors these days."

"No worries," I said, finding a chair amidst the clutter. "We appreciate your willingness to meet with us."

"I'm not entirely comfortable with what you want to talk about," she said, crossing her arms as she settled into her chair. "Such things are best kept private."

"Tell us only what you feel comfortable sharing. We understand you worked as a caregiver here," I said, handing her a document Mack's librarian friend discovered for us."

"I worked there as a registered nurse until my retirement a few years back."

I handed her a picture of Alicia O'Leary. Citing confidentiality, she skillfully evaded our questions. "Like I said, things like this are private."

Frustrated, I handed her a picture. She quickly diverted her eyes. I didn't blame her. "No, Mrs. MacRory. Look at it," I urged. "The dead woman in the image is Karen Boyle, Alicia O'Leary's daughter. We understand that Alicia's condition would make it pointless for us to inform her, but there are matters of Karen's estate that might need to be settled."

She rose. "I know who it is. I recognize her. That isn't the entire reason you're here, is it, though?"

"No, it isn't." I handed her another picture. "The woman in this picture calls herself Dianne O'Leary, but if you research her, the records of her past are quite confusing. The resemblance, though, is unmistakable," I said, handing her a more pleasant picture of Karen Boyle. "And we think this man was involved, somehow."

She feigned ignorance when I handed her a picture of Connla O'Grady, but her expression betrayed her. "Whiskey?" she said.

"It's a bit early for me, but thank you."

"It's a bit early for me, too," she sighed, "but I'm going to anyway." She returned to her chair. "I guess I knew this day would come. Yes. I know him."

"Connla O'Grady."

"Connla," she said, sipping her drink. "He kept my worthless bastard of a husband employed, off and on, for many years. Just enough to keep foreclosure away, but never enough to get anywhere. That's why, when Connla came to me with a financial proposition, I didn't feel we had much choice but to take it."

"What proposition, Mrs. MacRory?"

"I felt so sad for her," she said, handing me the picture of Alicia O'Leary. "Connla was old enough to be her father, but for some reason she was so taken with the man. Over the moon, they'd say, even though she was old enough to know better."

"Wasn't she married at the time?" interjected Mack.

"Oh yes, and what a mess it was. Married, and with a wee one at home. And there the poor thing was, pregnant by a man that wasn't her husband. Not that it doesn't happen, of course, but at that time people weren't quite as accepting as they are now."

"Karen was born late in 1975," I said. "When did all this happen?"

"Connla came to me in the middle of 1977. He bought the whole damned nursing home as part of the cover-up. It kept on operating as though nothing happened, except there, at the end of one wing was his pregnant girlfriend. They had the whole area blocked off for construction, so nobody was the wiser. What a bloody mess," she said, shaking her head. "It was a rough pregnancy. She was over forty at the time, and at several points, we thought she was going to lose the baby. She spent most of the last two trimesters in bed. Anyway, her child ended up getting raised as an orphan. To his credit, though, Connla set up a trust fund for her, and made sure she made it all the way through University. I was there, too, off and on, playing the role of a distant relative, just to keep an eye on things."

"Do you think the woman in the photograph is Alicia O'Leary's child?"

"The resemblance is there, no doubt, but it isn't the best picture in the world. Short of DNA, the only way to tell would be to get a look at the back of her knee. She took a nasty spill off her bicycle as a child. It left a deep, diamond-shaped scar, about two centimeters across. I'm sorry. I don't think there's much more to tell."

* * *

"What are you doing?" The sudden turn of my car onto a side street surprised Mack.

"I want ice cream," I said. "We just passed a little shop that sells it."

"This is rather random," Mack said, raising her left eyebrow. "Who are you, and what have you done with John Costa?"

"Truth is, I feel like we've hit a dead end. There's *something*, Mack. Dammit. I just can't put it together. Maybe changing things up will help me figure out what it is."

"I'm game," said Mack, as we rounded the corner. "The place looks charming, actually."

"I rather doubt they have some of those crazy flavors you like."

"I'll muddle through somehow," she said, rolling her eyes as we entered the shop.

As I feared, the selection of flavors was limited, but with some clever mixing and garnishing, Mack was able to build a suitable treat.

"Vanilla!" she said, exasperated. "All that, and you get a dish of vanilla."

"I just need a change of scenery," I said, sliding into the small, corner booth. "Besides, some of us can enjoy the simple delicacies of life without the need to over complicate things." I stuck my tongue out at her.

"Okay. Really. Who are you?"

"Oh, nobody, really," I said, grinning. "Just the person that has, once, after all these years, turned the tables on you, Jillian MacDonald!"

* * *

I became aware that I was staring into my empty ice cream glass, my spoon repeatedly tracing the same path around its interior.

"Are you able to see the future in that thing?" Mack said.

"Sorry. I was just thinking."

"And?"

"I have an absolutely crazy idea. It's so stupid that I'm not even going to say it out loud just yet."

The twinkle returned to Mack's eyes. "That's never stopped you before…"

"Is the library still open?"

Mack glanced at her phone. "It should be, for another twenty minutes."

"Come on, we need to hurry!"

* * *

It took ten minutes to get to the library, and we sprinted from the parking lot to the front door. After a brief search, I found the elderly librarian.

"What on earth?" she whispered.

"I'm sorry, but I have one more question for you."

"We're ready to close," she said. "Get on with it!"

"When you showed me the picture of Connla O'Grady in the pub, you mentioned that the younger woman in the picture wasn't the only one."

"I did."

"Just so I understood you correctly, you're implying that he had other romantic entanglements."

"That he did, Mister Costa, but the one I showed you is the only one I ever saw in person. The others we knew from rumor, but given the sources, I would call the information reliable."

Dammit. It wasn't the answer I was hoping to hear. She continued before I could say anything.

"The pub you visited wasn't his only haunt, you know."

"Are any of them still around?"

She studied me, peering over the rim of her glasses. "Let's take a quick look."

* * *

"Now, do you see why I like libraries so much? Those old town records and photographs aren't available online yet; it might be years before they're digitized and indexed. The only way to find them…"

"Yes, Mack, I know… in a library."

"I'm just waiting to hear it, John."

"Hear what?"

"That I am, as usual, absolutely correct."

Avoiding answering, I pulled the list compiled by the librarian out of my pocket. "Three pubs on the list, Mack. Which one shall we visit first?"

She rolled her eyes. "You pick."

"I'm terribly at things like this! If I pick, we'll find what we're looking for at the last one on the list. Assuming, of course, that what we're looking for exists at all, which I doubt." I sighed. "How about we just go to the pub closest to our hotel first and go from there."

"A pub crawl! Sounds like a plan…"

* * *

True to form, the first location we visited was a fun, but time consuming and fruitless venture. We searched every picture on the wall, but couldn't find Connla O'Grady in any of them. The owner was willing to show us a stack of pictures tucked away in a small closet, but they revealed nothing of interest.

"At least dinner was good," I said, finishing the last drops of my Guinness. "Ready for the next one, Mack?"

"Sure."

A brisk walk on a rainy evening took us to the second pub on the list. It was quiet, cozy, and sparsely populated.

"Are you wanting food?" the young lady working behind the bar said. "If so, our kitchen closed about thirty minutes ago."

"No, just in for a few pints."

"You're American, aren't you," she said, smiling. "What brings you to Mullingar? On holiday?"

"Doing a little family tree research," I said. "Mind if we take a look at some of the pictures you've got hanging here?"

"Oh, no bother at all," she said. "The whole back wall is covered with them. Looking to catch a glimpse of a relative, are you?"

"It's a long shot, but while I'm here, I might as well take a look."

"You have a picture of who you're looking for? I'll help for a bit if you'd like."

"I don't want to cause you any trouble."

"Not a worry! If anyone wants a pint, they'll let me know."

It didn't take long before the barkeep announced, "here, do you think this is him?" She pointed to a dusty picture, high and near the back corner.

I scrambled over to take a look.

"Here," she said, pulling a chair over, excitedly. "Climb up and pull it down if you'd like a better look."

Without hesitation, I hopped onto the chair, and carefully removed the picture from the wall. I placed it on a nearby table where the light was better. As I studied the image, my lips curled into a smile. "Mack, what do you think?"

She stared at the image, looking back at me wide-eyed. "Son of a bitch," she muttered. "When you're right, you're right!"

With the barkeeper's permission, we took several photographs of our newly discovered treasure before returning it to its perch high on the wall.

"Thank you," I said, slipping a stack of bills into her hand. "This should cover our drinks quite nicely, and buy a round for everyone. You keep the rest."

* * *

"It certainly explains a few things," Mack said, as we made our way back to the hotel, utterly oblivious to the heavier rain that had started during our stay at the pub.

"It does. More importantly, it gives us something we've not had until now: an ace in the hole."

"Now we just need to figure out the best time and place to play it."

CHAPTER SIXTEEN

"Where on earth have you been, Mack?"

"Oh, here and there," she said, grinning.

"All morning? It's almost lunch time."

"I didn't want to wake you this morning, so I slipped out quietly."

"Out with it, Mack."

"I just went for a walk…"

"Mack!!"

"Okay, okay! I was applying for a job."

"You were doing what??"

"You heard me, John. I was applying for a job."

"I can't even begin to figure you out, Jillian MacDonald…"

"I'll tell you if you promise not to be angry with me."

"Deal."

"Something Mrs. MacRory said bothered me. When Alicia O'Leary arrived, she was already married and, I expect, using the Boyle surname. Given her unfortunate circumstances, I would expect her to have used a false name while she was here. That way, if anyone stumbled onto what was going on in the nursing home's wing, she'd still have a decent chance to protect her identity."

"Yes, makes perfect sense."

"And she was raised as an orphan, right? But under what name? There is no way that it would be with either the Boyle or O'Leary surname — both are too obviously traceable should someone get inquisitive. But yet here she is, on record, using the O'Leary surname."

"I don't follow you, Mack…"

"She wouldn't have been raised as an O'Leary, John. At some point, I think it is likely she purloined the name used by her deceased Aunt. But how did she know that she had a deceased Aunt?"

"A deceased Aunt named O'Leary! I'm with you now. There had to have been some contact; somewhere along the line, she figured out who she is and who her mother is."

"Bingo! And that is why I had to go apply for a job at the nursing home where Alicia O'Leary lives."

"And… you lost me again," I said, running my hands through my hair.

"I needed a way to get on their network."

"Mack… get on their network to do *what*, exactly?"

"To get a look at their visitor logs. Remember, you promised — no yelling."

"I'm going to conveniently pretend I'm not hearing any of this…"

"Are you going to pretend not to hear what I learned?"

I sighed. "No. Go on."

"Take a look," she said, opening her laptop and directing my attention toward its screen. "Look at who has been visiting Alicia O'Leary every four weeks, almost like clockwork."

"Karen Boyle?" I frowned as I studied the screen. "But…"

Mack interrupted before I could continue. "Many of these visits corresponded to times when Karen was with us. It couldn't have been her, but it could have been Dianne O'Leary with a fake ID. In fact, I looked back at least five years, and I'd be surprised if *any* of the visits were really Karen. Ryan Boyle, Karen's father, didn't visit, either. Not once."

"Hardly the actions of a loving husband and daughter. I don't suppose her next visit is coming up any time soon."

"No such luck," Mack said. "If she stays true to her schedule, she won't visit again until next week."

I settled back into my chair. "I don't feel like waiting around. Another week on that damned rollaway bed, and I won't be able to stand up straight."

"There's no need for us to wait around," she said, a coy smile forming at the corner of her mouth.

"What did you do?"

"The visitor log includes a mailing address."

"It could be fake."

"Possibly, but I don't think so. I had a friend do a quick search, and the property is registered to Kristos Antonopoulos."

"Ulster Maritime Group," I muttered.

"One and the same," Mack said, beaming proudly. "If you're ready to head back north, we could stop by for an unannounced visit. Their place is on our way."

"Walking straight into the lions' den, Mack?"

* * *

"A few more days, and everything will be ready for you," Jim Finnegan said. "Molloy has the core legal points drafted and awaiting your review. I have three companies lined up that can screen the phone calls. The Police Service has worked with all three in the past, but it's up to you, of course."

"Okay, Jim. We're on our way back."

"Grand. I'll set up a meeting for tomorrow."

I glanced into my rear view mirror. "Dammit."

"What's wrong?"

"We've picked up a tail, Jim. I noticed him a couple of roundabouts back. This isn't your doing, is it?"

"Unfortunately, it isn't. Drive to the nearest Garda station. Ring them up on the way, and let them know what's going on."

"My thoughts exactly. I'll have Mack take a look at the map and find one. Sorry, Jim, gotta go. I'm going to need both hands on the wheel."

* * *

The driver of the car following us maintained a patient, but persistent, distance from our vehicle. When we reached the outskirts of a small town, I ducked into the first available petrol station. The car continued on its way, indifferent to our presence.

"Maybe I'm imagining things, Mack," I said, operating the station's cappuccino machine.

"I don't think so," she said. "The passenger was keeping a close eye on us as they passed," she said. "I tried to catch video of them as they drove past us."

"Good one, Mack. I thought you were just engaged with something on your phone."

"That was the general idea," she said, tapping the screen. "Oh well." She wrinkled her nose.

"What is it?"

"I only caught part of the license plate. Better than nothing, I guess. What's the plan?"

"We passed an intersection near the outskirts of town. If we backtrack, can you find us an alternate route to get back to the main road?"

"Yes, via smaller roads. Shouldn't be a problem."

"Thanks, Mack. Figure it out, then ring up the nearest Garda station and let them know what's going on."

* * *

Our detour took us through some narrow back roads on a course that ran roughly parallel with the original road. A few miles north of town, we emerged onto the original road.

"Looks clear," I said, glancing in my rear view mirror.

My words were proven to be hasty only a few minutes later.

"Dammit. He's back."

This time, the driver was being anything but subtle. He turned on his headlights, high beams, and accelerated. As he closed on our rear bumper, I pressed the accelerator pedal.

"Hang on, Mack. This could get interesting."

I overtook a slower vehicle; our follower did likewise, closing the distance to our rear bumper. After several gentle corners, the road straightened, and started a long, gentle descent. Both lanes were clear. Already near the posted speed limit, I accelerated.

The car behind us did likewise, but then pulled into the right lane as if to overtake. A glance into my mirror revealed his plans were otherwise. The passenger window rolled down. An armed man, face obscured by a ski mask, leaned out of the window.

"He's got a gun. Get down, Mack!" I mashed the pedal to the floor, and the engine roared. Bullets kissed the rear of our vehicle.

I knew I couldn't allow him to pull parallel to us, so I steered the wheel to the right, attempting to block his path. Our vehicles touched, and I fought to maintain control. The other driver did likewise, sharply decelerating and losing momentum.

As we rounded a sweeping corner, the explanation for the lack of opposing traffic appeared. In the distance, a line of cars formed behind a slow moving dump truck. In our lane, a tire delivery van would soon become an impediment, as it was traveling below the posted limit.

With our pursuer lagging, I sensed an opportunity and slammed the accelerator pedal to the floor. The transmission shifted to a lower gear, and the car jumped forward. I switched lanes; the oncoming traffic closed on us at an alarming rate. Our pursuer matched my actions, regaining his speed.

We pulled along side the tire truck, the distance between us and the oncoming dump truck dropping at an alarming rate. At the last possible moment, I darted back to the left. The car fish-tailed briefly before I regained control.

Our pursuer was not so fortunate. All I saw in my mirror was his vehicle leave the road. Dirt flew as he lost control. The vehicle rolled several times before coming to rest on its roof.

"Call the Garda, Mack, and make sure they get an ambulance out here."

"Already done," she said, her voice shaking. "I've been on the phone with them the entire time. They're on the way."

* * *

"You're lucky, Mister Costa," the officer said as he examined our vehicle. "Your car, on the other hand, isn't doing very well. One of the bullets penetrated the petrol tank. It's damned fortunate that it didn't catch on fire."

In the heat of the moment, I hadn't noticed the quantity of gunshots, but my car was struck at least five times. The rear bumper and quarter panel were heavily damaged.

"Unfortunately," he said, "we're going to have to detain you until we ascertain the facts of the situation, although they appear to be quite obvious."

"Understood. The men that were chasing us — what is their condition?"

"The driver is off to the hospital. The passenger wasn't so fortunate; he's off to the morgue."

* * *

The Garda had many questions, and the process extended well into the afternoon before they were finally satisfied.

"Please be advised," the officer said, "that you may be called upon to testify at a future date. The driver is facing a rather significant list of charges."

"Of course. What is the disposition of our vehicle and belongings?"

"Your vehicle has been towed here," he said, handing me a business card. "The situation with the petrol tank has left it inoperable. I'm sure they'll be able to assess it for you in the morning. I will be more than happy to take you to collect your items from it."

"Mack, what is Finnegan's ETA?"

"He's at least three hours away," she answered, wrinkling her nose.

"Three hours?"

"Don't get mad at me, John, I'm only repeating what he said. He mentioned something about being busy for a bit longer, then he'd leave to get us."

"Busy? Was he playing golf?"

Mack shrugged. "It didn't sound like he was on the golf course."

"Oh well, at least we've got time for a nice dinner."

* * *

"Several things are bugging me, Mack," I said, sipping a Guinness.

"Is one of them the fact that nobody in Ireland is going to rent you a car? This is two, now…"

"Only one," I protested. "This one is repairable. I think. But seriously…"

"What is it?"

"How did they find us, Mack? It was like they knew exactly

where we were the entire time, in spite of your best efforts to route us away from them."

She nodded, raising her right eyebrow. "I've been bothered by that as well. I expect they planted a tracking device on our car. Problem is, I have no idea when the might have done so."

"Possibly someone we talked to in Mullingar tipped them off."

"Perhaps," Mack said. "If we could find the device, maybe that would reveal something."

"What are our chances of finding it?"

"If I had all of my equipment, I'd say nearly one hundred percent. Here? Not quite as high."

"How high?"

"Twenty-five percent… or less… On the other hand, it is zero if we don't look."

"Point taken."

* * *

"What, exactly, are we looking for, Miss MacDonald?" Finnegan said, surveying the damaged car.

"Anything out of the ordinary, possibly magnetically attached."

"Okay, but I only have one spare flashlight."

"You take it, Mack," I said, "You know what you're looking for better than I do. Besides, I'm going to try something."

"I don't like the sound of that," Mack said, frowning. "What, exactly, do you have in mind."

"I'm going to see if I can poke the bear a bit. I've saved every single number Shanagh Grady has used to call me. I'm going to start calling them."

"John," Mack said, "every one of those numbers is going to end up as out of service or disconnected."

"Perhaps. Remember, though, she's lost her ace hacker."

"And replaced him with Geryon," Mack interjected.

"The alliance is still young," I said. "Humor me."

"Suit yourself," she said, rolling her eyes before turning her attention to the vehicle.

* * *

The first eight numbers I tried were exactly as Mack predicted, but the ninth rang endlessly before I eventually moved on to the next one on my list. My heart almost stopped when I heard her voice on the other end of the line.

"My, this *is* a surprise, Solicitor," she said. "Oh, sweet, misguided Giovanni, have you finally come to your senses?"

"No Shanagh. I'm calling you to let you know that, once again, you've failed."

"Such hostility," she said, her voice nearly lyrical. "I'm afraid I don't follow you."

"First your bomb failed, and today, so did your hit men. One is in custody, the other is in the morgue. Every time you fail, we get a little closer to finding you."

The tone of her voice changed, dropping to a quiet monotone. "I was not behind either event, Solicitor. You do me no good as a corpse. At least not yet."

I laughed. "You're pathetic! You don't even have control of your own organization. Maybe I should be speaking to the person who is *really* in control, because it sure as hell isn't you. Keep this line active in the unlikely chance I need to reach you." I hung up the phone before she could answer.

CHAPTER SEVENTEEN

"You're absolutely insane, John," Finnegan said, smiling, "but I like it."

"I hope I didn't overplay my hand," I said, still shaken from the encounter.

"Well, no use in worrying about it now. What's done is done."

Mack was still entranced by the front right wheel well of the vehicle. "Got it!" she announced.

"What is it, Mack?"

"Not entirely sure, but it isn't part of the vehicle, and was pretty well hidden. It had to have been placed there sometime when the car was parked for a long stretch. Perhaps in Mullingar, perhaps sooner. I won't know until I get a better look at it."

"Let's get the hell out of here before someone gets curious about what we found," I said.

We climbed into Finnegan's car and headed north.

* * *

"Giovanni," Mack said after a prolonged period of silence.

"Huh?" I said, slightly startled.

"She called you Giovanni. Not Solicitor, not John, but Giovanni."

"I didn't think you were listening."

"I'm always listening."

"I'll keep that in mind. I didn't think much of it, figuring she was just making fun of the Italian portion of my heritage."

"I'm not so sure, John. Shanagh picks her words carefully, all while speaking far more literally than one would expect. That's why I'm always after you to record her calls."

I could tell there was more. "Mack!"

"Something Shanagh said to you one time."

"Mack!!"

"Okay, okay! She said you were a *useful member of our little family.*"

I frowned. "She says all sorts of crazy things like that, most notably that I'm somehow her employee."

She wrinkled her nose. "Suit yourself, but I found her choice of words interesting."

"Hear her out, John," Finnegan interjected. "On her own, she's reached many of the same conclusions as our analysts."

"Fine," I sighed. "She must've gotten wind of the fact that I purchased a diamond to go in a wedding ring. I was planning to ask

Angela to marry me after she was exonerated. Shanagh had me pegged as love-sick from the beginning, even referred to herself as a future mother-in-law."

"I remember," Mack said, "but she used the word *family* long after any hope of matrimony faded. I did a little looking into your family tree, trying to see if any of the branches share a common root with Shanagh."

"I hope you've had better luck than I've experienced. I can find bits and pieces of my mother's family, and that's about it. Someday, Mack, I'm going to visit Cork and stay there until I've exhausted every clue I can find."

"Modest success," she said, "but nothing to indicate a connection."

"As I expected," I said.

"I also did some digging into your father's side of things."

"Why?" I laughed. "If there's a connection, which I doubt, it would be on the Irish side of my family."

"I agree," she said, "but there *is* a Giovanni Costaglioli in your tree…"

"Really? I've never heard of him, and I've traced that line back five or six generations."

"True, but you've only traced your direct line. Giovanni was your great-grandfather's brother, making him your second great uncle. His branch of the family stayed in Italy, although I've not been able to find any record of them after World War II."

"Giovanni is a very common name, Mack. I think you're grasping at straws."

"Possibly," she said, unconvinced, "but I'd like to keep working on it."

"Sure, but don't let it keep you from matters that are more pressing."

"Such as?"

"Helping me get in touch with Geryon…"

* * *

When we finally made it to our rooms in Antrim, fatigue was calling, loudly. I could tell from the sound of her coffee maker in operation, however, that Mack had no intention of sleeping. She was intently examining the device retrieved from our vehicle, and seemed oblivious to my presence.

Before turning in, I made the mistake of catching up on my e-mails. The first to catch my attention was from information-broker Jerry Keynes, and warranted an immediate call.

"Jack!," he said, "I'm surprised it took you this long to call."

"Sorry, Jerry, but I've been busy dodging bullets."

"I hope that's a figure of speech."

"Me, too. What do you have for me?"

"I was able to convince Ryan Boyle's lawyer to let me look at a few of his belongings. He couldn't release any of them to me without the executor's signature."

"Can we get the necessary signature?"

"You tell me, Jack. You're listed as the executor of the estate, such as it is."

"That's an interesting turn of events. If you send me their contact details, I'll get it taken care of."

"Done," said Jerry. "However, I still have some information I think you'll find useful. Our normal fee, I expect?"

"Our normal fee."

"Ryan Boyle kept some journals; I felt bad for the guy after reading through one of them. Reminds me a bit of you, Jack."

"How so?"

"The poor guy was surrounded by nefarious women his whole life, from the sound of things. Things were fine until their child, Karen, was born. Then something changed, and his wife started to grow distant. Well, it turns out, she was having an affair with, of all people, Connla O'Grady."

"Is there mention of another child, Jerry?"

"Christ, Jack, always in a damned hurry! Yes. It seems there was an illegitimate child involved when Karen was still a toddler. Alicia, his wife, wanted to keep the child, but Ryan refused. This made things a living hell for a few years, even to the point that Ryan worried about Karen's safety. He wanted to separate, but felt it was better for his child if he stayed around. The sad irony in the whole thing is that, in a later journal, Ryan lamented the fact that his daughter turned out to be like her mother. He even suspected Karen of somehow being involved in the Strabane bombing, even though she was living in the United States at the time. And, for the record, he didn't trust either Shanagh or Angela Grady."

"Wow."

"Yeah. Surrounded by beautiful danger. Reminds me of you, Jack."

"Well, there's only one of that crew remaining."

"You're missing one. I count two dangerous women in your circle."

Face flushing, I closed the door so that Mack couldn't hear. "What the hell is your problem with Mack, anyway?" I growled.

"She's too good to be true, and I don't trust anything that seems too good to be true. Especially if it's a woman."

"Mack has saved my bacon more times than I care to mention. Hell, Jerry, with an attitude like that, it's no wonder you're single!"

"Just setting a good example for the rest of us. Not my fault people aren't smart enough to listen. Look, either she's the greatest thing on the planet, and you're the dumbest man that ever lived for not putting a ring on her finger, or she's waiting for the right moment to clean you out, and you're the dumbest man that ever lived for keeping her around. Either way, it should serve as a constant reminder as to why I call you Jack."

"Yeah, yeah, I know. Short for jackass."

"You got it, buddy."

* * *

A gentle knock on the door distracted me.

"Why the closed door?" Mack said, as I invited her in.

"I was on the phone with Jerry Keynes, and I didn't want it to distract you."

"From the color of your face, I expect he was saying all sorts of wonderful things about me."

"Sorry, Mack. I don't know why he's got a burr up his ass about you, but he does."

"Oh well," she sighed, "I can't control what other people think of me. Here," she said, her demeanor changing as she handed me a small, plastic object, "this is really interesting."

"This came off our car?"

"It did, and its damn clever stuff."

"Tracking?"

"Definitely."

"It can't find us here, can it?"

"No," she laughed, "I removed its batteries the moment I found it. Take a look inside," she said, beaming.

"Okay. Looks like a circuit board to me, Mack. How does it work?"

"Like I said, it is very clever. It works a bit like the location service on a cell phone. This chip provides GPS functionality," she said, tapping a small, square of plastic with dozens of small, metal legs protruding from all sides. "This one will talk to wireless networks." Her finger highlighted another area of the circuit board. "Nothing really unusual there. I expect it is programmed to find open wireless networks and check-in with whomever is monitoring. But the real cleverness of this device is here," she said, moving her finger to a previously unmentioned area of the circuit board.

"What does it do?"

"It's a small radio transmitter. This bit over here is the antenna, and these cylindrical objects wrapped in wire actually generate energy from the motion of the vehicle to keep the batteries charged. Between the wireless networks and the GPS coordinates, they would have a good idea of our location. With the addition of this transmitter, they could tell exactly which vehicle we're in, even if we were in heavy traffic."

I studied her expression. My eyes narrowed. "What, exactly, are you saying, Mack?"

"Take another look at that circuit board. Look at it closely."

I studied the device, but had no idea what I was looking for. "I'm sorry," I said, handing it back to her, "I don't understand what you're trying to tell me."

"Look at the workmanship. This isn't a hacked cell phone, and it isn't a kit someone bought to learn electronics. This board has at least six layers of traces, and the numbering on the integrated circuits is unusual. This isn't consumer technology, John, it's military."

"Dammit."

"Yes, indeed. Even worse, I think it is related to this." She showed me the screen on her computer. "One of the newer toys in the west's proverbial war on terror."

"What the hell is that thing?"

"A shoulder-fired missile, with a twist. The tube is reusable, but, thanks to some new materials, is half the weight of predecessors and nonmetallic. It would be trivial to smuggle these things. Same for the electronics," she said, changing the picture on her screen. "All modular. There's even a rumor that the launcher can be operated with a properly configured cell phone if the normal electronics are damaged or missing."

"You're not telling me things that are going to make me sleep any easier tonight…"

"The tricky part would be getting your hands on these beauties." A few clicks, and a new picture appeared. "This is the business end of the operation, so to speak. Armor piercing, head packed with polymer-based explosives of some sort, I'm sure. Range of three, maybe four miles. Could be more if there is a new propellant involved. This thing is designed to take out anything from a light armored vehicle all the way down to…"

"A car…"

"A car. And this little beauty is the other half of the deadly team," she said, holding up the device discovered on our car. "A low-level operative could be issued one of these to attach to the target's vehicle. Each transmitter carries a unique code, so when the target gets in range…"

"The person carrying the missile launcher selects the target and fires," I said, finishing her sentence.

"Yep. The GPS gets the missile most of the way there, the tiny transmitter does the rest, making it a precision operation. If one of these would've hit our car, we'd both be dispatched to the hereafter instantly."

"Do you think we were meant to find this thing?"

"No. It was well hidden. Whoever did it knew what they were doing."

"Why the chase? Why not just blast us when we got within range?"

"I have no idea. Maybe we traveled a route they didn't expect. Possibly something else prevented them from springing the trap. Either way, we're damn lucky to be alive."

"You said each device has a code, right?"

"Yes. I'm working on recovering it. Once I do, though, I'll need to get help finding where it came from. I don't think I'll be able to track it down without raising the attention of Geryon."

"You think this is their work?"

"Likely. I don't think any of our other suspects could get their hands on this technology, with the possible exception of someone inside the U.K. military."

"What about someone inside the Police Service?"

"Unlikely that they could get it directly, although…"

"What is it, Mack?"

"You just gave me an idea. I need to find out if anything like this has been seized and held as evidence. According to Kelly Hamilton, our friend William Hayes has officially applied for the position that would put him in charge of securing a significant portion of the Police Service's impounded evidence."

"Maybe he's already gotten the job, and the world just doesn't know of it, yet. Talk about the fox guarding the hen house!"

"Assuming our suspicions are correct."

"They are, Mack. I can sense a dirty cop a mile away."

CHAPTER EIGHTEEN

"The script looks perfect," Finnegan said, handing it back to me.

"So what's wrong? I can tell something's bothering you, my friend," I said.

"We may have to delay this just a bit." His eyes were focused elsewhere.

"Why?" Disappointment rushed over me. We had spent days perfecting the script and choreography of a television show where I would announce a significant reward for information leading to the arrest of Shanagh Grady. Finnegan was an active and enthusiastic participant. Now, he seemed deflated.

"Somehow, Hayes has gotten wind that we're up to something. I don't think he knows the specifics, but word has it that he's furious."

"Who cares? Let the crooked bastard stew! He can't stop me, can he?"

Finnegan sighed, flopping into a nearby chair. "No, he can't.

What he can do, however, is control staffing, resources, and the flow of information to the people that would actually investigate any promising tips that come out as a result of the reward. He could apply a few well-placed roadblocks, enough to make any legitimate tips go stale by the time we investigate them."

"I can hire private investigators, off-duty police officers. Hell, Jim, I've provoked Shanagh Grady. We *have* to move!"

"Trust me, John. There are some good reasons to wait."

"Like what, Finnegan?" I growled. "What kind of dirt does Hayes have on you, anyway?"

Finnegan's nostrils flared. "What the hell are you on about, Costa?" he said, springing from his chair. "Who do you think you are making a comment like that? Bollox!"

"Who do I think I am? I *think* I'm your friend."

He paused, his expression easing. "Yes," he said, quietly. "You *are* my friend."

"Then talk to me! We both know Hayes is corrupt; it's damned obvious. What I don't understand is why the brass doesn't see it."

"The brass sees good arrest numbers, good morale within his command, and a dedicated police officer. His grandstanding about departmental corruption is laughable, given what I know about him, but I can't prove it. The leadership wants proof, not circumstances and innuendo. If I go to one of them with my suspicions, it will inevitably get back to Hayes; he's got too many friends and connections for it to remain secret. If it gets back to Hayes, bad things happen."

"What kind of bad things? Does he have something on you? Maybe we can make it go away…"

Finnegan laughed. "No, nothing like that. But if he put his mind to it, he could find the names of my confidential informants. I'm sure

Shanagh Grady and others like her would like to collect a pound or two of flesh from some of them. And then there are the people that I've helped to disappear over the years; new identities, credentials, you get the idea. Witnesses, mostly, but a few others, too. The longer I'm suspended, the more time he has to search for my secret files. If I'm reinstated or sacked, things become a lot more complex for him."

"And ergo the standoff."

"In a manner of speaking, yes, although he holds the upper hand. I only have hearsay; my files, on the other hand, are real."

"So the only way to turn the tables would be to find something tangible on William Hayes."

"Yes, but he's been awfully good at covering his tracks."

"Perhaps we haven't looked far enough back," I said, smiling.

Finnegan's eyes narrowed. "Go on…"

"Mack, can you pull up the Index Reference document, please?"

Mack nodded, and shortly the document fragment appeared on her computer:

```
	William Hayes (born 16 December 1954, Portadown, Armagh)
	74-0102* 97-0048*
```

"You are certainly full of surprises," he said, smiling. "What have you found out about them?"

"The first was a Loyalist attack in eastern Tyrone, one of your first cases where you were the primary investigator."

His expression grew distant. "Oh yes. I remember the case. There was an ambush, and a bomb that malfunctioned; some sort of an issue with the timing device, if memory serves me correctly. We thought the whole thing was in reprisal to an attack on some Orange men a few weeks prior."

"What we were able to learn," I said, "was that you turned up a promising witness, only to have the information quashed by Hayes."

"That isn't exactly how I remember it," Finnegan said, frowning. "I got a call from a man who said he had some information about the bomb. He was able to give me a few details of its construction that we hadn't released to the press. Hayes thought it was promising, so he ran with it. The man in question turned out to be mentally unstable and the information was a false lead designed to waste our time. It wasn't too uncommon for us to be intentionally misled, and at the time, I just chalked it up to my inexperience. Do you have reason to believe it was something else?"

"Quite possibly. When Preston pulled the file for me, there was no corroborating reason for discounting the witness."

"Unusual," Finnegan said. "That certainly wasn't standard procedure, and likely what caused the Index Reference document to come into existence. I wouldn't be surprised if my file didn't reference the same case."

"I see it was unsolved when this reference was created," I said, noting the existence of the asterisk after the case number. "Do you know if it was ever closed?"

"No idea."

"And the other one?"

Finnegan winced. "I know all about that one." He folded his arms. "Bastard," he muttered.

"Sorry."

"Not you, John. Hayes."

I could tell that Jim was struggling. "I'm sorry, because I'm going to ask you what happened. We need to know, I think."

Finnegan's lip quivered. He rose, staring out the nearest window. "Early in 1997, I got a tip about an upcoming attack. The informant was reluctant, so it took a lot of time and gentle coaxing to get what we needed. It was worth it, though. Our source turned out to be deep within an organization we now know was Shanagh Grady's."

"Strabane?"

"Yes," he said, a solitary tear running down his cheek. "Our source was desperately trying to warn us of an upcoming attack against the Royal Ulster Constabulary. Hayes stepped in and sent my bother, Gregory, in to investigate. A veil of secrecy dropped around the whole thing, and I was out of the loop. Of course," he said, collecting himself, "we know the rest. My brother was a skilled law enforcement officer, but something like this needed a task force. Hayes sent my brother in with a dolt of a partner and precious little else. I don't know if poor Greg was sent there to die, but he certainly wasn't sent there to succeed."

"Dammit. It seems we all know the identity of the fox in the henhouse, we just can't do anything about it."

"Why do you say that?" said Finnegan.

"Preston couldn't find the fully linked documents, and the one on the computer screen is a fragment; the rest of it looks to be destroyed. We're stuck."

"Maybe not," he said, "although we're running out of options."

"What do you have in mind?"

"Look at that document again," he said, pointing to the screen. "Would you say it is a copy of an original or a copy of a copy?"

"Hard to say. Mack?"

She shrugged. "The quality is quite poor. It could be either."

"Not everything the Constabulary recorded was digitized," Finnegan said. "With the arrival of the Good Friday accord, it was thought that the risk of certain documents going public, even fifty years in the future, could potentially ignite old disagreements."

"So the wrongdoing was covered up…"

"Not exactly. Some, perhaps, but in many cases, the reasons were far more altruistic than you give us credit for. There were always negotiations going on, always peacemakers at work on both sides, sometimes from unlikely places. It was thought best to prevent digitization and the risk of the wrong thing getting out. But that isn't to say the records don't exist."

"They're preserved somewhere?"

"Yes, in an archive. That's the good news. The bad news is that it is incredibly difficult to get in."

"We have to!" The excitement in Mack's voice startled me.

"I appreciate the enthusiasm, but…"

"No," she said, "you don't understand. There's something we've been missing."

"What is it, Mack?"

"I have this thing for numbers, you know. I can't ever forget them, even if I try."

"Yes…"

"74-0102. For some reason, it sounded familiar, so I started digging, and I just now found it." She paused. "This is the point in the conversation where you tell me how amazing I am."

"Mack!"

She rolled her eyes, and turned to Finnegan. "I swear, he doesn't appreciate me."

"Mack!!"

"All bloody right, already! Three years ago, we uncovered a similar Indexed Reference document when we were investigating the Strabane bombing."

"Yes," I said, interrupting. "It was a character assessment of Angela's father, Sean Grady."

"Correct! It listed the members of his immediate family. Case 74-0102 appeared under Connla O'Grady's name."

"You *are* absolutely amazing, Mack!"

She smiled, taking a heavily-flourished bow.

"Now, Jim, how the hell do we get in to the archives?"

He sighed. "I'll tell you, but you aren't going to like it."

"Why?"

"Because it is going to be expensive," said Mack.

"That, and we're going to have to break a few laws along the way."

I grimaced.

"And it will probably be dangerous."

"Cut to the chase, Jim."

"Maybe something else will come to me, but right now, I can only think of one way to get this done. If we get caught, there's a distinct possibility of prison."

"How much prison?" I said, eyebrow raised.

"Three years... possibly five... definitely no more than ten. Unless..."

"Unless *what?*"

"Unless we get shot in the act."

"Comforting..."

"Oh, that's not the half of it. I'm too well known, and you're far too likely to be recognized unless we can work up an incredible disguise. That leaves Miss MacDonald and Miss Hamilton, and even that's risky."

"I don't know, Jim. I'm not sure this is such a good idea..."

"I'll do it!" Mack said, before I could finish my sentence.

* * *

Kelly Hamilton arrived at our meeting heavily disguised, this time passing quite nicely as a middle-aged woman. She almost left after Jim Finnegan's first sentence.

"You want us to do what?" she said, eyes widening.

"We are going to collect some documents from the Constabulary archives," he said, calmly.

"You realize, of course, that they have armed guards, along with some of the better security systems in Northern Ireland. It's a tough nut to crack, as the saying goes."

"We're not going to try to crack the nut," Finnegan said. "That would be bloody impossible."

"Then how, exactly, do you plan to go about this wee bit of insanity?" Kelly asked.

"We're going to walk in, complete with orders and credentials, and take them."

"Of course," I interjected, "the orders will be fake, as will the credentials. And, in the interest of disclosure, by *we*, he means you and Mack; possibly me, too, depending on your ability to disguise me."

"Well," she sighed, flopping back into her seat, "that makes it all a bloody beezer then, doesn't it?"

"A what?" Mack whispered.

"A beezer, Mack. It means a good thing, but in this case, she's being a bit sarcastic."

"You think?" said Mack, rolling her eyes.

"We wouldn't ask if it wasn't important," I said. "Before you answer, let me get you up to speed on things."

Kelly listened patiently as I explained the situation. When I was done, she remained silent for several awkward minutes before speaking. "Who are you going to get to handle the physical credentials and orders?"

"We were thinking of this guy," I said, showing her a name on my phone.

"Expensive, but top notch work. I can make sure they're in the system, but I've never been to the archives or handled such a request. A first-timer wouldn't be sent with orders as important as these."

"I can brief you on the protocols and the layout," Finnegan said. "They recently installed a new digital fingerprint system; I hope that doesn't complicate things."

"No worries," Kelly said. "Actually, it might help us. People tend to be overly reliant on technology. When our fingerprints scan successfully, and our orders appear in the system, it will reduce the scrutiny on our credentials. I worry more about an old-school technophobe taking too much interest in us than I do about anything else. That could get sticky, as the saying goes."

"The whole thing could end badly, no doubt," Finnegan said. "If anyone wants out, speak now, and they'll be no hard feelings."

Nobody spoke.

"Very well," he said. "Let's get to work."

CHAPTER NINETEEN

"One thing terrifies me," Mack said.

"What's that?" I said, glancing up from the morning paper.

"I still can't do an Irish accent to save my life, and in this situation, it might be exactly that!"

"I'll work on it with you, but I want to show you something first. Take a look at the email I just received." I handed her my phone. An expression of surprise crossed her face as she read the message:

Dear Mr. Costa,

Please ring me or email at your earliest convenience. I would like to arrange a meeting. We have many things to talk about.

All the best,

Dianne O'Leary

"Are you going to meet with her? It could easily be a trap."

"Perhaps after I record the show this afternoon, I could meet with her. I have to admit, my curiosity is piqued."

"And curiosity killed the cat," Mack said, wrinkling her nose. "Please tell me you're going to take me with you."

"If I say no, you're going to come along anyway, aren't you?"

"Naturally."

* * *

I had no idea that filming a ten minute television spot would consume the entire afternoon. Our director, a spry, energetic man from New York set a frenetic pace. He was a believer in perfection through repetition, a trait that I initially admired, but came to loathe by about the seventh take.

"You look like a talking two-by-four," Mack said, wrinkling her nose.

"You're not helping," I protested. "This isn't as easy as it seems. I'm surrounded by nothing but green walls and strangers."

"Relax, and pretend you're talking to me."

"Then I'll appear like an *annoyed*, talking two-by-four," I said, winking.

She rolled her eyes. "Suit yourself," she said.

"I think your friend has a great idea," the director said. "We'll put her behind your camera, and you can focus on her pretty face instead of this ugly bastard," he said, tilting his head toward the man operating the camera. "Again!"

It took three more takes to convince Mack to stop making me laugh. There was method to her madness, though, as I finally was able to relax enough to produce a usable take.

"You went off script once or twice," the director said, "but it felt natural, and we can use it."

"Good. What happens now?"

"We're going to digitally add the set, including a clock on the wall. It will look and feel exactly like a live show."

"Mack, is everything else ready?"

"All set. Once they're done, we'll have the final digital copies in our possession, and the cast and crew will be on their way to the docks."

In addition to the director and crew, we hired seven aspiring actors and actresses to accept fake phone calls throughout the show. All were carefully screened, but for additional assurance that our subterfuge would persist, I rented a luxury yacht where they could enjoy an extended pleasure cruise, free of internet or cell phone service.

* * *

"I don't like this one bit," Mack said. "Why are we meeting her at her house? Now it really smells of a trap."

"Her vehicle is in the shop," I said. "Finnegan knows where we are. If something goes wrong…"

"He'll know where to find the bodies," Mack said, rolling her eyes.

"At least we'll die in a nice house," I said, pointing to the generous home of Dianne O'Leary.

* * *

I was momentarily left speechless when the door opened. A small gasp from Mack confirmed what I was feeling: Dianne O'Leary's resemblance to Karen Boyle was remarkable.

"Come in, please," she said, motioning for us to enter. "I have tea brewing."

"You have a lovely place, Miss O'Leary, or is it Mrs. Antonopoulos?"

"Please, call me Dianne. And it's O'Leary. Please, sit down; I'll explain everything."

"Thank you," I said, as she handed me a cup of tea. "I'm sorry if I'm staring, but you bear a tremendous resemblance to a close friend."

"Women take after their mothers," she said. "I read about the unfortunate death of your friend. I'm sorry for your loss."

"Thank you. So, our suspicions that your mother is Alicia O'Leary are correct, I take it."

"Quite true," she said. "I was told that I was orphaned when my mother died in a traffic collision. I grew up thinking my name was Siobhan O'Connor."

I smiled. "Interesting. I prefer what you're going by now, though. How did you decide on it?"

"I stayed in touch with Linda MacRory — I believe you've met. She finally let it slip that my mother's last name was O'Leary. I did some research and discovered that a woman named Dianne O'Leary died under conditions similar to those described to me. When I was of legal age, I changed my name to match the woman I thought was my mother. Imagine my surprise when I discovered that my real mother was still alive!"

"I think your name is lovely," said Mack.

"Thank you," Dianne said. "Mister Costa, I understand you've been asking about Ulster Maritime Group."

"I have."

"Maybe we can help each other, then."

"Possibly. What do you have in mind, Miss O'Leary?"

"An exchange of information. I'll tell you what I know about the dealings of my company, and you tell me about my father."

"I never met your father. All I know of him is what I've learned from research."

"That's far better than what I know. You see, I don't even know his name. Mrs. MacRory refuses to tell me about him, and there's no official record of anything." She rose, turning away from me. "Just so you know you're talking to the right person," she said, extending her well-toned leg outward and exposing the back of her knee, "here is the scar."

The diamond-shaped scar that Linda MacRory described was there. "That must've hurt. How did you get it?"

"Whilst riding my bicycle," she answered, returning to her chair.

"I don't think your father was a very nice man, I'm sorry to say."

"I gathered that from the way Mrs. MacRory reacts when I mention him."

"Dianne, your father's name was Connor O'Grady, although he went by the name Connla Grady. He was born in Cork in 1919, but his family moved to Mullingar about a year later. He volunteered for service in World War II, which is where he got his start as a businessman, of sorts."

"Of sorts?"

"Ostensibly, he ran a contracting business with his partner and friend, David A. Brennan. His real business was smuggling guns and munitions from the Middle East into Ireland, ostensibly to support the efforts of the various IRA factions in the North. He was good at it; so good, in fact, that he branched out to become a global organization. He did it through a series of small, interconnected, but often disparate businesses. Each operated, for the most part, legitimately, called on occasionally to perform various tasks."

"I call it micro-smuggling," added Mack. "No single business is significant enough to draw the attention of the authorities. No single shipment is big enough to spark a wide scale investigation. But when combined, the effectiveness is stunning. The whole thing is quite brilliant, really."

"It doesn't sound like much, but the value of the diamonds Connla smuggled in is worth nearly a billion pounds in today's market," I said.

"So all this unpleasantness that has been on the news, the Grady gals, the woman who was murdered, the whole bit…"

"Yes," I said, quietly. "Your family. Shanagh Grady married Connla's son. Angela was their daughter, and although you're only about a year older, you would have been her aunt. Karen Boyle was your half-sister."

She rose, rubbing her fingers on her temples before running them through her hair. "You know," she said, fighting tears, "you read all these stories about people who were adopted finding their families and having happy reunions. Maybe I should have left mine alone."

"I'm sorry," I said.

"Don't be," she said, collecting herself. "I asked, and you answered — fair play to you. But what does all this have to do with me? Am I in trouble? In danger?"

"That's what I'm hoping to find out, and why I've been asking about your business. Its profile is similar to others in Connla Grady's network, and the initial loan that got things started was provided by a finance company connected to the Grady organization."

"Oh no," she said, returning to her chair.

"So, to answer your question," I continued, "if your business is involved with Shanagh Grady, then you're probably in trouble, although to what degree, I don't know. In danger? Possibly. Shanagh Grady hated your mother, which is one of the reasons Karen was murdered. It isn't beyond the realm of possibility that her hostility could extend to you, if she knows about you."

"Do you think she does?" Dianne O'Leary's voice was trembling.

"She knows about Ulster Maritime Group, that much is certain. When Mack was kidnapped, she spent part of her captivity in a ship that your company was repairing. That's how we learned about it."

"Kristos runs the business," she said. "Always has."

"Your husband?"

"When I was about twenty years old, a pair of lawyers showed up at my door. Seems that I had inherited a shipping company from the same mysterious, rich relative that sent me money and gifts whilst I was growing up. What the hell did I know about running a shipping company? Any company for that matter. I just wanted to sell the bloody thing and be done with it. They assured me, though, that it was being competently run, and that my involvement could be minimal."

"Let me guess — your husband, Kristos Antonopoulos, was running the company when you inherited it."

"Yes, but we're not married, Mister Costa, and never have been. People assume it, but we've never so much as been on a date."

I glanced over at Mack who raised her eyebrow in response.

"We're a little confused about the ownership of your company. When we initially researched it, we assumed Mr. Antonopoulos was the owner."

"That was something the lawyers set up. He is the legal owner of Ulster Maritime, I inherited its holding company. They did it because, at the time, the shipping business was male-dominated. Besides, I had no interest in the day to day operation of the company. I still don't, really. They trot me out every now and then when they need some publicity, otherwise, I'm the perfect example of a silent partner."

"Your silence seems to have done well," I said, glancing around.

"Yes," she laughed, "some of this is from my company income. More of it is from my other venture."

"And that is?"

"I'm a writer, Mister Costa. I use a pseudonym, and I doubt you've heard of my books."

"Oh? What do you write?"

"Formulaic romance novels. They're utter rubbish, but stick a man with a rippling chest on the cover, and ladies devour them, one after another."

"How many have you written?"

"Thirty, with three more in the queue ready to go."

"Wow! You know, your sister was quite an artist. It's a shame you never got to meet her…"

We spent the next hour sharing stories about Karen Boyle, carefully avoiding the unpleasant events that led up to her death. As our visit concluded, I handed her a business card.

"There are several names on the back. The first is a reliable solicitor, should the need arise. The second is someone who can arrange for personal security. I recommend you call him as soon as we leave, and mention my name when you do."

"I will," she said.

* * *

"How much of that did you believe?" Mack studied my face.

"Some of it, I think. She was rather quick to throw Kristos Antonopoulos under the bus, wasn't she?"

"I noticed that, too," she said, wrinkling her nose. "I also found it interesting that she denied their marriage, yet I was able to find a license when I searched the records."

"Could have been faked, I suppose. It would be well within the Grady's modus operandi to do something like that, especially if it benefited them."

"True," she said. "You held up quite well, by the way."

"What do you mean, Mack?"

"The incessant flirting."

"Flirting? I didn't notice."

"You didn't notice the coy eye contact she made with you, or how she twirled her hair?"

"I noticed the bit with the hair, but I attributed it to nerves."

"Nope," Mack said. "Flirting. Unabashed flirting."

"Not interested."

"If she knocks on your door, claiming she's scared and alone, we'll know she's involved," she said, rolling her eyes.

I sighed. "That does seem to be a theme in my life lately, doesn't it? I think I've just about had my fill of Irish ladies, thank you."

"Perhaps an American gal is what you need."

"Nah," I said, shaking my head. "I think I'm going to give up and get a cat. One that sits there, staring at me, quietly plotting my death. Dammit. I'm hungry. Dinner?"

"Of course," she said, giggling quietly.

CHAPTER TWENTY

It was a pleasant surprise to hear the voice of Laura McConnell, the general manager of my pub and perpetual graduate student.

"Good morning, Mister C!"

"Laura!" I said, staring at my clock, "what are you doing up so early in the morning?"

"I'm heading back to my apartment for a few hours of sleep. Today's the big day!"

Dammit. I had become so engrossed in the search for Shanagh Grady that I'd forgotten the date. My pub, damaged heavily by an intentionally set gas explosion, was set to reopen. "And so it is," I replied. "Are you opening at the usual time, or later?"

"You forgot, didn't you, Mister C?" I could hear a twinge of disappointment in her voice.

"I did. I'm sorry."

"We're opening for dinner, complete with live music and lots of hoopla. We've been closed longer than I wanted to be. Hopefully, the regular crowd will return."

"If the hoopla involves free stuff, they'll be back."

"It does," she said, laughing quietly. "Would you like a tour?"

"Certainly," I laughed, "but I'll have to take a rain check until I get back."

"I was thinking more along the lines of a video call."

"That works. Now, how do I do this?"

Finally, after a few failed attempts, her face appeared on my screen. An immediate glance told the story.

"Wow! The kitchen looks bigger."

"It is," she said, proudly, "and more efficient thanks to a streamlined layout. I ordered a new computer system, too, to track the orders."

"But where did the extra space come from? You didn't lose tables, did you?"

"Relax, Mister C! The damage extended into the adjacent business, too. They opted not to reopen, and I got additional square footage at a significant discount. Check it out!"

She walked through a doorway and into the main bar area.

"We are able to serve twelve more patrons at the bar, and I've doubled the number of taps. But here's the part I'm really proud of…"

She turned her phone so that I could see the full extent of the renovations.

"It looks absolutely wonderful. Very authentic."

"Thank you. We've included some modern amenities, too: upgraded WiFi, our own app..."

"Wait. We have an app?"

"Yes. People can use it for everything from reserving a table, to carry-out orders, to requesting a refill. You'll like this, too."

She turned on some lights, revealing a small stage.

"A stage?"

"Yes, and where we've located it, people on the other side of the pub can still enjoy a quiet conversation."

"Clever. Speaking of which," I said, "where's my normal corner?"

"Bad news on that one," she said. "There was some structural damage in that area. The contractor had no choice but to add some reinforcements. Unfortunately, they consumed most of the area where your booth was. There's a wall where it used to be."

"Oh well," I sighed, "nothing lasts forever. I'm sure I'll find a new spot. Get some rest, and drop me a note later letting me know how things go."

"Will do, Mister C. Hope to see you soon. We miss you!"

* * *

I barely had time to catch my breath before my phone was ringing again. This time, it was Charlie Hannon. Charlie, the detective I'd hired during the initial investigation of the Strabane attack was curmudgeonly, foul-mouthed, expensive, and worth every penny.

"A damn good thing you referred your friend to me, it is."

"You lost me, Charlie. Who and what are we talking about?"

"Dianne O'Leary," he grunted. "I hope she can pay my damned

bill."

"I don't expect it will be a problem for her, but what on earth is going on?"

"She made us go through the whole damn house, inch by inch. Then her car. Good thing we did, too. Someone attached one of those tracking gadgets like Miss MacDonald found on your car. God knows how long it's been on there."

"Interesting. What did you do with it?"

"We took the batteries out of it, just like Miss MacDonald instructed. I'll bring it by later today."

"Sounds good. What about Dianne? You have her someplace safe, I presume."

"Safe?" he guffawed. "She's not interested in hiding, Costa, she's on quite a tear. Her business partner is on holiday in Greece, or something like that, and if I were the poor bloke, I'd stay there."

"This is going to sound like a bizarre question, but does all of it seem sincere to you?"

"She's as serious as a heart attack. I'm told she's already sacked one person at her company, and hired a team of auditors to go through the books with a fine-toothed comb. I'd say she's bloody serious."

"Thanks, Charlie. Keep me informed, will you?" I winced at my own words, knowing that each phone call would come with a corresponding bill.

* * *

"What is it, Mack?" She had that look on her face, and I couldn't wait to hear what she was going to say.

"Has your car been repaired yet?"

"Yes, and it arrived yesterday."

"Where is it?"

"I made arrangements with Charlie Hannon to park it somewhere safe. You look like the cat that swallowed the canary. Spill it."

"Today, I'm going to give a reminder of why you keep me around."

I laughed. "Mack, you don't need to remind me!"

She handed me the tracking device. "Behold!"

"Umm... Okay..." It looked no different to me than when she had removed it from its hiding place inside my vehicle.

She retrieved the device, raising her eyebrows and winking as she did. "The genius is on the inside."

"I believe you, Mack, but what does it all mean?"

"Remember that I told you that these things have a mechanism to phone home?"

I nodded.

"Well, this otherwise mild-mannered fellow eventually revealed his secrets to me. I'm irresistible that way, you know."

She tried batting her eyelashes, but failed, miserably. I rolled my eyes in response.

"This little guy encrypts everything it sends," she said, quickly turning serious again. "The encryption prevents someone who might intercept the traffic from reading it. So even if I had software monitoring every router on the internet collecting traffic from this thing, it would take years to decipher a single message. By then, the data would be absolutely useless. But that's only if we don't have the key. In our situation," she said, tapping on the device, "we have the key. It's right here, in this little device. The trick was finding it, and figuring out the algorithm it uses to talk on a network."

I was starting to understand what she was telling me. "And with the key?"

She smiled, "and with the key, a smart person could reverse engineer the software used to monitor the location of these things." She pointed to a map that appeared on our television, which she had commandeered to serve as another monitor. "So, there's good news and there's bad news."

"Out with it, Mack!"

"The good news is, there's a zero in the upper left hand corner of the screen."

"And that means?"

"My software hasn't found any active nodes. In other words, there aren't any devices that are phoning home. Either we have all of them, or nobody with a tracking device is moving. They go dormant if they haven't moved in twelve hours, to preserve battery life."

"And what's the bad news?"

"Actually, there are two bits of bad news…"

"Mack!"

"Okay, already! The devices listen, too, and have the ability to generate a new key. We were lucky; the one we have still has the original key. Perhaps they didn't know to change it, maybe they forgot, but there could be ten of them active right now, and I wouldn't be able to see them because they're running a different key system."

"Charlie is going to bring us the one from Dianne O'Leary's car. Will you be able to tell if its key is original?"

"Yes, but that still doesn't help if there are others out there."

"I get it. And the other bit of bad news?"

"My software works with a simulated tracker, but I've not been able to test it with the real thing. The only way to know for sure is to activate one of the trackers we have in our possession. And we can't do that…"

"Without risking an *up close and personal* meeting with one of those shoulder-fired missiles."

"Precisely, John. I do have an idea about that, though…"

"If it involves me being live bait, I'm not particularly interested."

"The system has one weakness. Actually, less of a weakness than an intentionally designed limitation."

"And that is?"

"It doesn't understand elevation, largely because it doesn't need to. It was designed specifically to attach to land-based vehicles, so its data stream only includes latitude and longitude figures. The missile uses the radio frequency transmitter for the final piece of the puzzle, which brings me to my idea…"

"And that is?"

"Setting a trap."

"I like it, but aren't they going to know something is odd if one of the trackers suddenly starts chattering miles away from its previous location?"

"Yes," she said, her voice dropping. "That's why we can't test my theory using this one." She slipped the device back into her pocket. "How much do you trust Dianne O'Leary?"

"Not much. Why?"

"We may not have any choice. If we activate this one, and there is an attack planned against us, we won't have time to get out of a populated area. God forbid they actually have one of those missiles and fire it; a lot of people could get killed."

"I'm with you there, definitely."

"But Dianne O'Leary's house is on the outskirts of a rural area. What if she were to go for a drive in the country?" Mack smiled, deviously.

"Even though I don't trust her, I still won't ask her to be bait."

"Not her. Us, but with her tracking device."

"Sounds too much like live bait to me, Mack," I said, frowning.

"It isn't without risk, but I have an idea that should minimize it."

"I'm all ears, Mack."

"I've been thinking over the events that happened on our way back from Mullingar. The people who were chasing us didn't have a missile, and the Garda haven't been able to locate any trace. That tells me they were using the device only to track us, not as a homing beacon. Otherwise, why try to kill us?"

"Good point. Maybe they only have one missile, and they couldn't get it in range fast enough."

She wrinkled her nose. "I don't think so. They knew we were in Mullingar, where we were, and had enough time to plant the device."

I nodded. "True."

"What this tells me is that we weren't the primary target."

"Then that would make the primary target…"

"Dianne O'Leary," she said. "The arrival of Charlie Hannon's men has made her a much more difficult target, but I don't expect them to give up. That's where my idea comes in…"

"Talk to me."

"We're going to need three things," she said, clicking the mouse on her computer. "We're going to need a couple of officers from the Police Service that we can trust; Finnegan should be able to help. And we're going to need permission to be here," she said, pointing to an area on the map.

"What is that place?"

"A quarry. I imagine that you'll be able to come up with a financial arrangement with the owner that will permit us to be there on Sunday, when it's closed and not in operation."

"I suppose so…"

"We're going to need one of these, too."

"A drone? Do I even want to know why?"

"Probably not… And you definitely don't want to know how much of your money I spent on it."

"Mack!!"

CHAPTER TWENTY-ONE

"That is, undeniably, the worst attempt at an Irish accent I've ever heard," Kelly Hamilton said. "If she can't do this, our goose is cooked, as the saying goes."

"I told you," Mack said, clearly discouraged.

"What if she simply doesn't speak?" I asked, trying to be helpful.

"No such luck," said Finnegan. "At the very least, she'll be expected to give her name, commanding officer, and so forth. No way around that."

"Perhaps we're approaching this from the wrong angle," I said. "Mack, can you do any sort of accent? Anything at all?"

"I've been told that I do a passable Scottish accent."

I laughed. "You're kidding, right?"

"Not at all," she said. "I played an online game for years, and most of the original founders of my guild were Scottish. I heard enough about Glasgow to last a lifetime, too. I could probably pass for having lived there, unless I ran into an actual resident."

"It could work," Kelly said, casting a glance at Finnegan.

"Let's hear you," Jim said.

Mack rattled off several sentences, then, on Kelly's prompting, a few more. It sounded Scottish to me, but my ear lacked the acumen to know if it would stand up under scrutiny.

"Can you do it under pressure?" Kelly asked, "because it isn't bad, but there were several times when it felt close to slipping back to your normal accent."

"I don't know the answer," Mack said. "I've never used it when it really mattered. It was something fun we did online, nothing more."

"We're going to have to go with it," said Finnegan. "We can list Belfast as your place of birth, but Glasgow as your residence until you returned for University, or something along those lines. That should explain the accent."

"Now that we've got that sorted," I said, "we need the names of several reliable Police Service officers; people you trust, Jim."

"I can do that, although it might be nice to know what you've got in mind, John."

"We're going to take a drive in the country, Jim."

* * *

Adnan Jasik seemed unhappy to see us, but had no objections to the cash I paid him to facilitate the meeting.

"Emil," he growled, "doesn't like talking. What he likes even less? Questions."

I understood, and dutifully kept my mouth shut as our car

meandered through the streets of Belfast.

"Is everything ready, Poppy? Emil doesn't like surprises or last-minute changes."

"Everything is as it should be," Kelly said.

Her words seemed to settle Adnan. He drove silently for another ten minutes before turning into a narrow street. "Last on the left," he grunted, pointing toward a row of doors, "but around the corner and down the stairs."

We stepped out of the vehicle, and he quickly drove away.

"He'll be back," Kelly whispered. "Now, follow me and keep quiet, you two."

* * *

The front room of the apartment, if it could even be called that, was barely the size of a moderate walk-in closet, and a blanket tossed across a makeshift curtain rod hid whatever was beyond. Given the general squalor of things, I dreaded what it might be.

"You have the money?" he said, studying Kelly closely.

"Money on the delivery of the product," she said.

"I don't like this one," he said, pointing his thumb toward me. "You pay first."

"I don't care if you don't like him," she growled. "He's the one with the money. We do things per the agreement, and maybe he'll pay you instead of breaking your neck."

I tried to remain stoic, even menacing, as I assessed the man.

"Follow," he grunted, pushing the blanket out of the way, and disappearing into the room beyond. Without hesitation, Kelly and Mack joined him. I was the last to cross the threshold.

The small, but neat, kitchen surprised me, as it was in stark opposition to the front room's disheveled appearance. The bedroom that connected to it was, likewise, meticulously organized and spotless. He opened the door into a narrow closet, brushing aside the clothes hanging within.

He pounded twice on the back wall. To my surprise, it slid open, revealing a hidden room. A large, scowling man studied us as we entered.

"Hello, Poppy," he said in a heavy Eastern European accent. "Or should I say goodbye, perhaps?"

She acknowledged him with a slight nod of her head. "Emil," she said. I wanted to know what the hell his comment meant.

"You have the details?" he said, hand outstretched.

Kelly handed him a flash drive.

He moved to a computer, plugged in the device and examined the contents.

I took the opportunity to study the room. Clearly, it had one purpose: the creation of false identification cards. Attached to the computer was an expensive camera aimed at a nearby wall. On the wall hung a blue backdrop, the type commonly used in licenses. A nearby table held several printers.

"Number forty-seven," Emil said.

The smaller man slid open the third drawer of a flat file, a cabinet similar to what an artist might use to store paper. He removed a new background, replacing the one that hung on the wall.

"Are you sure of this, Poppy? These will get you into places where people carry guns, and aren't afraid to use them."

Now I understood the meaning of his earlier comment. My stomach quietly protested our situation.

"Just shoot the damn pictures, Emil," she said.

He raised his eyebrows, and returned his attention to the screen of his computer. "You first," he said to Mack, motioning toward the chair.

Mack removed her jacket, revealing a crisp Police Service uniform. Her hair, straightened and died jet black, was pulled back neatly. Subtle makeup and brown contact lenses completed the illusion. It was am impressive transformation. Kelly Hamilton followed, her disguise equally convincing.

"A few minutes now," Emil said, connecting one of the printers to the computer. It whirred to life, and it wasn't long before Kelly Hamilton was scrutinizing two Police Service identification cards.

"Impressive," she said. "Your reputation is intact, my friend."

On her cue, I handed him a thick wad of cash.

* * *

"Bastard!" Kelly said, as we drove.

My stomach sickened. "Is there something wrong with the identification cards?"

"No. They're perfect. Absolutely perfect, right down to the embedded chips and the holograms."

"That's good, isn't it?"

"For us at this moment, it is, but not for the Police Service. Emil sells his services to the highest bidder. There's no telling who else is buying Police Service credentials and using them for God knows what. He's got to have a source on the inside, either at the Police Service, or at the company that produces the stock used for the cards."

"Why don't you arrest him?"

She laughed. "He's probably packing for a move to another location as we speak. Not only that, but I can't risk my cover. I have a reputation to maintain, as the saying goes."

* * *

Finnegan studied Mack's disguise closely. "Flawless," he said. He handed Mack several pages, stapled together. "Here is your back story. Study it. John, here's a copy for you. Quiz her on it until she knows it, cold. One slip and you're headed for prison. If you're lucky, that is, and don't end up with a bullet in your heart."

He turned to Kelly, handing her an official-looking document and a sealed envelope.

"Your orders," he said. "Make sure they get in the system."

She examined the pages, raising her eyebrow. "Signed by Assistant Chief Constable Walsh. Impressive forgery, I have to admit. Expensive, no doubt."

"Indeed," Finnegan said, "but we can't afford to take risks."

"Of all the people to forge," Kelly said, "why did you have to pick her? There's going to be hell to pay when this gets back to her. And it will, you know. She signs so few of these kinds of things."

"True, that," Finnegan said, "but she's so thorough and picky that her signature won't draw as much scrutiny. At least that's the plan. As for the consequences, well, I'll handle that when I get there."

"So when does all this happen?" I said.

"Forty-eight hours, coordinated with the airing of your appeal to the public. That's all ready to go, correct?"

"It is."

* * *

I met Dianne O'Leary at a secure location arranged by Charlie Hannon. One glance, and I realized she was livid.

"I'm going to end up in prison," she said.

"I hear you've been on quite the mission lately," I said. "I take it you've found some things going on within your company that are as I feared?"

She nodded, her jaw clenched.

I continued. "I think it is premature, however, to talk about prison. Have you spoken to the solicitor I recommended yet? He's quite astute, and I'm sure there are plenty of deals to be made at this point, especially if you're coming forth with evidence."

"Oh, I'm not worried about that. I'm worried about the murder charge after I find Kristos. I'm going to put a bullet in that feckin' eejit's brain when I find him! Look at this," she said, handing me a three-ring binder stuffed with copies.

"What is all this?"

"This is just what I've found so far," she said, "and I'm not even an accountant by trade."

"Do you have an accountant you can use to audit the books?" It took only a moment to realize that I had inadvertently struck a nerve.

"The Greek bitch conveniently disappeared," she said, her lips barely moving. "I made a few inquiries. Care to guess where she is?"

I shrugged. "I'm sorry; I don't really have any idea."

"Off to Greece, probably to be with Kristos. Seems they've been carrying on for quite a while now, right under my nose."

Her anger gave way to sobbing as the truth dawned on me. "You loved him, didn't you?"

"The damn wanker used me," she blubbered, fighting to catch her breath. When her composure returned, she continued. "It seemed like a match made in heaven. I was a university student, and I knew absolutely everything there was to know. Or so I thought. I'd just inherited a fair sum of money and a shipping company, and I was all set to sell it and move to France. But there he was: handsome, well-off, and already running the business — quite well, by all accounts."

"And you fell for him…"

"Like a ton of bricks," she said, fighting off tears. "My friends kept warning me that I'd meet men that were interested in me only for my money. In his case, he already had plenty of money, so why would he want mine? Seemed like a safe bet, it did. I should've known something was bloody squiffy when he wouldn't marry me."

"What excuse did he give you?"

"Some nonsense about keeping our assets separate; proof that his love was genuine. I feel like a bloody damned fool."

"I know the feeling, all too well, unfortunately. I wish I had some sage advice for you, but honestly, I've not sorted out my own thoughts on the matter yet. I know it hurts, though, and it doesn't go away quickly."

"It was all a damned illusion, right from the beginning, and its all in the binder, Mister Costa. The most recent is at the front; I expect it will interest you the most. My company was involved in the kidnapping of your friend, at least peripherally. The ship was brought in for repairs. Kristos faked some problems with it so we could keep it a few weeks beyond the original schedule. There are some rather questionable deals involving South America in the works right now." She slid the binder across the table to me. "This copy is yours. As I find more, I'll share it."

"Thank you. We'll definitely look through this. I do have another favor to ask of you…"

"Name it."

"We would like to borrow your car this coming Sunday."

She looked confused. "Certainly."

"We discovered a tracking device on it, similar to the one that was surreptitiously attached to our vehicle while we were researching your childhood in Mullingar. My theory is that someone, probably Shanagh Grady, was desperate to keep us from meeting — likely so we wouldn't discover what is in this binder. It was good fortune that your car ended up in the shop, or else we might not be talking now."

"Why is that?"

"The tracking device is actually a homing mechanism for a shoulder-fired missile."

She paled. "And one was found on *my* car?" she said, voice shaking.

"Yes. We deactivated it, of course, but I'd like to see if anyone is still interested in eliminating either of us now that you've discovered the truth about Kristos. If so, we've got a plan to trap them."

"You're welcome to my car if it will help, but the whole thing sounds bloody dangerous."

"My assistant has a plan, but we're going to need you to play along in setting the trap. And we need your car."

"It's yours," she said, handing me the keys. "Mister Hannon's men have been nice enough to provide me safe transportation. I'm sure they won't mind continuing to do so. What do I do in the interim?"

I handed her a document. "Continue on with the same routine you've done for the past few days, just like this meeting never happened. Study the papers I just shared, and don't mention a word about what we're doing to anyone."

CHAPTER TWENTY-TWO

"Kelly," I said, "can you get me in touch with Geryon?"

"I can give you a couple of email addresses and a few chat servers you could try. No guarantees, of course."

"Would you be able to tell if the response is real, or someone pretending?"

"Possibly. Tell me one thing, though…"

"What is it?"

"Why are you wanting to make contact? Seems like you're just asking for trouble, as the saying goes."

"I want to convince them that their new partnership will end up being a liability. We're going to appeal to the public, which will put the spotlight on Shanagh. That will make her a less effective force, at least in theory. Have you noticed?"

"Noticed what?"

“Shanagh hasn’t called in days.”

“It could be the calm before the storm.”

“Good point. I should’ve kept my mouth shut!”

Kelly rose, a smile crossing her face. “Your idea has merit, though, all laughing aside. Perhaps what you need is a little leverage.”

“What do you have in mind?”

“We’ve been monitoring a few bank accounts that we think might be intermediary pools for Geryon to clear illicit funds. Mostly the conversion of shadow currency into something real, I’d say. If we could seize several of them, or at least temporarily shut them down, it might reinforce your message. I don’t think it would do much to their operation globally, but it’s something.”

“Isn’t that going to take a while?”

“The technology is all set,” Kelly answered. “We just need an official blessing to do so.”

“That’s what I was afraid of,” I said, returning to my chair, discouraged.

“It would be grand if we knew someone with the connections necessary to produce such a blessing.”

All eyes turned to Jim Finnegan, who pretended not to hear us. After a few moments of deafening silence, he grunted. “Fine. I’ll make it happen.”

“How much is this going to cost me?” I asked.

“This one is on the house,” he said. “I’m owed a favor or two; I’ll cash one in.”

* * *

Everything was happening all at once, and my nerves were

getting the best of me. Mack was putting the final touches on her disguise, and undergoing a final round of quizzing from Finnegan. She passed with flying colors.

"You look the part, Mack" I said. Her uniform was crisp, and her demeanor felt cold and professional — exactly what we needed.

"Move along, citizen. Nothing to see here," she said, deadpan. Finally, after an awkward pause, she wrinkled her nose. "I don't like my hair."

Her hair, normally wavy and red, was straight and black; normally hanging freely over her shoulders, it was pulled back into a tight ponytail.

"It's only temporary," I reassured. "Now, for the last time, are you sure, absolutely sure, you want to do this?"

"I'm sure, but I don't think you are," she said, taking my hand. "You're always the one telling me to stay within the law. I can't imagine this is sitting well with you."

"It isn't, but too many lives are at stake, and I just can't think of another way."

"You're taking less risk than you think," added Finnegan. "The rich can always buy their way out of problems, anyway. Worst that happens is you two get a slap on the wrist and sent home."

"Can't buy my way out of a bullet in my best friend's heart, Jim."

"True that," he sighed, "but, in truth, the chances of that are fairly low. Nearly zero, in truth."

I knew he was trying to make me feel better. My mind appreciated his efforts; my stomach remained unconvinced.

* * *

Watching my televised appeal for tips and information leading to the arrest of Shanagh Grady wasn't helping distract my preoccupied mind. I found myself scrutinizing every aspect of my performance, hating my voice, and wanting to crawl under a rock. Five minutes in, and I was contemplating calling the station to stop the broadcast. Strong words from Jim Finnegan and a glass of whiskey put a quick end to the foolish notion.

I was too focused to notice the ringing of my phone until it was too late. I cursed as it went to voice mail. Moments later, it rang again. The Pavlovian response to answer it nearly won, but something stopped me. I stared at the incoming number, a smile formed as my brain finally made the connection.

"Jim," I said, "Shanagh is calling."

"You're not going to answer it, are you, John?"

My eyes narrowed. "Of course not. I'm doing a live television show, remember?"

There was a longer pause before the phone rang again, showing the same incoming number on the screen. Once again, I ignored it.

"Oh, I bet she's unhappy with you," Finnegan said, sipping his whiskey.

"Care to find out?" I said, smiling as the icon signaling the arrival of a voice message appeared on my screen. Before I finished speaking, the counter changed to show a second.

He nodded.

"And now there are two for us to listen to," I said, tapping the screen, playing the recorded message.

I'm disappointed with you, Solicitor. Even though you're too stubborn to see it, there are too many that believe in the cause to ever betray me.

Her voice was calm, almost lyrical. Dammit.

"I guess my gamble didn't pay off, Jim."

He raised his glass. "Well played, though," he said. "Give the next message a listen."

I pressed the button. Shanagh Grady didn't speak, but I could hear my broadcast in the background. Although I couldn't hear every word, I knew precisely where in the script it was:

Please do not be fooled. Shanagh Grady claims to support the cause of freedom. Shanagh Grady claims to support the cause of a united Ireland. The truth is, Shanagh Grady supports only perpetual violence and her own wicked self-interests. Throughout the Troubles, her organization supplied weapons, ammunition, and explosives to both sides, indiscriminately. As long as people were killing each other, she was profiting, and therefor, happy. In the Bosnian conflict, her organization supplied both sides. The same holds true for the Middle East today. You will not betray your beliefs if you share information with us.

Then she spoke, her voice quivering:

"You've just sealed your fate, Solicitor, and that of your little red tart. You're going to beg for the sweet release of death, you damned traitor! How dare you! You lying, thieving bastard!"

She then descended into a torrent of profanity. A brief silence followed, then she spoke again, urgency decorating her voice. "Talk to me, damn you, Giovanni! Answer me!"

Finnegan and I stared at each other, wide-eyed.

"Could be your disappointment was premature," he said, rising. "It may have been staged for our benefit, but I'm not taking any chances."

"It sounded genuine to me, like she might be coming unhinged."

"Better safe than sorry," he said. "Excuse me for a moment; I need to ring someone up."

I nodded, sipping my whiskey as he stepped into the hallway. Moments later, he returned.

"We have to assume we're at a dangerous point right now," he said. "She may lash out, attacking random targets. Or she may press, all out, against you and Miss MacDonald. Are you sure I can't interest you in protection? I know, for a fact. that there are members of the Police Service willing to stand in as doubles for both of you. In fact, they would be honored to so do."

"I can't ask anyone to do that, Jim. With William Hayes still in the picture, we wouldn't be safe, anyway."

"Point taken. I think, though, it would be wise to move again. I have a cousin who's out of the country on business, then the lucky bloke is going straight onto holiday. The place is out in the countryside, too. Might be a nice change."

"Are you trying to chase me away, Jim?"

"No, but I am trying to keep you alive."

"I'll start packing."

* * *

It was another hour before we heard the arrival of a vehicle. Shutting the lights out, we carefully peered out of the window. A familiar vehicle came into view.

"All clear, Jim." I said, relieved. "It's Mack and Kelly."

We barely had time for the routing exchange of pleasantries before we were in the car, heading back toward the city.

"I thought you said his place was in the country, Jim."

"It is, but it's on the other side of town. Patience, my friend…"

"Aren't you going to ask how we did," said Mack, unable to contain herself any longer.

"The important part is that you both made it out alive," I said.

"Of course we did," said Mack, "and we made it out with the documents." She proudly tapped the briefcase that sat on her lap. "Everything went exactly as planned, oh worried one!"

"The signature worked exactly as hoped. Nobody dared to question it. I'm still worried that there'll be hell to pay, as the saying goes," Kelly Hamilton said.

"I'll deal with that when the time comes," said Finnegan. "Give a listen to the voice mail that Shanagh left during John's broadcast."

I played the messages. They quickly cast a pall over the vehicle.

"Sounds like she's coming unhinged," Mack said.

"That's why we're headed to a new location. That, and we have a lot of work to do. Between the documents from the archives and the binder Dianne O'Leary gave me, we're going to be busy."

"There's one more thing that you forgot," Mack said.

"And that is?"

"If your appeal for information works, we may become inundated with leads. Even with screening, it could be a daunting number. The potential of earning a million pounds is going to bring people out of the woodwork."

I sighed. "You're right, of course. I hope your cousin's place has something we can use as an office."

"I don't think that will be a problem," said Jim.

* * *

A series of turns took us to a narrow, rural road. As we reached a grove of trees, Jim made a final turn.

"Are you sure you've got the right place?" I said, staring at the gate in front of us.

"That, I am," he said, pulling forward to an intercom. Cameras watched from every angle as he pressed the silver button. A moment later, a humorless voice came over the speaker.

"Name and business."

"James Finnegan," he said. "Here on a social call."

There was a moment of disconcerting silence before the voice said, "Proceed."

The gate swung open, and we drove forward. "I said he was my cousin, not my poor, destitute cousin," Finnegan said, smiling broadly. "You'll be able to appreciate the place better in the morning."

"What, exactly, does your cousin do for a living?"

"He's some sort of muckety-muck with a big, American chemical conglomerate. I wasn't entirely sure he'd go for this, but he did. Said something about political uncertainty being bad for business, and agreed, straight away."

"You trust him, I take it?"

"I do, but I've already had a friend of mine sweep the place for bugs and so forth."

"I bet that job took a while," Mack said, looking out the window.

As we turned the corner, climbing a gentle incline, the generous proportions of the house came into view. Two large, serious men awaited our arrival.

They spent what felt like an undue amount of time scrutinizing our identification, but eventually let us enter. "The guest rooms are up the stairs and to the right," one of the men grunted. "Only area off limits is the office," he said, pointing to a closed door immediately to our left."

"We will need a place to set up some computers and work," said Finnegan.

"Boss said you're welcome to use the library."

"Library?" said Mack, her eyes twinkling. "Jim, is your cousin single?"

Jim laughed. "As a matter of fact, he is."

"Enough, you two," I said. Apparently, my voice was louder than I intended it to be, because they seemed startled. "Sorry. I'm tired, and I want to get settled in. I guess today has me a little overwhelmed."

"Understandable," said Kelly Hamilton. "A shower and a good night's sleep sounds absolutely grand!"

"Agreed," said Mack, collecting her bags and following Kelly up the stairs.

Jim waited until they were out of earshot. "Did I detect a hint of jealousy in your voice, John Costa?"

"No," I said, chuckling. "You detected hints of exhaustion. See you in the morning, Jim."

CHAPTER TWENTY-THREE

Still clinging to sleep, I made my way downstairs. The well-stocked kitchen was vacant, but showed signs of recent use, including a freshly-brewed pot of coffee. I poured a cup, and started to assemble a simple breakfast.

I was halfway through my cereal when the voice of Jim Finnegan caught my attention.

"Good morning, John," he said. "I see you managed to find the coffee already."

"Where is everyone?" I said, still longing for more quality time with the mattress.

"Already hard at work in the library, he said."

"Dammit. I didn't mean to oversleep. Why didn't anyone wake me?"

"You had a rough night. None of us had the heart to wake you first thing this morning."

"I did?"

"Several of us heard you. Sounded like you were having a nightmare."

Vague recollections of the night flashed through my memory. "I'm sorry," I said, sipping my coffee. "I hope I didn't make sleeping difficult for everyone else."

"No. Nothing like that. More concerned than anything else. Is everything all right, my friend?"

"A restless mind, I think, leading to disturbing dreams. Mostly dreams of Angela; reliving those horrible moments in the warehouse when she died in my arms; wondering if I could have done anything different. The scene keeps replaying, Jim. Sometimes, I worry about myself…"

"I'd worry if you *didn't* have something like this happening, especially with all you've been through."

"Maybe I should finally get around to dealing with the elephant in the room: the letters and her last wishes. I guess I keep avoiding it because it represents finality — the acknowledgment that she's gone. I'm not quite ready to admit that to myself, Jim, because some little part of me feels that she's still here with me. I know… it's bloody ridiculous, but that's how I feel."

He rose, staring out the kitchen window. "Perhaps your mind is somehow working through things. If you're not ready, you're not ready."

"Well, enough feeling sorry for myself," I said, rinsing my cereal bowl. "There's real work to be done. Is everything ready for tomorrow?"

We started walking. "Yes," he said. "I have four members of the Police Service who are willing to help, and another who will take you and Miss MacDonald to Dianne O'Leary's late tonight."

"Perfect," I said, as we rounded the corner into the library.

"Good morning, sleeping beauty," Mack said.

"Sorry if I kept anyone awake," I said, my voice still raspy. "Where do we stand?"

"I've started working on Dianne O'Leary's documentation," Kelly said, motioning to a large table almost completely covered with papers. "There's a lot here, and its going to take the better portion of the day for me to get it organized logically."

"The same holds true for the archives," Mack said.

"Any data coming back from the broadcast?" I asked, sipping my coffee.

"The first batch of it should be arriving within the hour, and then hourly after that, assuming there are any tips worth relaying."

"It sounds to me like I would provide the most help by staying out of the way," I said. "How is the internet situation?"

"Actually," Mack said, looking up from what she was reading, "it's amazing. High speed, reliable routing, stable quality of service."

"Knowing my cousin," Finnegan said, "he's probably paying for some special tier of service that normal mortals can't afford."

"In other words," I said, "it is good enough for me to attempt to communicate with Geryon."

"Of course," Mack said. "Just use the precautions I showed you, and all will be well."

* * *

I spent the better part of the morning fishing around in various chat rooms, but received no responses.

"A good start," said Kelly. "It can take time."

I nodded. "What have we gotten from the broadcast?"

Mack looked up from what she was doing. "We're not off to the the best possible start," she said, sighing. "We've had a few reported sightings, but so far nothing credible has turned up. Five from the Belfast area, and two from the Republic. One even came in from Stavanger, Norway!"

"One person," Kelly added, "told us that you were a member of the Illuminati, and that he was reporting in for duty as needed in the upcoming struggle. And, lest we forget, one sighting of Angela Grady in Dublin, complete with short, black hair and a pet Irish Wolf Hound." She stopped abruptly, catching herself, one sentence too late. "Oh, damn me!" she said. "I'm sorry, Mister Costa."

My expression undoubtedly betrayed the sharp pain that cut through my spirit. "No. It's all right," I said, rising. "I should have been prepared for something like that happening. Keep me informed if anything credible comes in, please."

* * *

I sat alone in the small solarium attached to the back of the kitchen, picking at my lunch.

"Quite a view, isn't it?" Mack asked, her hand gently resting on my shoulder.

"I honestly didn't notice," I said, glancing up. The terrain sloped away from the back of the house, making the solarium a balcony with a panoramic view of the Irish countryside. A small lake hid just beyond a narrow grove of trees. I smiled at Mack, nodding.

"She didn't mean anything by it, just a momentary lapse of good judgment."

"I know it, Mack. I feel bad about the way I reacted. I'll say something after lunch."

"That would be good," Mack said. "I expect she'll do the same."

I rose, moving near the window and taking in the view. "Those hedgerows," I said, pointing off into the distance, "are well over a hundred fifty years old. They divided plots of land farmed by various families. There was a time, right around our Civil War, when most of this acreage would have been growing flax to support Belfast's linen industry. Not any more, obviously. From the look of things, this house included, the area is undergoing gentrification."

She looked at me, smiling, but with a confused expression. "How do you know all of this?"

"One branch of my mother's family came from Ballygowan, a small town not too far from here."

"I never knew you had ancestry in the north. I assumed it was all from around Cork."

"The family never spoke much about them, especially since they were Presbyterians, God forbid," I chuckled. "Somehow, it all worked out, a Catholic man marrying a Presbyterian woman. Love conquers all, I guess. Speaking of which, I could sure get used to this view!"

"Well," she said, "Finnegan tells me the house will be coming on the market within the next year or so; sooner, if someone were to express interest."

"He shouldn't have any trouble selling it, unless the price is unrealistic."

"I expect you're right," she said.

I looked at my watch. "Oh! I've got to call Dianne O'Leary. Time to bait the trap…"

* * *

"Remind me to punch Jim Finnegan in the face when we get

back," I groaned. "Being stuffed into the back of a delivery van is hardly my idea of a good time. Is that contraption of yours going to survive the trip? All this damn jostling!"

"I hope so," Mack said. "I don't like it either, but we had to find a way to get to Dianne's house without drawing any attention."

"It'll draw plenty of attention when they have to rent a forklift to pry my stiff muscles out of this damned sardine can. Even worse if we get caught crossing private property dressed like this," I said, referring to our black clothing, complete with ski masks.

"Shut your damned gob and quit complaining," the driver growled. "Two more turns and we're there."

"See?" I said. "Things go much faster when one can enjoy a stimulating conversation en route."

"Eejit," the driver muttered, making the last turn and stopping the vehicle.

* * *

We waited until the driver tapped the side of the truck twice. After waiting the prescribed amount of time, we clambered out of the back. Mack retrieved her drone, painted black for the occasion, while I grabbed the suitcase stuffed with the other components necessary to bring her idea to life. We eased the door of the vehicle closed, and crossed the street.

"Here!" I whispered, pointing to the short stone column that supported a driveway gate. "Number twenty-one. Dianne's back yard is adjacent to this one."

"Go!" Mack said, "there's a car coming."

Dammit. We made a sharp turn into the driveway, jogging to get out of view of the street. We only made it a few steps before a motion-activated floodlight illuminated the entire area.

I almost froze, but Mack smacked me sharply in the back of the head and took off running, full out.

Burdened by the suitcase, I couldn't keep up as she dashed along the driveway and out of the illuminated area. It was only a momentary respite, though, as a second floodlight illuminated the back portion of the driveway. The light proved helpful, as I saw Mack sprint through a narrow gap between two trees at the back of the property line.

Or so I thought.

The property was deeper than expected, and I found it necessary to cross an open section of lawn. Mack had, once again, slipped into the shadows and out of my view, so I had no choice but to proceed blindly. Finally, my eyes adjusted and I was able to make out my next obstacle. Dammit. There was a hedge marking the real property line.

I slowed, taking a moment to look for a gap. Finding nothing, my mind quickly assessed my alternatives. Before I could decide, a light turned on in the house behind me. I held the suitcase in front of my face, closed my eyes, and plowed headlong through the hedge. I stumbled out the other side, falling several times before regaining my balance and composure.

"Over here," Mack whispered from the darkness.

I made my way over to her location. "The back door is supposed to be unlocked. Let's go!"

Crouching to remain below the height of the surrounding hedges, we approached the back door of Dianne O'Leary's house. I reached out, turned the knob. Much to my relief, the door opened. We slipped inside, closing and locking the door behind us.

"Stop right there," a voice said. The sound of a shotgun racking froze us in our tracks. "On your knees," she commanded, "hands on your head, interlace your fingers." We complied.

A narrow, dim beam of light hit my face, lingered for a moment, and then moved to Mack.

"Collect your things and come this way." The beam widened, illuminating the floor just enough for us to collect our belongings. We moved forward, following the beam through a doorway. The door closed behind us.

"Close your eyes. I'm going to turn on the lights."

* * *

"You're bleeding," the woman said, pointing to my leg.

In all the excitement, I hadn't noticed. "I must've scraped myself going through the hedge."

"That's more than a scrape," Mack said. "Let's get a look at that." She rolled up my pant leg, exposing a series of gashes. "Those might need to get stitched," she said.

"No time for that, Mack." I said, just now aware of the throbbing pain in my leg.

"I can't find where Miss O'Leary keeps her medical supplies," the woman said, handing me a wash cloth. "Apply pressure with this while I look again."

"Just get a bed sheet and cut it into bandages," I said. "I'll reimburse her for it."

"You need a doctor, John. The cuts are ragged and dirty, and several of them don't want to stop bleeding. Not to mention the risk of infection."

"I'll go when we're done with the drone, and not a moment sooner. Help me get to the bathroom so I can wash this off."

"I see now where your reputation comes from," the woman said, tearing fabric and wrapping my leg. "That should let you get to the bathtub. Miss MacDonald, give him a hand, please. I'll fashion some more bandages whilst you do."

"Thank you," I said, wincing as I got to my feet. "You seem to have us at a disadvantage, though."

"Not by design, Mister Costa. Bella Rourke," she said, extending her hand, "Police Service, and playing the role of Dianne O'Leary for this evening's show. Now, enough with the pleasantries; let's tend to that leg."

CHAPTER TWENTY-FOUR

"How's the leg?"

"Hurts like hell, Mack, but I think I'll make it. Tell me something…"

"Of course…"

"You don't have a scratch on you. How, exactly, did you do that?"

"We've been over this before, I think…"

"We have?"

"Yes…. Because I'm a woman, and I'm smarter than you. Let me look at that leg," she said, examining the bandages. I winced as she peeled back the layers of cloth. "You went to the wrong side of the hedge; there was a gap on the other, and I just stepped through."

"Story of my life," I sighed. "What's the prognosis, doc?"

"For better or worse, you'll live. I'd still like you to get to the doctor later." She busied herself changing the bandages.

"I will, if we're around to go to the doctor," I said.

"Have some faith, Doubty McDoubts-a-lot!" she said, frowning.

* * *

The sound of Dianne O'Leary's phone started our subterfuge in motion. The call, designed to sound authentic, was, in reality, carefully scripted and each voice prerecorded independently. Placed to her traditional, and likely compromised, landline, the call was designed to draw out our would-be assassins.

Mack sprung into action, playing each clip of Dianne O'Leary's voice in the exact timing and sequence the script demanded. At the other end of the faux conversation, Kelly Hamilton was doing the same for my voice.

"Hello?"

"Hi Dianne, John Costa here."

"Good morning."

"I was hoping we could see each other today. I've learned some additional details in the past few days, and one of them should interest you in particular."

"I've discovered a few things, too. I think you'll find them enlightening."

"I'm in Comber, staying in a lovely bed and breakfast. Care to meet here?"

"Sounds grand. My car was just in the shop for some repairs. I need to take it for a drive, and this gives me the perfect reason."

"Noon-ish, then?"

"Perfect. I'll ring you when I'm nearing town. And Johnny, I hope you've cleared your entire afternoon…"

"Clear, all the way through tomorrow morning…"

"Oh! I like the way you think, Solicitor. I'll bring the wine…"

I turned to Mack, smiling. "I hope Shanagh hears that last little bit, personally. She hated Karen. I can't imagine what kind of rage she'll fly into if she thinks I'm romantically involved with Dianne."

"I can imagine," Mack said. "I got a taste of it when they kidnapped me, and have no desire to see it again. Poking a bear is harmless until the bear decides it doesn't want to be poked any more. I really hope you know what you're doing, John."

"Me, too, Mack."

* * *

I could barely recognize Mack's drone — she had made so many changes. Most notable were the bits of copper mesh and foil attached, spanning the four arms that supported the propellers.

"What did you do to that thing?" I said. "It looks a bit like the lunar module from the Apollo days."

"The copper foil?" she said.

"Yes. It looks cool, but what purpose does it serve?"

"Honestly, this is one of the bits of this whole contraption I'm not sure about. I'm a bit concerned about the added weight, too, but this worries me more."

I stared at her, waiting for what followed.

"If I explain it to you, are you going to understand?"

"Probably not, but I'll listen and try."

"Fair enough," she said, laughing lightly. "The problem is with the homing transmitter, the part that uses radio waves to signal to the missile precisely where the target is. It is designed for attachment to something that has a large surface area of metal, such as a car or truck.

It uses it as a ground, in effect. The plastic drone doesn't have anything like that, so I'm trying to create it. Like I said, it works on paper, more or less, but I can't really test it."

What followed was a brain-melting lecture that included terms like *impedance, standing wave ratio, and capacitance.* I listened patiently until she reached the conclusion. "So — bottom-line it for me, Mack."

"Bottom line? It might work perfectly. There's a chance that it will work, just with reduced transmission range."

"That's still good, right?"

"Maybe. I have no way to know how the actual missile is designed, but if it can't find a strong enough signal, there's a possibility it will revert to other technologies to find a target."

"That's still good, right?"

"No. That's bad. The whole damned thing is classified, but rumor has it that the alternate targeting mechanism is a simple heat-seeker. And the hottest thing in the area…"

"Will be our car."

"Correct."

"That's not good."

* * *

"We're on the clock, people!" I said, noting the time.

"All set here," Mack said.

The rear seat of Dianne O'Leary's car had been removed, specifically so Mack and I could remain unseen on the trip out of Belfast. My sore muscles and injured leg didn't appreciate the situation, but I knew there wasn't much choice in the matter.

"When I turn this thing on," Mack said, "there's no turning

back."

I nodded, and she flipped the switch. Bella Rourke eased the car out of the garage and on to the road.

Mack's notebook sprung to life a few moments later, as our location appeared as a moving, red dot on the screen. "Things are at their most dangerous when the device can find plenty of wireless networks on which to send our coordinates."

I raised my eyebrow. "Like in the city?"

"Yes," she said, unconcerned.

"Like we are right now, Mack?"

"Yes." Still unconcerned.

"Mack!"

She paused, peering at me with a look of utter annoyance. "Do you think for a minute I'd put innocent people at risk? Notice the color of the dot, John."

"Yes. It's red. I can see that..."

"The tracking device sends back coordinates, as I mentioned previously, but it also sends back a confidence factor as part of the payload. If it doesn't have a good signal, can't see the GPS satellites, and so forth, the confidence level drops. Right now, the dot is red because it isn't certain of our location."

"No signal?"

"No," she said, smiling. "I made a few improvements to the software. I can control the confidence level it is sending back. Has the dot moved since we started talking?"

I looked at the map on the screen. "No. It hasn't."

She tapped a key on her computer. Moments later, the dot

jumped forward, turning yellow momentarily, then back to red. "Just so they don't lose track of us."

"Clever, Mack, but I don't see exactly how…"

"The system won't fire unless the missile has sufficient confidence or it can see the radio frequency homing signal, at least according to the rumors on some technology forums. In other words, I'm trying to force their hand. I'm not going to give them anything usable until we're ready."

"But what if…"

"They get close enough to lock in on the signal?"

"Yes."

"That's where my friends come in," said Bella Rourke. "We're not on our own today, Mister Costa. Finnegan's got quite a few friends in the Police Service, and his friends are your friends. Anyone makes an aggressive move on us, they'll be taken out. We're nearing the point, Miss MacDonald. Best give them a good look at us."

With the tap of a few keys, the dot turned green. My stomach churned. "How will we know if one of those damned missiles gets launched at us?"

"The border of the screen will start flashing red, at least that's the theory."

* * *

It felt like an eternity before Mack switched the dot back to yellow, and then to red. The change brought momentary relief, but it was short lived. Moments later, Dianne O'Leary's cell phone, borrowed specifically for this purpose, rang.

"Time for car troubles," Mack announced. She readied her computer to direct another staged conversation.

"Hi, Dianne."

"I'm on my way, Johnny, but my engine light came on. Not sure if it is anything serious or not."

"Dammit."

"True, that! I just had this bloody thing in the shop. Cost me three hundred quid, and now this!"

"Have you noticed anything different with the car? Sluggish? Noises?"

"No. Nothing out of the ordinary. I'm going to slow down a bit just in case."

"Good idea. Call me if anything happens. I can come get you."

"Thanks. I will."

"Show time!" Bella said. "I'm making the turn now, then out comes the steam." I heard an electrical switch click.

On cue, Mack called me from Dianne's cell phone. This time, it went to voice mail.

"John, it's Dianne. The bloody car is overheating. I've pulled off the road and into a quarry. Doesn't look like anyone is working here today, though. Was hoping one of them could check it for me. I'm going to look around and see if anyone is here. Ring me when you get this."

I heard the crunch of gravel under our tires as we eased off the road.

"I'm going to drive in a ways," Bella said. "Stay down for a bit longer you two!"

A few nervous moments passed before she spoke again. "We're parked between a lorry and a shed. That should give us enough cover to get the drone deployed and get the hell away from the car. I don't want to be anywhere near it if your contraption doesn't work, Miss MacDonald, no offense intended."

"No offense taken," Mack said, handing me her laptop. "John, when I tell you, click okay. Not a moment before."

"Got it," I said, my hands shaking more than I was willing to admit.

We climbed out of the car. Mack busied herself with the drone, while Bella, pressed against the side of the lorry, surveyed the area.

The motors of the drone whirred to life. "Okay, John," Mack said, "click the button."

I did, and within a few seconds, the dot representing our location turned green. "Green dot," I whispered.

"Good," Mack said.

"We need to get away from this damn car," Bella said. "Let's see if that old cement lorry is unlocked." She pointed to our right.

The cement truck had definitely seen better days, and had likely been relegated to a source of parts. Much to my relief, the door to the cab was unlocked. We climbed in. The interior smelled damp and musty, but it was tolerable, and the location couldn't have been better if we had planned it.

"Watch the screen, John," Mack instructed. "Don't take your eyes off it, and let us know if it turns red."

"Take the drone slowly along the access road," Bella whispered, "as if she's driving around looking for someone." Her radio chirped before she could continue. "We've got company," she said. "There's a car moving in from the west, lingering along the perimeter fence."

"I'm going to move the drone to a better spot," Mack said, pressing the controls forward.

"More company," said Bella, her hand cupped over her ear. "There's a second car approaching the main entrance. How's your position, Miss MacDonald?"

"Right where we want it," she said.

"Good," Bella said, "Now we wait and…"

"Red screen!" I shouted.

"I see it," Mack said, calmly. "From the west. Relaying coordinates."

The drone's screen went black, and the earth shook from the explosion that followed.

"I'd say your contraption worked, Mack," I said, shaking all over. "Why did the screen just turn red again?"

"Crap! Get down!" Mack screamed. The earth shook again, and dust obscured the sun.

Bella Rourke sprung into action, drawing her firearm. She said something, but my ears were ringing too badly to hear. I motioned frantically, pointing to my ears and shrugging. "Stay here! Lock the cab!" she shouted, directly into my ear.

I pushed the plunger, locking the door behind her as she slipped out of the vehicle. I did the same to the other door, pulling Mack down to the floor with me.

The wait seemed interminable and terrifying. The incessant ringing, thankfully, was starting to fade, and I contemplated peeking out one of the vehicle's windows. The idea was immediately dashed as the sound of gunfire erupted outside. Rounds struck the side of the cement truck. I pulled Mack underneath me, trying my best to shield her. A bullet smashed through the passenger window, and then, silence, followed by the sound of someone testing the lock on the door.

CHAPTER TWENTY-FIVE

The door's locking mechanism had either given in to the ravages of time, or it was broken when the vehicle was interred. I heard the latch mechanism catch, and the door started to open. Not waiting to see who our visitor was, I slid up onto the seat, flat on my back, then kicked the door with all my might.

It traveled a short distance before striking someone. The unknown man grunted as the rebound of the door threatened to close it. I kicked again, and the door hit solidly, sending the man off the cab.

Not stopping to think, I jumped out of the cab. The man, bleeding profusely from a deep gash in his forehead was on the ground. A handgun lay a few feet from his hands, and he was scrambling to reach it. My foot met his outstretched arm moments before his fingers could close on the firearm's grip. The force of my kick sent the gun flying.

He rolled over, and attempted to rise, but before he could, I drove a powerful kick into his midsection. Then another and another, as rage welled.

"Costa!" Bella Rourke's shout stopped me, as the man crumpled to the ground. She emerged, weapon drawn, from behind the cement truck, a second, handcuffed man in tow. She sat him down, roughly, near the back of the cement truck. "Constable MacDonald," she said to Mack, who emerged safely from the cab of the truck, "please keep an eye on this bastard. If he even looks at you the wrong way, shoot him."

"Glad to see you're all right," I said, drawing a deep breath in an attempt to quell the rushing adrenaline. A strange look crossed her face. "What is it?"

"Oh, God, no," she said, examining the second man. "I know him." I didn't quite grasp the meaning of what she was saying or the look of pain in her eyes. "Oh, Sammy, I'd rather of let the American kill you than find you like this. What are you doing here, you stupid bastard? You're a disgrace to the uniform!" She rolled him over, roughly, cuffing his hands.

"He's Police Service?" I said, a sick feeling overcoming me. "I'm sorry."

"Don't be," she snapped. "He's here without his badge or uniform, and with an unlicensed gun, no doubt. Bastard's no better than the trash in Maghaberry prison; I can't even bear to look at him."

"Finnegan," the man grunted, blood still oozing from his gashed forehead. "Must see Finnegan…"

"The only thing you're going to see is the inside of a jail cell," Bella growled.

"I'm a dead man if you take me in," he whispered.

"Better, that," she said, her eyes aflame.

He glanced around, nervously. "If I'm alive, I can give you Hayes. I'm useless to you, dead."

"Sam, you eejit…" The sound of cars arriving interrupted us. A man emerged from the first vehicle, exchanged a few words with Bella, collected our other prisoner, and drove away. The second vehicle followed.

A man emerged from the third car. He looked familiar, but I couldn't recall if we'd even been introduced. "Do you want me to take this one in?" he said.

Bella and I exchanged glances, and I gently shook my head.

"No, she said, "he's helping us. This is to maintain his cover." She helped Sam up, removing the handcuffs. "How'd we make out?"

"We got two others," the man said, "plus the launcher and another two unspent missiles." He paused, looking around. "You're going to have one hell of a bill to pay," he said, laughing and slapping my shoulder before returning to his vehicle.

Dammit. He was right. Dianne O'Leary's car was a smoldering heap of wreckage. The nearby shed and lorry were also extensively damaged and I had no idea how much carnage the other explosion created.

"No worries," I replied. "If it helps us put an end to this, it's well worth it."

* * *

We sat the man in the kitchen, removing his blindfold.

"He needs a doctor, but refuses to allow us to take him to a hospital," I said.

"My cousin has a private physician," Finnegan said. "Perhaps I can find the number and ring her up." He motioned me to follow him. Once out of earshot of our new guest, he continued. "We're ready to leak the story of a vehicle crash to the press," he whispered. "They will report that the driver, Dianne O'Leary, was taken to the hospital with life threatening injuries. Of course, it will be Bella Rourke, waiting to spring our trap should it become necessary. Any reason to change our plans?"

"No," I said, "not that I can think of. Shanagh Grady and Geryon both tend to be thorough, and are probably expecting us to do something."

"Good. Speaking of Geryon, I believe that Miss Hamilton has something to share with you when you're done questioning our new guest. I'll ring up the physician now."

* * *

"Hayes said you'd be a pushover, Costa," Sam said, wincing as the doctor examined his ribs. "A bit naff, that!"

"I'd prefer to get X-rays," the doctor said, "but he has repeatedly refused."

"No!" Sam said. "Stitch me up, and send me on my way."

Frustrated, the doctor shrugged, and removed several items from her case. "I'll give you something for the pain, and then suture your gash."

Sam cooperated, more or less, using every lull as an opportunity to flirt. The tall, slender, dark-haired doctor, born of Indian parents but raised in Dublin, was clearly unimpressed. I pondered interceding, but she had the situation well in control, dashing his hopes at every turn.

"Keep an eye on him," she said as she left, her voice barely audible. "If he starts coughing up blood, get him to a hospital straight away. Same if he starts to lose color or complain of feeling light headed."

"I will. Thank you for coming out on such short notice. He's involved with a Police Service operation, so discretion is of the utmost importance."

"I understand completely," she replied, accepting my generous payment. "I was never here."

***

"Hayes had me early on," Sam said, sipping his Scotch. "I was involved in an incident in Newtownards late into my first year. I was in the wrong, and there should have been hell to pay — maybe even the sack. Hayes made it all go away, and I've been in his damned pocket ever since. No way out, short of dying, of course, with all that hanging over my head."

"I'm sorry for your misfortune, but how, exactly, does this help us?" I said, drinking a Guinness.

"Our job today was to eliminate Miss O'Leary by any and all means possible. If you were caught up in it, all the better. Does the name Kristos Antonopoulos mean anything to you?"

"Should it?"

"I'd expect so, since you two seem to have a mutual interest."

"And that is?"

"Dianne O'Leary."

"Tell me more, Sam..."

"I've worked some security jobs for Hayes, and most of them have been for this Kristos fellow. I've provided security on occasion, but mostly I've been helping to make sure things go smoothly with his shipping operations, meaning that things make it onto and off of the docks without unnecessary scrutiny."

"From customs, you mean," Finnegan said.

"Correct," Sam said, returning his empty glass to the table. "There's something big going on, though, and soon. I don't know all the details, but I've overheard bits and pieces about trucks and a large shipment of merchandise."

"Merchandise?" Finnegan said. "Is Antonopoulos bringing drugs into the country or something?"

"No, nothing like that. They're talking about an outbound shipment, and apparently, they are planning on some passengers as well. Beyond that, I don't know anything."

"Why kill Dianne?" I asked.

"I'm not entirely sure, but ever since you went to Mullingar, Hayes has had nothing else on his mind, and Kristos couldn't care less what happens to her, at least from what I've overheard. He's bad news, that one. He brought those little rockets in, smuggled right out of the Middle East, they were. How he got them is God's guess."

"Are there any more of them out there?" Finnegan said, leaning forward in his chair.

"You got all that we were given," Sam said, "but that's only what I know of it. Look — if you go after Hayes, I'll testify, but you've got to protect me. That means you make me disappear, dead and gone. I know you can do it, Finnegan. You're the best at it."

"Get all this written up," Jim said, finishing his drink. "I'll get things in the works."

* * *

"We have everything arranged to seize those accounts that we think are used by Geryon, but I wanted to hold off until you saw this," Kelly Hamilton said, pointing to the screen of her computer. "It looks like Geryon might be willing to talk, or at least listen."

The entry in the chat room looked nondescript, but Kelly and Mack assured me that it held a secondary meaning.

"We were thinking that you could use our impending action as leverage, possibly to prove a point," Mack said.

"What do you have in mind?"

"You're hoping to convince Geryon to rethink their partnership with Shanagh Grady, right?"

I nodded.

"We collected our information via a number of different mechanisms, mostly electronic. Geryon will expect that, of course."

"Of course…"

"If you tell them the breakthrough was due to a leak in Shanagh's organization, they will have no way to know whether or not you're telling them the truth. Carelessness, compromised computer, loose lips — use your imagination."

A smile crossed my face as I started to understand what Mack was telling me. "Not bad," I said, raising my eyebrows. "Any idea how much seizing the accounts will hurt them?"

"Uncertain," Kelly answered, "but every little bit helps. The message is more important than the actual damage we do to them."

"Works for me," I said. "When do we do this?"

"Right away if you're feeling up to it. The longer we wait, the bigger the chance that the accounts will be closed or go dormant."

* * *

Several hours passed, filled with pointless online conversations and waiting. Kelly and Mack encouraged me to continue even though fatigue was rapidly setting in.

"Mack, don't these hackers ever sleep? Now that I'm asking, don't *you* ever sleep?"

"I can sleep when I'm dead," she said. "In the meantime, it is just an inconvenient three or four hours out of my day."

I was formulating a clever reply when Kelly motioned for me to look at the screen. "This is promising," she said. "Respond to this one." She pointed at a line of text on the screen.

I engaged in another round of banter, occasionally injecting phrases provided by Kelly and Mack. It seemed hopeless, especially as others gradually left the chat room.

"This is pointless," I said, "everyone is leaving."

"Stay with it," Kelly said. "Five more minutes."

I rolled my eyes, but complied. Without warning, my connection to the room failed. A few seconds later, my system automatically rejoined the room, but I was the only name listed. My finger nearly pressed the power button, but before I did, text appeared on my screen.

MasterCrowley: Understand you want to talk.

Mack and Kelly clustered around my screen. "We need to find out if that's the real Master Crowley," Mack whispered.

"Who is Master Crowley?"

"One of the four known ring leaders of Geryon," replied Kelly. "We need to ask him something only an insider would know. Let me think for a moment…"

MobBoss: I do, if you're who I think you are.

MasterCrowley: Who do you think I am?

MobBoss: Someone important. Someone who can make decisions.

MasterCrowley: I am all of those things. What do you propose we talk about? The weather?

Kelly Hamilton narrated my next few lines, helping me though the technical jargon and the chat room protocol.

MobBoss: The weather is deadly dull. I'd rather talk about a certain stock market that went off line a few years back.

MasterCrowley: Unfortunate computer glitch.

MobBoss: My friends tell me there are no such things as computer glitches, that the real story isn't what the public knows.

MasterCrowley: Trunking protocol failure.

MobBoss: That's what the public was told. You'll have to do better if you want me to believe you are who you claim to be.

MasterCrowley: The public was told some of the truth, not all of the truth. The protocol didn't fail. It worked exactly as it should; we just made it do what we wanted it to do – which was cripple the markets.

MobBoss: Sure, but to what end?

MasterCrowley: To help some short positions we held. The markets backed up, and investors got nervous, all to our benefit.

MobBoss: Interesting, but you're not telling me anything I don't already know.

MasterCrowley: We were able to forge the time stamp for a routine trunking table update. We replaced the table with one of our choosing. This included redefining some data paths in a way favorable to us. Specifically, some highly sensitive Mercantile accounts were in our hands for about six days.

Kelly tapped me on the shoulder, nodding her head.

MobBoss: Acceptable.

MasterCrowley: What do you propose?

MobBoss: A truce, at least long enough to listen to what I have to say.

MasterCrowley: I'm here. Not promising anything else.

MobBoss: You have recently formed an alliance. I'm here to warn you that you have cast your lot with someone who is deeply unstable. Shanagh Grady will be your undoing.

MasterCrowley: We share a mutual interest. We want your money, she wants you dead. Seems like an ideal arrangement.

MobBoss: So it would, but if I'm dead, you'll not get a cent of my money. The government will take most of it, and the rest will be untouchable.

MasterCrowley: Which is why you are still alive. We understand that the order of things is important.

MobBoss: But does your associate? There have been three rather serious attempts on my life recently, both thanks to your associate. Even worse, she tried to deny one of them. So either you did it, misunderstanding the necessity of my continued existence, or someone in her organization is a loose canon.

MasterCrowley: There are always those within any organization that do not meet the standards required for continued employment. I'm sure the offenders will be dealt with.

I nodded at Kelly. She sprang into action, tapping furiously on her keyboard. Mack did likewise. I waited for her signal, insides churning. It was less than thirty seconds before she signaled for me to continue, but it felt like hours.

MobBoss: It doesn't end there. You may want to look at some of your intermediary accounts. Your new partner's carelessness led to what just happened. If you decide to reconsider my offer of a truce, you know where to find me.

Shaking, I pressed the computer's power button.

CHAPTER TWENTY-SIX

Geryon's response was quick, but indirect. They created outages for a regional airline that extended several hours before the issues were corrected. The news attributed the issue to a power failure, but we knew better.

"We hit them a little harder than expected," Kelly said. "I don't know if they got careless, or we got lucky, but I'm sure they're none to happy, as the saying goes."

"Either that, or it was a trap," I said, unconvinced.

"I don't think so," Mack replied, sipping her coffee. "There is a lot of chatter within the black hat community speaking negatively of Geryon's reputation right now. Reputation is everything, John. They wouldn't risk it to set a trap for us."

"Still, I think caution is called for."

"Of course, oh careful one!" Mack said, rolling her eyes. "We've got a few tricks of our own."

I knew better than to ask any questions that would trigger an eye-glazing technical answer, so I changed the subject. "Have we learned anything from the archives?"

"Funny you should ask that," Kelly said, smiling. "There's a bit in here we thought you'd find quite interesting. We were able to track down a few details about reference 74-0102."

The image on one of the larger monitors changed to show a scanned document. The other monitor displayed a map.

Kelly continued. "In 1974, there was an attack on three men just outside this little town in eastern Tyrone. The men were, ostensibly, republicans, and one died as a result of the explosion. The attack, thought to be by loyalists, was in reprisal to events that happened at a pub a few weeks prior. Finnegan investigated the case, under the supervision of William Hayes."

"Yes," I said. "Not to be a killjoy, but we knew this much already."

"But here is what we didn't know, and why we risked life and limb to get these files," Mack said, as the screen changed.

Kelly continued. "We were able to pull the entire document chain from the archives, and I think you'll find this quite illuminating."

I stared at the screen, reading every word. The contents caused me to sink into the nearest chair, perplexed.

"Does this mean what I think it means?" I said, my face likely contorted into an unflattering expression.

"It means exactly what you think," Mack said, smiling broadly. "Finnegan was working with an informant, and was making some significant progress, at least until he got a little heavy-handed with one of the suspects."

"It wouldn't surprise me to learn that Hayes pressured Finnegan into getting a bit rough," Kelly added. "At the time, Finnegan would have been inexperienced, and likely to defer to a senior officer."

I nodded. "The solicitor who worked for the Grady family during the initial investigation into Strabane was able to get Finnegan censured, at least enough to let Angela get out of the country. He portrayed Jim as out of control, and as a police officer that intimidated witnesses and suspects. Is this the same case?"

"Yes, one and the same. William Hayes interceded, proclaiming that Finnegan's informant was unreliable and unstable. Between that and Finnegan's heavy-handed approach, the investigation effectively ended, and the case remains unsolved. But the really interesting part is on the next page," Mack said.

She clicked her mouse, the screen changed, and I was left speechless.

"The call from the informant triggered the creation of a series of reference documents. In the archives, as you can see, they're not redacted. Finnegan's informant in 1974 was none other than Sean Grady! He tried to warn them about one of Connla's schemes."

"You're telling me that Sean Grady, Angela's father, was prepared to rat out his dad?"

"Not prepared to," Mack said. "He did."

"Probably the only thing that saved his life was the fact that he reached out to Finnegan instead of William Hayes," Kelly added. "The way informant data was compartmentalized at the time meant that Hayes couldn't get his hands directly on the names."

"How did Hayes manage to get the informant flagged as unreliable if he didn't have access to the name?"

"Likely by calling in a favor, probably from this man," Kelly answered. The screen changed, and a name I didn't recognize appeared in its center.

"Who is he?"

"He was one of the people in the records department at the time," Kelly said. "There are several inconsistencies in the archives, and all of them are his entries. He died under rather mysterious circumstances a few months later. I can't say with certainty, but it is hard to call it a coincidence."

"Sounds like the work of Connla Grady," I said. "I'm a bit confused, though. The Indexed Reference document we found on Sean Grady during our initial investigation was newer. I think Tom Preston deemed it to be from 1996 or 1997."

"Just a newer link on the same chain. 1974 was just the first entry we traced back to Sean Grady. There were two that followed, one in 1976 and another in 1977. Then they stop, abruptly, until 1996 when the entry you previously discovered was created."

"Interesting," I said, scratching my head. "The gap matches his marriage, and Angela's childhood."

"Even more interesting," Mack said, "is that the 1996 entry for Sean was in relation to case 96-0096. Remember that one?"

I recalled it all too well, and the annoying churn in my stomach returned at its mere mention. "All too well… There was an attack on some Constabulary paramilitary vehicles. Angela and her mother were considered persons of interest. Eyewitnesses seemed to place Angela in the vicinity, but nothing was ever proven. If I recall, Finnegan was more interested in Donny Cassidy, one of the people later involved in Strabane."

"We think that Sean tried to warn them. The 1996 attack, in retrospect, looks like it was a rehearsal for the Strabane bombing. There were striking similarities in the explosive and timing mechanism used," Kelly said. "Unfortunately, by 1996, Sean had enough baggage to make him a less-than-reliable informant. Guilt by association, as the saying goes."

"Not to mention the black mark from 1974, thanks to Hayes," I said.

"True, that," Kelly said. "Sean Grady was born under a cruel star. I don't think he was a bad person. Take a look at this."

The screen changed again. This time, it was a report on the death of Sean Grady.

"Interesting," I said, studying the screen. "An otherwise healthy man dies, unexpectedly, of a heart attack. Sounds eerily similar to the demise of the corrupt coroner from County Tyrone. Do you think Shanagh got wind of his attempts to reach the authorities?"

"Entirely possible," Mack said. "Only Shanagh knows the answer to that.

I arose from my chair, stretching. "This is all very interesting, but I'm not sure how this helps us. Perhaps I can press Shanagh a bit about the suspicious death of her husband. As far as Hayes is concerned, though, we have nothing but circumstantial stuff. Good, but not actionable."

"You haven't seen the best part, oh skeptical one!" Mack said. "Here is the report on the death of Sean Grady. Take your time. I'll still be awesome when you're done," she said, winking at me.

I read the document, end to end, sat down, then read it again. "This poor man was murdered." I muttered.

"Digitalis, we think," Mack said. "By all rights, there should have been an investigation, but look who stepped in to quash the idea."

"Hayes," I said, reciting the name highlighted on the screen.

"He did it by changing the official report that came back from the coroner," Kelly said. "Here is what was on file…"

"Death by heart failure, likely due to previously undetected conditions. Strangely familiar, once again."

"Indeed it is," said Mack. "He did a good job of covering his tracks, too."

"One thing he didn't count on," Kelly said, smiling broadly.

"You and Mack?"

"Well, that too, but I was really referring to the new transactional system that was installed in 2004."

"I'm not sure what you mean by that, doubly so because Sean died in 2003," I said.

"A transactional system," Mack lectured, "tracks all of the changes made to a record, like deposits in a bank account. If an entry is made in error, it can be backed-out and fixed. If a transaction fails to work, it can be replayed until it does."

"In our situation," Kelly added, "an older system for keeping and tracking official records, including coroner's reports, was in transition at the time. An older, mainframe-based system was being upgraded to a transaction-based distributed system. That's where Hayes made his mistake."

"You two seem terribly excited by all of this, but I'm not sure I understand why."

"The old system was transactional, too. However, when old records were moved to the new, only the most recent version was preserved. All of the changes that lead up to the final, official version were lost. It was done to save money on the migration."

"But if the new system didn't arrive until 2004…"

Kelly smiled. "It didn't arrive officially until 2004, but several departments were part of an early pilot program starting late in 2002, including the office of the coroner. Whoever Hayes engaged to falsify the records mustn't have realized this."

I glanced back and forth at them, frowning, as I attempted to understand exactly what they were telling me. "Bottom line it for me, Mack."

"Hayes changed the records on the wrong system — the *old* system, to be exact. He probably knew that when the records were scheduled to be converted, his alterations would become the official record."

"What he didn't know," Kelly added, "was that the coroner's office was doing double-entry as part of their pilot. Because of Hayes' changes, the new system and old system were out of sync when the final cut-over to the new system took place. Fortunately for him, the conversion algorithm was designed, intentionally, to accept the final record from the *old* system as official. Discrepancies like this were commonplace, because the people responsible for doing the double-entry rarely had enough time to do everything they were being asked to do. They prioritized data entry into the old system, and double-entered as time permitted. As such, nobody would have noticed or cared that the two systems didn't agree."

Mack picked up the conversation. "Hayes was in the clear, except for one pesky detail: the new system's transaction records were preserved. And this is where *we* got lucky."

"I was able," Kelly said, "to access the transaction logs and re-create the original report along with a timeline of the changes. Good thing for us, this was one of the records someone actually bothered to enter into both systems."

"He altered the cause of death," I said, looking at the document. "The coroner recommended an investigation, too. Hell, he even altered some of Sean's medical records. This is actionable, folks. We need to call someone…"

"Already in the works," Mack said, smiling. "Finnegan has already been in contact with Assistant Chief Constable Walsh. He should be meeting with her right now, if everything is going according to plan."

"This is what working until half four will get you," Kelly said. "I could use a bit of a nap, though."

"Not a bad idea," said Mack, finally appearing human.

"Get some rest," I said. "You've earned it a thousand times over. Between this and what Sam provided us, I expect Hayes will be an unhappy man very soon. I just wish I could be there to see the look on the bastard's face."

* * *

It wasn't long before an unexpected wave of fatigue hit me. The past few weeks of my life were an adrenaline-fueled blur, and it was catching up to me. I retreated to my room in hopes of a short nap.

The pillow was a willing accomplice, but my racing thoughts made sleep an unlikely partner. After staring at the ceiling for what felt like hours, I opened the small box that contained Angela's letters. The envelopes were as they had been when Finnegan handed them to me after her death. Even the position of the rubber bands holding them remained unchanged.

I removed one of the rubber bands, allowing me to thumb through them. They were in chronological order, each dated to show a time period. I took a deep breath, and slipped the top, and earliest, letter from the stack. Finding it sealed, I retrieved a nearby letter opener, and slid its blade along the seam. And then I froze, unable to will my hand to remove the letter that awaited within.

Finally, my muscles agreed, and I unfolded the letter:

My dearest Johnny,

It is over. Confession signed. Sentence handed down. Early this morning, they tossed me into a black cage and brought me to prison. I miss you, and would give anything to see you, although I expect you would rebuke me, and rightfully so. I hate myself for what I've done. Be well, my love.

A handful of entries followed. Most were nothing but my name followed by the date. Each line tilted progressively more downhill. Turning to the second page, I found two longer entries:

Johnny,

I'm all in bits. I'm having dreams, terrible dreams, and my memories are confusing. They have assigned a woman to talk to me, and we speak daily, but it doesn't change anything. Something about her is familiar, but I can't, for the life of me, put my finger on it. It won't matter soon, anyway. This existence, pointless as it is, is more than I deserve. Nor do I deserve anything from you but hatred.

Angela

My dearest one,

I've written some wishes for when I'm gone. You are mentioned within. I can only pray that they reach you and that, someday, you find it within your heart to carry them out. If not, I understand. I told you many lies, and I did things that are unforgivable. I never lied when I told you that I loved you. I did, and I always will. Goodbye, Johnny.

Love,

Angela

Her writing, especially in the last few lines, was weak and barely legible, the words often trailing off into shaky, descending lines. The tears welling in my eyes made it even more difficult.

A final entry on the back of the second page was all that remained in the first letter. Summoning my fortitude, I turned the page.

Dear Johnny,

I did not have plans for this day to arrive. Yesterday was to have been my last, and by all rights it should have been. A simple, undeserved act of kindness changed everything. Finnegan paid me a visit late in the day and conveyed your message. You are truly an amazing man, John Costa. Thanks to you, tomorrow will arrive, as will the days that follow. I will try, each day, to be the woman you hoped I was, the good soul you saw within, even when others doubted.

I wish you peace, my love.

Angela

Hands trembling, I refolded the letter, and returned it to its envelope.

CHAPTER TWENTY-SEVEN

My nap was a dismal failure, again interrupted by the recurring nightmares that had become an increasingly frequent visitor. I sat in the solarium, watching the wind move the raindrops on the glass.

The gentle hand of Jillian MacDonald touched my shoulder, momentarily startling me. "The same nightmare?" she whispered.

I nodded. "They're becoming so frequent, I'm worried that one of these days, I'll fall asleep while driving or doing something important." I stood, stretching gently. "I guess I shouldn't be surprised, especially since I read the first of Angela's letters immediately before drifting off to sleep."

Mack's green eyes studied me. "Pretty rough, I take it?"

I nodded, fighting back tears. "I'm always back at the warehouse, fighting with Paddy Bannion, Shanagh's henchman. Funny, but when I'm awake, the details of what happened are hazy. I know, overall, what went on, but the ancillary details are blurry. In the dream, though, everything is crystal clear, almost like I'm watching it from outside my body in slow motion. At least that's how it seems when I wake up. Crazy, huh?"

"I don't think so."

"And I always wake up feeling like there was something I could've done differently. Maybe if I'd have just been a step or two faster, or if I'd dodged his knife and had my full strength…"

She hugged me, tightly. "I know it hurts," she said, easing out of our embrace, "but healing is often an uncomfortable process, whether it is physical or emotional. I think you've taken a good first step, though."

"What if the nightmares don't stop, Mack?"

"Have you considered talking to someone about them, like a professional? Sometimes just bringing it to the surface will help you sort things out."

"Jesus, Mack, a shrink would have a field day with me. What's the term you use to describe me sometimes?"

She smiled, shyly. "A hot mess?"

"That's it, among others. I'd be headed for a padded room in no time."

"You have a point there," she said, winking. "Your mind might be having trouble reconciling something."

"What do you mean?"

"Sometimes, when I'm working on a technical problem and I can't find the solution, I'll dream about it until, magically, the answer arrives."

"But your mind is a marvel, Mack. Mine is just an addled old bowl of porridge by comparison."

"No it isn't!" she said, wrinkling her nose. "We just have

different strengths. That's why we're such a good team, in spite of the fact that you're a hot mess."

I scowled at her, pretending to be irritated, but I couldn't hold the illusion. Laughter followed, only to be interrupted by the chirping of my cell phone. Dammit. The brief respite my mind was enjoying evaporated.

"You're not going to believe this," I said, showing her the message.

There are things Finnegan isn't telling you.
I can and will.
Is a deal possible?
W. Hayes

"What are you going to tell him, John?"

"Let's see how serious he is." Mack watched over my shoulder as I typed my reply.

Many things are possible.
But you tried to have me killed.
Why should I deal, especially when I'm holding most of the trump cards?

A chirp signaled the arrival of his answer.

Just business, not personal.
You may hold more cards, but you don't hold all of them.

I drive a hard bargain, Hayes.
Give me a sample of what you've got

And you'll call off the dogs?

If the information is good enough and arrives in time, yes, at least as much as I can. Otherwise, you're out of luck.

I can give you Shanagh Grady's locations. Is that good enough for you, Costa?

It is if it's real, but you could easily be blowing smoke up my ass.

True, but I have little reason to at this point. I'm a liability to her now. And I can tell you some interesting tidbits about your girlfriend, things Finnegan is keeping from you.

She's dead and gone. What does it matter now?

Sometimes the dead still have tales to tell that are of interest to the living.

"What do you think, Mack?"

"He's probably desperate to save his skin. Might be worth

listening to."

I nodded, and tapped my reply:

`I'll meet with you, but somewhere public.`

`Connswater Shopping Centre. Text me when you get there, but don't wait too long.`

* * *

"Why are you waiting?" Mack said, glancing at her phone.

"I'm finding an alternate route. If it's a trap, I don't want to reveal the direction I came from or how long it took to get there."

Mack smiled. "Pretty good for a hot mess."

"I surprise myself, sometimes. Try to get Charlie Hannon on the phone, and see if he has someone on his payroll who is in the area and can watch my back. Yes, I'll pay, and no, I don't care what it costs. Did I actually say that out loud, Mack?"

"You did," she said, forcing a smile. "Be careful."

"I will, Mack" I said, studying her.

"I mean it," she said, frowning.

* * *

My route took me well south and west of my destination. I pulled into a parking spot at a branch bank just outside the perimeter of the Connswater Shopping Centre and checked my phone. Several texts, encouraging me to hurry, awaited me. A third instructed me to proceed directly to an electronics shop upon arrival. A quick check of the map revealed it was directly across the Connswater River, and only moments away.

I eased my car onto the road, only to be startled by the rapidly approaching sound of a siren. Glancing in my rear view mirror, I saw the ambulance make its turn. I pulled over to the left, allowing it to pass. A sick feeling churned in my stomach when it pulled into the parking lot of the electronics store.

The medics ran through the front door, and I wasn't far behind them. A man was slumped in a chair near a display of tablet computers. I worked my way closer.

The medics took his vital signs and immediately were on their radio. I couldn't hear what they were saying, but their actions betrayed urgency. Finally, as they moved the man out of the chair and onto the floor, I could see. It was William Hayes.

He was still alive, but obviously in dire straits. The medics attached an oxygen mask and started to work. Hayes glanced over at me, clearly recognizing me. Against the wishes of the medics, he waved to me to move closer.

"I'm his friend," I said. "He's trying to tell me something. Maybe it will help."

He had removed his oxygen mask and was fighting the medic to keep it off. I moved in, trying to stay out of their way, but it was nearly impossible.

"Kristos…"

"Properties…"

His words were short, gasping utterances, repeated emphatically.

"Kristos!"

"Properties!"

He paused, breathing deeply before managing to speak again.

"Dublin"

"Fin…"

Before he could say any more, the medics shoved me out of the way and reattached the oxygen mask. Hayes gave up any pretense of resisting them.

"Tachycardia," one of the medics said into his radio, followed by Hayes' dangerously high heart rate.

"Digitalis!" I shouted. "He may be poisoned!"

They looked at me strangely, but relayed my information to the hospital.

"Establish an IV," the radio barked. A police officer, who had arrived sometime during the chaos, moved me back before I could hear any more than a passing mention of lidocaine and charcoal.

"Do you know this man?" the police officer asked.

"I do," I replied. "That man is Police Service Superintendent William Hayes. We're working together on a case."

My answer served its purpose. "Stick around," the officer said, his attention turning quickly to his comrade.

I nodded.

"You'll do no such thing, an unfamiliar voice whispered in my ear. "Charlie sent me, and we're going to get out of here."

"But…"

"No arguments," he said. "We don't need some of Hayes' boys showing up and deciding this was all your fault. Trade coats with me until you get to your car. Put on this cap."

Using the small crowd of gawkers that had formed to shield us from the distracted officer, we slipped out. We quickly exchanged coats, and I drove away.

* * *

I barely made it through the front door before my phone rang.

"Hayes didn't make it," Finnegan said.

"Dammit. He was trying to make a deal with me; information in exchange for some help escaping the net that was closing around him. I figured most of it was bluster, but he did claim to know Shanagh's whereabouts."

"So a dead end, is it?"

"Not entirely. I got a few words out of him before the medics hauled him away. Speaking of which, I might need your help with a pesky constable."

"Oh?"

"I told the medics Hayes might have been poisoned with digitalis. That, apparently, caught his attention, and he wanted me to stick around for questioning after they transported Hayes to the hospital. I slipped out before he could ask me anything."

"I could see how that might upset him. I can take your statement if it becomes necessary."

"Does that mean what I think it means?"

"It does," he said, his excitement barely concealed. "I've been fully reinstated. Of course, my first order of business is to investigate the death of William Hayes, since it is considered suspicious."

"He was murdered, no doubt about it. I didn't like the bastard, and the feeling was mutual, but that doesn't mean I wanted him dead. Doubly so since he was willing to make a deal. Hopefully, this time the records won't be altered, and the guilty will be found."

"There will be plenty of scrutiny this time around, that I can assure you."

"And Connla's treasure?"

"Safe and sound," Finnegan answered, "so that's another bit that's in our favor."

* * *

"Mack," I said, sipping my after-dinner Guinness, "how far have you gotten with the records Dianne O'Leary provided us?"

"About halfway through, give or take," she said, drinking wine. "Why do you ask?"

"Hayes mentioned Kristos in his final words to me. *Kristos* and *properties* — he said it twice, then something about Dublin. That was all he managed before they hauled him away in an ambulance. Is there any evidence that Kristos owns property in Dublin?"

"Not that I've found. He owns properties here, in South America, and in Greece, but there were no records of anything in the Republic. Like I said, though, we're only halfway through."

"What about Dianne O'Leary? Does she own any property in Dublin?"

Mack opened her notebook, tapping its keys feverishly. "No. No record of anything in the Republic for her, either. She owns her house, a small warehouse, and a cottage in Scotland, and that's about it. She's reinvested a lot in her business, but most of her assets are traditional investment vehicles."

"How much is she worth?"

"Oh, ten million pounds or so. Now, Kristos, on the other hand, is a different story…"

"Oh, do tell, Mack."

"He's worth several hundred million, conservatively, with holdings ranging from shipping vessels to speculative gas drilling ventures, and damn near everything in between."

"Where did his money come from?"

"Still working on that one, John. One thing is certain, though: it didn't come from Ulster Maritime Group. He did a masterful job of keeping it floating in and out of profitability, while poor Dianne shoveled her money into it. The company revenues tracked even with inflationary changes. Dianne's net worth, on the other hand, steadily decreased."

"So given long enough…"

"He would have drained her completely, unless, of course, she found out along the way and tossed the bastard out on his ear, which, it seems, is exactly what she's doing."

"Oh? This sounds interesting…"

"In spite of being in hiding, she's still on a rampage at Ulster Maritime. Twelve people were summarily sacked yesterday. They weren't even given the option to clean their office. Instead of being walked out the front door, they were walked into a conference room, right into the waiting arms of the Police Service. Here," she said, pointing to the screen of her laptop. "A video made it onto the internet last night. It's a bit shaky, but you get the idea."

The video that followed was drawing more attention for its narration than its content. Shot by an unidentified woman, it was filled with over-the-top reactions as people were led out and whisked away by the Police Service in waiting police cars.

"She's not messing around," Mack said, refilling her wine glass.

"So I can tell," I said, chuckling at the narrator's monologue.

"This isn't the half of it, John. Over the past week, Ulster

Maritime Group has invalidated at least a dozen contracts with firms tied to Kristos Antonopoulos. Every outgoing and incoming shipment has been subject to a secondary, and in a few cases, tertiary search. Shipments en-route are going to be seized by customs on arrival for additional scrutiny."

"Good for her! Old Connla's probably turning over in his grave as we speak."

"True, and I'm sure Kristos is none too happy, either. Many of his companies were enjoying sweetheart deals from Ulster Maritime, all at Dianne's expense, of course."

"He'd better hope she never gets her hands on him!"

"Agreed." She rose, collecting her wine glass. "I'm going to take a short nap, and then dig into the remaining bits of the documents Dianne shared. Need anything while I'm up?"

"No, but thank you, Mack. And get some rest! This stuff will all keep until the morning."

"We've gone over this before, Sleepy McSleeperson. I can rest when I'm dead, which I'm not. So deal with it!" She stuck her tongue out at me.

* * *

I knew reading more of Angela's letters would inevitably lead to another encore by the recurring nightmare, but they beckoned, nevertheless. I poured a tall glass of whiskey and settled in with plans to read as many as I possibly could.

Careful to preserve their chronological order, I slid one of the rubber bands off the stack, and retrieved the next letter. Like most that followed, it spanned multiple days, and provided a glimpse into the monotony of prison life. Nevertheless, Angela's tone improved steadily, as did her handwriting. She seemed to draw fulfillment from her job, menial as it was, and shared achievements, often trivial, proudly.

By the sixth letter, however, I noticed an unsteadiness in her hand.

Dear Johnny,

One of these days, I'll summon the nerve to dispatch these letters. I'm sure you'll be utterly thrilled to learn about the wiring changes in the laundry and the lovely ray of sunshine that reached the yard yesterday. Maybe we could discuss Ulysses by correspondence, if you're so inclined.

My doctor has changed my medication, and I don't think it is working as hoped. My mind seems in a fog, and, as you can see, my hands are shaking. I mentioned it, but she'll hear nothing of it, insisting that I continue. I'm not permitted enough access to the internet yet in order to research it, so I can't even tell you what it is.

I've not broken a single rule since I've been here, but this is going to be a first. I'm going to stop taking this wicked stuff, against doctor's orders. I'm not sure what they'll do to me if they find out.

Love,

Angela

I drifted off to sleep clutching the letter.

CHAPTER TWENTY-EIGHT

"You're up early," Mack said, smiling. "Coffee?"

"Yes, please. Now — tell me you've gotten some rest."

"Actually, I ended up sleeping most of the night, unintentionally. I guess I needed it. I'm sorry — I'll work on the rest of Dianne O'Leary's documents today."

"Do what you can, Mack. Where's Finnegan?"

"On his way to headquarters with Kelly. They're talking about reestablishing our command center there now that he's been exonerated."

"Probably not a bad idea, but I sure like the beds and the view better here." The offices and accommodations provided by the Police Service were functional and convenient, but spartan.

"It's still for sale, you know…"

"That's the second time you've mentioned that, Mack."

"Oh? Is it? Maybe I'm getting old, and repeating myself all the time like you do." She winked at me. "I've got to get back to work."

"Not so fast, Jillian MacDonald! You've got something on your mind — now, out with it!"

"Okay, Pushy McPushington! I just thought that, after all this is over, you might enjoy having a place here, and this one seems to suit you quite well. Don't you think it's about time you let yourself enjoy life a little bit?"

Her answer surprised me. "I hadn't really thought about it, Mack. Almost everyone and everything I know is there, though, not here."

"It would give you a chance to keep up with your friends here, too. And don't you have family in Cork?"

"I do, but..."

"Well, there you go! All the more reason."

"Mack!"

"What?"

"That isn't the reason, and we both know it..." I peered over imaginary glasses, pretending to scowl.

She sighed. "All right... There's a Senior Analyst position in the elite Cyber Crimes division of the Police Service. Kelly says I'd be perfect for the job, and Finnegan promised to put in a good word for me. It would be an incredible opportunity, perhaps once in a lifetime. I'd get to work with the latest equipment, and train with some of the best cyber crime experts. I kinda like it here, too. But I don't think I'd want to do it without you around, at least some of the time. How else will I stop you from sending millions to those poor, unfortunate Nigerian princes who keep sending you emails?"

Her words caught me totally off guard, and for a brief moment, a tinge of sadness shot through me. "I'd never want you to pass up a once-in-a-lifetime opportunity on my account, Mack. If it's something you want to do, by all means, do it."

* * *

Mack's strange and unexpected revelation was yet another thought swirling in my agitated mind. Fighting to regroup, I dialed Dianne O'Leary.

"Good afternoon, Mister Costa," she said.

"I trust all is well with you, Dianne. Do you have a moment?"

"I do. I'm set to meet with my solicitor later this afternoon. We have some more documentation to turn over, and more negotiations. Oh, hell, who am I fooling? I'm trying everything I can to avoid having to go to prison. Have you heard the latest from Greece?"

"No, I haven't."

"Kristos apparently turned over a crate of documents that implicate *me!* There is talk that the Greeks will issue a warrant for my arrest. I hope I have enough documentation to the contrary to fight it. To make things more interesting, the bastard disappeared shortly thereafter, citing concerns for his safety. He better hide, because if I ever find him…"

"I'm sorry."

"I wish I'd been left an orphan, and never heard of Connla Grady or his damned company!"

"It does seem to carry a poison with it. Do you happen to know if Kristos owns any property in or around Dublin? An informant hinted about it, but we've not found any record of any. Perhaps there's something we're missing."

"Dublin? No. I don't think so. We were there a few times, but I don't think Kristos liked it very much. I can look, but I highly doubt it."

"Thanks, Dianne. Anything you can find is appreciated."

* * *

I wanted to talk to Mack, but word arrived that we would be moving back to the Police Service facility in Belfast. "It's safer, and we have better access to equipment and data," Finnegan said. "It will be ready for us the day after tomorrow."

I nodded, less than thrilled with the prospect of sleeping on what amounted to a glorified military cot. "Any word on Hayes?"

"Massive heart failure. Early toxicity results are consistent with digitalis toxicity, but we won't know with absolute certainty until the entire screening is back. Off the record, though, he was poisoned, just like you thought."

"I'll get busy packing, then tomorrow we can throw a day-long party and thoroughly trash your cousin's place."

Finnegan smiled, and started to say something, but the ringing of my phone interrupted him. I didn't recognize the number. "Probably Shanagh," I said, tapping the screen.

A computer-generated voice greeted me:

Good afternoon. After careful consideration, we would like to continue discussions of a truce. Please meet Master Crowley as you did previously. He is available immediately, and doesn't like being kept waiting.

"Presumptuous," I whispered to Finnegan as I hung up the phone. I guess I'll listen to what they have to say.

* * *

True to his message, Geryon's hacker was waiting for me. Mack stared over my shoulder as I typed:

MobBoss: Understand you are amenable to additional discussion.

MasterCrowley: Circumstances seem to indicate that it would be wise to do so.

MobBoss: Your new partner has lost a key ally, and with it, your chances to steal the treasure he guarded are all but gone.

MasterCrowley: An unfortunate turn of events. Only your wealth remains.

MobBoss: It is not available to either you or your partner.

MasterCrowley: Our associate seems to believe that you will give it, willingly.

MobBoss: Additional proof that she is not stable. She will be your downfall if you continue your relationship. Are you aware of the circumstance around the death of her ally?

MasterCrowley: Enlighten us.

MobBoss: She was unable to control him, so she had him murdered. It should be clear from her actions that self-preservation is her only motivation, and that she is operating from desperation at this point. Otherwise, she would have been sensitive to his importance in achieving your goals, and found another way to rein him in.

MasterCrowley: Your reputation for eloquence and convincing arguments is well earned. What terms do you propose for our accord?

MobBoss: You cease and desist aiding Shanagh Grady or her organization in any way. Likewise, you take no action, electronic or otherwise, against me or any of my associates.

MasterCrowley: And in turn?

MobBoss: I will focus my pursuit solely on the capture of Shanagh Grady and the dismantling of her organization. I will not pursue Geryon unless the terms of this accord are breached.

MasterCrowley: And does your assurance extend to the Red Wizard?

I glanced up a Mack, who nodded.

MobBoss: As long as the Red Wizard is in my employ, she will abide by the terms of our agreement.

MasterCrowley: Then we have an accord. Please give my respects to the Red Wizard who is, no doubt, watching over your shoulder.

MobBoss: I will relay your message.

I looked up at Mack. "Do you think I did the right thing, making a deal with the devil?"

She sighed. "I don't think you had much choice. We can't fight a war on two fronts, John."

"The lesser of two evils, I suppose. Either way, what's done is done. Did you find anything in the rest of Dianne's papers?"

"Just more of the same, but nothing new, and nothing related to Dublin properties."

"Any properties at all?"

"Nothing we didn't already know about. A few more things that the Police Service will be interested in, likely the Greek authorities as well, but all of it is related to shipping contracts and shady deals at customs."

"Thanks for trying. What's up next, Mack?"

"Packing, I suppose," she sighed. "We have some new data from the tip hotline to analyze, too. I'll get started on that when we get settled in Belfast."

* * *

My packing efforts started half-heartedly, but picked up steam as the afternoon progressed. I reached a stopping point, and retreated to the kitchen for a cup of coffee. A phone call, again from an unrecognized number, arrived just as I had poured.

"Good afternoon, Solicitor." Shanagh's voice sounded rough, but had regained its wicked edge. I gathered my energy, and met her head on.

"Shanagh. Are you calling to make arrangements to surrender? Because if not, we have very little to talk about."

"Oh, we have plenty to talk about, Giovanni."

"I suppose we could replay your recent list of dreadful failures. That ought to keep us talking long enough for Mack to trace your location, and dispatch the authorities."

Mack, who was searching the refrigerator, perked up at the mention of her name. She came over to listen in on our conversation.

"Failure is a word that I reserve for you, Solicitor. I prefer to think of recent events as the rising and falling tides of war."

"Mostly falling, in your case. In spite of your best efforts, I'm still here, Mack's still here, and the authorities are learning more and more every day from the records of the Ulster Maritime Group. Whatever large shipment you were working on with Kristos Antonopoulos isn't going to happen."

"There are many fish in the sea, and many boats in the ocean."

"And now, your recent alliance has disintegrated."

"What do you mean?" She coughed, deeply, and from the chest.

"I've made a truce with Geryon. You'll not be getting any assistance from them starting immediately. It's just a matter of time before we track your cell phone, your data, and find your location."

"I know you'd like to think otherwise, dear Giovanni, but it isn't of consequence. Their contributions were minimal, anyway, and their usefulness to me has passed. I do find their lack of loyalty to be disappointing, a fact that I will not soon forget."

"They didn't seem to think that their usefulness to you was at an end."

"I cannot control their misconceptions. Oh, boy-o, I do so love our little conversations. I'm going to miss them."

"You can write me from prison, if it makes you feel better."

"No," she laughed, "our time together is running short. It won't be long now before I claim your fortune and your life."

Unlike previous calls, she seemed to be in control of her emotions. It was a worrisome change.

"Your confidence is laughable. You had to murder one of your key players because he was out of control. You're pathetically weak. A better leader can control people like that."

"His loss could not be helped. One does not defy Siobhan O'Connor and not pay the consequences."

"You even messed that up, Shanagh. He talked before he died, you know. He talked, and gave us vital information. We're closer now that we've ever been."

"You're only closer to death, Solicitor, which shall surely come. But not until I've kept my promise. The little red tart will die while you watch."

"Your argument is with me, not her."

"Although you pretend otherwise, you are a man full of lies, sweet Giovanni."

"How so?"

"William Hayes didn't talk, and you know it. He gasped a few, nonsensical words that you're still struggling to understand."

Dammit. How did she know that? A sick feeling washed over me as Shanagh Grady continued.

"Such a lovely house you're enjoying, and the tart loves it, too. Great view — you should buy it for her. Perhaps as a memorial, because she won't be around to enjoy it."

The reality suddenly dawned on me and I reached for Mack, trying to tug her toward me and down. I heard the sound of glass shattering, followed by a pot crashing to the ground in the kitchen. She slumped forward into my arms, blood spreading through her shirt.

"Call 999!" I screamed as Finnegan appeared in the doorway, "Mack's been shot!"

CHAPTER TWENTY-NINE

"Get something to help me stop the bleeding," I cried. My feelings were somewhere between panic, rage, and helplessness.

Finnegan and Kelly left to give chase to the assassin, leaving one of the security guards to assist. They mentioned something about the man having experience, but I felt as if they'd abandoned a hopeless situation. The guard, a tall, brutish man, grunted and tossed me several towels from a drawer in the kitchen. My heart was pounding as I pressed them firmly against the wound. With my free hand, I desperately searched for a pulse.

"Calm down," the guard said, easing my hand to the side, and checking her pulse. "Take deep, slow breaths; you're on the verge of hyperventilating." He stared into the distance, a reluctant smile forming at the corners of his mouth. "She's got a good strong pulse. Let's get a look at that wound."

It took a bit of convincing to get me to ease off the pressure so he could examine the wound. Finally, I allowed him to take over.

"Lucky girl," he said, smiling at me. "You don't know very much about gunshot wounds, do you, Mister Costa?"

"No, not really." In truth, I had only seen one other wound in person. All of my previous experience was photographic evidence used in trial.

"I was a medic in Iraq," he said, applying pressure to the wound. "This is what we call a slap wound. The projectile ran along the surface of the skin, in this case enough to open a gash. But, thankfully for your friend, it didn't strike anything vital."

"So much blood, though."

"Yeah, they can do that," he said, "although this one looks worse than it really is. She'll need quite a few stitches, though, and it'll hurt like all hell for a while. Here, now," he said in a comforting tone, unexpected from one of his physique and profession, "she's coming around."

Mack groaned, looking at me with blurry eyes. "What the hell just happened? Why did you pull my arm like that? You ripped the damn thing out of its socket." She tried moving her arm, but cried out in pain. "Son of a bitch!"

"Don't move your arm, Mack. Someone took a shot at you."

"Your friend, he saved your life, he did, Miss," the guard added. The bullet ripped up your skin a bit, but you're going to be all right. Just have to get you stitched up."

"Somehow, they figured out where we were hiding, and got a sniper into position. Finnegan and Kelly are giving chase as we speak."

"Well," she said, wrinkling her nose, "maybe I don't like this house all that much after all."

"Understandable," I said, "especially since you died here…"

"Huh?"

"Oh yes. Being dead might be the only way to keep you alive, Mack."

She smiled. "I'm with you, but we have work to do!"

"I'm sure Kelly can come up with a suitable disguise. I'm thinking a frumpy, old librarian."

Mack laughed, interrupted by spikes of pain. I finally gave in, allowing tears of relief to flow freely.

* * *

"The bastard got away," Finnegan said. "What's the story in here?"

"Mack's hit, but it isn't as bad as it looks. We need to make her dead, though."

"But I still want to work," Mack protested.

"I can help with a disguise," Kelly said, checking on Mack.

"My cousin's doctor can take care of the wound, I'm sure," Finnegan said, grabbing his phone, "and I have a nephew that's in the undertaking business. We should be able to produce a reasonably effective ruse, at least for a few days."

"That may be all we need. Shanagh hinted that things will be over soon, which I presume will correspond to her leaving Ireland."

"We'll concentrate on possible exit routes," said Finnegan. "But first, we need to make you dead, Miss MacDonald."

* * *

The doctor arrived and immediately started tending to Mack. An ambulance arrived shortly thereafter. The medics talked to Finnegan, and departed after reporting that the victim had succumbed to her injuries. The doctor, on the other hand, was less eager to cooperate.

"This is a gunshot wound, and I'm required by law to report it," she protested.

"And we're here to collect your report as the law requires, Doctor Robertson," said Finnegan, showing his identification. Kelly Hamilton did likewise.

The doctor nodded, reluctantly. "I've written you a prescription for antibiotics, Miss MacDonald," she said, "to prevent any infection from setting in. If you start to run a fever, or the wound meets the criteria listed in my instructions, you need to see a physician right away. Understand?"

"I understand," Mack said.

"And you three," she said, glaring at Jim, Kelly, and me, "have the job of changing the dressing as scheduled. No shirking! It must be kept clean."

"One more detail," Jim said, handing the doctor a sheet of paper.

"I can't sign this!" the doctor protested. "It is against everything in my professional ethics to sign a legal document stating that this woman is dead when she's clearly quite alive!"

"We understand and appreciate your commitment to your professional ethics," Finnegan said, "but we wouldn't ask unless it was a matter of the utmost importance."

"You also took an oath to do no harm," I added. "My friend's life is in obvious danger. If the world thinks she's dead, we stand a better chance to protect her. Please. It's only for a few days, and then Kelly will make any and all records of this disappear forever."

The doctor looked at me, then at Mack, sighed, and grudgingly signed the certificate of death. "You may want to consult a plastic surgeon, Miss MacDonald, regarding the scar. They might be able to minimize it, if that's something you're interested in doing."

"For your own safety, doctor," Finnegan said, "it might be wise to take a few days of holiday if you can." He handed her a card. "This is the address of Shannon McLeod, my cousin. She lives in Galway, and is a member of the Garda. She'll be more than happy to have company for a few days, and will definitely be able to keep you safe."

* * *

Finnegan introduced us to his nephew, the mortician.

"I'm one of the few people who gets to ride in the back of a hearse and tell the story of it," Mack said as we loaded her onto a stretcher. "I'm not too sure about being zipped into a body bag, though."

"I'll leave it open 'til the last possible moment," Finnegan's nephew said, "then once we're safely in the car, I'll unzip it. Won't be closed but for a minute, I promise."

"We have to assume we're being watched," I said. "Now that Shanagh knows where we are, she's probably eager to discover the results of her handiwork. Mack, do you think you can play dead convincingly for about twenty seconds?"

"I imagine so," she said. "What do you have in mind?"

"As he wheels you to the hearse, I'll come running after for one final goodbye. We kill two birds with one stone: you get less time in the bag, and whoever might be watching gets a good look at you."

"It could work," Jim said, "but you've got to be absolutely still, Mack. Not a breath, not a sound."

"Of course," she said.

"I'll do a bit of fake blood and makeup," said Kelly. "You're a bit too lifelike at the moment."

"Our friends are here," Finnegan said, "we need to make this happen."

* * *

There were at least half a dozen Police Service cars on the property, if not more. A reporter, intentionally tipped by Finnegan, lurked at the periphery, snapping pictures and asking questions of anyone nearby. Nobody said anything until Jim arrived to grant her an exclusive interview. Under the pretense of privacy, he maneuvered her into a position where her camera could catch a fleeting glance of my final goodbye.

That was my cue, and the ruse started. I ran out of the house, stopping the mortician's progress as I begged for one final farewell. The shutter of her camera snapped repeatedly as my wish was granted.

* * *

With Mack's theatrical exit past us, I turned my attention to another nagging issue.

"Shanagh knew that Hayes wasn't able to tell us anything. How did she know that?" I said.

"The only way," Finnegan said, "is if she had someone there, perhaps even the assassin himself."

Kelly came into the room, carrying an object resembling a flash drive. "Ever seen this before?"

I examined it. "No, can't say I have. What is it?"

"You didn't plug it in to your computer, did you?"

"No. I've never seen it before. What is it, and where did it come from?"

"I found it in the pocket of your coat, the one hanging in the entry way. It's a bloody clever tracking device."

"Dammit. I wore that coat to meet Hayes," I said. "In the commotion, it would have been easy for someone to slip something in my pocket."

"On the bright side, I'm sure we can obtain the footage from the store's security cameras. Maybe our assassin is on there."

"Cameras! Of course!" I said. "I recorded the whole thing with my pen camera. Hopefully he's on there, too."

"Give me the files and I'll get busy," Kelly said. "Maybe this little thing has a few secrets to tell, too," she said, holding up the tracking device. "I'm heading in to Belfast tonight. I'll take good care of Mack until you guys get there tomorrow."

"Don't let her over do it," I said. "If she catches wind that you've got a project, she'll be hard to stop."

"Got it!"

* * *

In spite of being surrounded by security guards, I felt anything but safe, and struggled to get to sleep. Finally, I allowed myself to read more of Angela's letters.

Examining her handwriting, I could see the effects of the medicine wearing off as her penmanship returned to its normal level. A long string of mundane letters followed, describing the mind-numbing dullness of prison life. What they didn't explain was the conundrum that weighed heavily on my mind: why was Angela being drugged? What might she remember that Shanagh didn't want to come to light?

The most obvious conclusion was that Shanagh didn't want Angela to recall the real identity of her counselor. Gwen Carruthers, assigned to evaluate and manage Angela's psychological well-being, secretly worked for Shanagh Grady. She was exposed and captured when we discovered a previously unknown photograph that triggered Angela's repressed memories.

But if that was Shanagh's goal, why involve Gwen Carruthers at all? The risk of her mere appearance triggering memories and exposure seemed too great. There *had* to be another reason, but the letters provided no enlightenment.

Finally, in the wee hours of the morning, I neared the end of the stack. Only two envelopes remained, so I opened the next in the series.

My dearest Johnny,

I wish I would've sent the other letters, because with the recent events, I'm not sure any of them will ever reach you. This morning, well before the rising of the sun, guards arrived at my cell. I was chained and taken by helicopter to where I am now. That's all I can tell you, because I have no idea where I am. Something big has happened, though, because I hear a lot of hushed conversations, but always with an air of urgency.

The woman who is counseling me told me to take one day at a time, and I've done that. I've done my job. I've behaved. I've tried, every day, to be the person you thought I was, and it feels good. It doesn't chase away the suffocating loneliness, but it keeps me alive.

I don't know why they moved me here, and nobody will tell me anything. I have the strange feeling that I'm not going to survive this. I pray that, somehow, this letter eventually finds you. When it does, close your eyes, and think of us embracing, and of a time when inhibitions were cast aside in favour of passion.

Yours, always,

Angela

The back of the page contained columns of sequential dates, as if she was marking each day in the secret prison, but no words. The list continued partway onto the second page where it stopped and the final words on the page began.

Today, the prayer I thought least likely to be answered came to pass.

It is a divine gift I do not deserve.

I could tell from your eyes that today was painful for you. I don't mean to hurt you, but it seems to be an inevitability.

You do not deserve the pain that I bring.

If your heart lingers in darkness when your spirit and mind wish to soar freely, please release it. Be happy, my love.

I drifted off to sleep, and the dream, the damned dream, arrived.

CHAPTER THIRTY

My arrival in Belfast was on the afternoon of a rainy, dismal day and lacked even the slightest modicum of fanfare. I slipped into the building after riding the final dozen miles or so ignominiously stuffed into the back of a bakery delivery truck. I waited until three police officers, appropriately disguised, started unloading the vehicle. Hopefully, midst the comings and goings, nobody would notice that one more worker exited the truck than entered.

Once inside, I was whisked away from the loading dock and into the back hallways of the building. After descending several flights of stairs and making numerous corners, we passed through a reinforced door that opened into a short hallway. At its end was a heavy door, designed to be opened only from the other side. The man, who was obviously the leader of the security team. pounded on it thrice and stepped back. It opened, and we were briefly staring at the barrels of four automatic rifles. They lowered immediately on the word of Jim Finnegan.

"This is normally a secret emergency exit, should a viable attack ever breach the building's security. Sorry about the ride here," he said, shaking my hand, "but Shanagh's message left us no choice."

"Message?" I frowned, confused.

"Yes," he replied, showing me the display of a tablet computer.

```
Inspector Finnegan,
I hope you have said goodbye to your friend.
His time grows short.
Even today might be his last.
```

"Well," I said, shaken more than I let on, "she does seem to be satisfied that she's down to a single target."

"We're focusing our efforts on the information Dianne O'Leary provided about Kristos' contacts in the shipping industry."

"Probably wise."

"If she's planning on leaving as quickly as it seems, we're searching for a needle in a haystack."

We rounded a turn and reached the doors of an elevator. Finnegan inserted his card, followed by a key and the door opened. The elevator carried us up to the floor above, and the familiar confines of our previous base of operation. After the security team verified my fingerprints and retinal scan, my credentials and keys were returned.

"All this time, I thought we were on the lowest floor," I said, my eyes scanning the technology-laden room, looking for Mack.

Finnegan smiled, but offered no additional explanation.

* * *

I was dreading unpacking, but several analysts, all of whom I recognized but didn't know by name, volunteered to help. They made quick work of getting me back in business.

"You'll need to reset your password," Kelly Hamilton said, as she brought in a small box and a stack of papers.

"Already done," I said, proudly.

"Not bad for a dead man!"

I wheeled around, and immediately started laughing.

"I'm so going to kill the both of you," Mack said in her full Scottish brogue, glaring.

"I just do what I'm bloody told," Kelly protested. "The whole thing was his idea." She pointed to me, unabashedly throwing me under the bus.

Kelly had done a remarkable job on the disguise. Mack's red hair and eyebrows were died black, with hints of gray lurking near her temples, and her skin looked aged and wrinkled. Even her fiery green eyes now appeared a muted slate gray. Her hairstyle, a simple, tight bun, and thoroughly frumpy uniform rounded out the disguise.

"D. Dalyrimple," I said, again choking back laughter. "What's the D stand for?"

"Deadly," Mack growled.

"Delphinia," said Kelly. "Delphinia Dalyrimple, sounds like the perfect name for our computer library services liaison from Glasgow, on loan to the Police Service."

"It definitely fits the character," I said, ignoring Mack's deadly stare. "Not sure why we need to maintain the disguise here, but whatever you think is best."

"I'm not too concerned about people on this floor," Kelly said, turning serious, "but this isn't the only floor in the building. We can't risk her being seen, especially since her demise has made the front page of the newspaper." She slid a newspaper across the table.

American Researcher Murdered.

Below the giant headlines was a grainy picture of me bidding a final farewell to Mack. "Not bad," I said, tapping my finger on the picture as I scanned the article.

Jillian MacDonald, computer research expert and business partner of American attorney John Costa, was shot dead while visiting friends in County Down. Known for her work in exposing Angela and Shanagh Grady for their role in the 1998 explosion in Strabane, MacDonald was working with authorities at the time of her death. Mister Costa, pictured above, was not available for comment. Authorities were tight-lipped about the murder, but a source close to the investigation indicated that several key suspects have been identified and that arrests are expected soon.

"I've got to rest a bit," said Mack. "I'm supposed to be taking it easy. I guess when you're my age, these things are expected."

"How old are you supposed to be, anyway?"

"About your age, I think," she said, her eyes searing me. She glanced around, and when certain nobody was watching, she stuck her tongue out at me.

"I'll send an entire crate of prune juice to your quarters, Miss Dalyrimple," I said.

* * *

"What's in the box, Kelly?" I said.

"The gadget that was used to track our location."

"You're sure?"

"As sure as can be," she said. "It works on principles similar to the missile's tracking device, but a bit less sophisticated. Still, good enough to phone home and give us away."

"Dammit. I should've been more careful."

"You can't hold yourself responsible. Here," she said, tapping the keys of her computer, "we've been able to retrieve the security camera footage of the event."

The large screen on the wall flickered briefly, then a video appeared.

"This is the footage from the entrance," she said as we watched people come and go. "Here comes Hayes; can't tell if he's suffering from the poison yet — he doesn't stay on the screen long. Here comes a group of people. Can't really see the two in the back, but there are other views of the store that might give us a better vantage."

A few more people came and went before we could see someone rush past the camera, mostly out of view.

"This is where Hayes truly started to have a problem… Here comes the squad… And there you are."

I sighed. "Not too helpful. Let's look at the other views."

We reviewed three more clips that were equally lacking. "This is the best one," Kelly said, bringing the image into view."

"That's more like it," I said, watching the scene unfold. "There! Freeze it!" I barked the command so loudly that I startled Kelly. "Back up, please…"

She did, and my blood ran cold.

"What is it?"

"That man," I said, referring to the image on the screen. "It can't be."

"Who is it?"

"Declan Clarke." Finnegan's voice startled us. "He's Shanagh Grady's ace henchman and assassin. John and Miss MacDonald tangled with him four years ago."

"How?" I said. "He was serving a life sentence in the United States. How did he end up on a security camera in Belfast?"

"It seems," Finnegan said, tossing a folder on the table, "that a computer glitch caused him to be processed for release about a week and a half ago. By the time the authorities figured it out, he was long gone."

"A week and a half ago? Why the hell are we just finding out about this now?" I pounded my fist on the table.

"It seems the news was slow to leak out, and even slower reaching us."

I rose, exasperated. "How, in this day and age, is that even possible? A man in the Yukon farts in rhythm to Jingle Bells, and the whole damn world is laughing at it 30 minutes later. A dangerous murderer walks free, and the news was slow to reach us?"

"I'm sorry," Finnegan said. "I can't explain it."

"No wonder Shanagh suddenly sounded confident. She's got her leading man back. Look at him," I said, turning my gaze back to the image on the screen. "He's looking right at the camera, sending us a message. We barely caught a glimpse of him in all the other cameras, only this one, and only when he wanted us to."

"Look at this," Kelly said, allowing the video to play. "He moves into the small crowd that surrounded Hayes. Right here," she said, slowing the speed of the video. "You're pushed back into the crowd, and that's where he slips the tracker into your pocket."

I looked at the scene, a chill passing over me. "He could've slit my throat, and nobody would've been able to stop him," I muttered.

"Unlike some of Shanagh's other muscle, Declan Clarke follows orders," Finnegan said. "I'd bet money that he was the one who shot Miss MacDonald. All told, we had half a dozen people watching that place, and he still managed to get in and out without being caught."

"He made the mistake of underestimating Mack four years ago. He won't make the same mistake twice. You're *sure* she's well protected here, Jim?"

"As well as any of us," he said. The tone of his voice didn't bolster my confidence.

* * *

It was early evening before the four of us could safely meet. Kelly Hamilton started with more disconcerting news.

"We're missing some of our files," she said.

"Which files?" Mack and I asked, nearly simultaneously.

"Files from the archives. God, there's going to be hell to pay, as the saying goes." Kelly was pacing. "These were the references from 1996 and 1997, too."

"Oh no," said Mack. "We've not gotten to those yet."

"Exactly," said Kelly.

"Not many people handled the boxes when we relocated your offices here," Jim said. "Each was signed for at every stop and transfer. I'll pull the signature logs and start there."

"I'll review the footage from our security cameras," said Kelly. "I can't believe it happened here, though. It had to have been somewhere in transit."

"We're at a bit of an impasse until we find them," Mack said, "assuming we find them at all. I've finished with everything Dianne shared, and I'm also done analyzing the latest batch of tips to arrive."

"Aren't you supposed to be taking it easy?" I lectured.

"That *was* taking it easy," Mack said, smiling.

"Have we learned anything?"

"If you're asking about a solid, eyewitness tip, no," she said, her voice falling.

"How many tips have the Police Service been able to investigate?"

"About ten percent of those that survive the screening process," Finnegan said, his voice equally unconvincing. "None of them have yielded any results, sorry to say."

"On the other hand, I have been able to run some statistical analysis on the tips we have received," Mack said, her voice more hopeful.

"And?"

"If one looks at sheer quantity of tips, the more populated areas produce the most. However, when filtered for quality, a different picture emerges." She connected her computer to one of the large monitors in the room. A map appeared with red dots of various intensity and size.

"They're spread out all over the place, Mack," I said, discouraged.

"And so they are," she replied, "and this is part of the reason the Police Service has only been able to follow up on about ten percent of them. And, of course, the quantity matches the general population of an area. The most tips come from Belfast, second most from Derry, third most from Lisburn, and so forth. It didn't occur to me, until recently, to create some additional groupings."

"What do you mean?"

"We assess the quality of a lead a number of ways, but that only shows part of the picture. I decided to group them based on the characteristics of the tip. For example, here are all of the tips that involve spaceships. I've filtered out quality and the date they arrived, focusing only on one feature of the tip."

The map changed, showing a few clusters of blue dots.

"So all we need to do is look for any spaceship landing pads that have been built in the area recently, right?"

Mack glared at me, but I continued.

"Can you correlate that with any missing flux crystals, or whatever it is spaceships run on?"

"Funny, Chatty McYacks-a-lot," Mack said, positively fuming. "But, almost in spite of yourself, you've managed to capture the spirit of the idea. It turns out, these dots are centered around facilities that provide outpatient treatment to adults with mild mental disorders. That's what I mean by groupings."

"Sorry, Mack," I said. "It looks interesting, I'm just not sure where we're going."

"Here are some maps I built using various commonalities in the statements given by our callers. This one shows reports of suspicious activity. This one shows reports of construction. This one shows reports of noise or unusual sounds..." As Mack announced each grouping, dots appeared and disappeared off the screen.

"So what are you getting at?"

"Simple," she said, smiling. "The best tips, and those reporting the types of activities we might expect, even when population differences are statistically considered, all come from one area."

"Belfast," I muttered. "You think she's hiding right here in the city?"

"I do," Mack said.

"Well," I said, taking a deep breath, "if you're going to hide a tree, a forest is probably the best spot. It's also going to make it damn hard to find her."

The lights flickered, briefly.

"What the hell was that?" said Finnegan.

"I think some of the lights in here must share a circuit with the elevator. Every time someone rides, the lights on this side of the room dim, briefly..." My voice trailed off as my mind started to focus. "Mack, for Shanagh and her team to do what they've done so far, they're going to need computers, right?"

"No doubt. A bunch of them, and good connectivity, too. And likely a satellite dish or two..."

"All of which take power. Can you look for anything in the reports related to power, wiring, or related?"

"I can do that," Mack said. "You might be on to something."

"I can look up reports of power theft," added Kelly.

"Good," I said. "It isn't much, but it's something."

CHAPTER THIRTY-ONE

The dream replayed violently during the night, undoubtedly stoked by Mack's brush with death. Several times, I woke up shaken and sweating profusely. Once, fighting the fog of fatigue, I scribbled something on a notepad near my bed before going back to sleep. Unfortunately, they made little sense in the morning. I stared at them, nevertheless, willing my mind to remember details, but nothing arrived.

IV
Syringe
Turkey

The words made no sense, try as I might. The impending threat of a headache pulled me away from the enigma.

* * *

Kelly Hamilton was my sole companion at breakfast, and words were sparse. Finally, she broke the ice.

"I've tracked our boxes all the way through the process from where they left the house through to delivery. Nothing was out of order that I could find. All shipshape, as the saying goes."

"So what are you telling me?" I said, nibbling on a scone.

"That either the documents went missing before they arrived here or after they were disbursed. It didn't happen in transit, that I can assure you."

"I oversaw the packing process personally. I remember, specifically, the archive files being packed and the box being sealed. All of them were there."

"That's what I was afraid of," she said, sipping her tea. "I can account for the delivery of sealed boxes to the correct recipient in all cases. Which means…"

"One of us is responsible."

She reluctantly agreed. "Seems to be."

An awkward silence followed. "Oh hell," I said, pretending to laugh, "I could have them. I've been such a mess lately it's entirely possible I packed them wrong and don't even realize it. Which ones were they, again?"

"The chain of documents surrounding 96-0096 and 97-0048. The first was the attack on a Constabulary armored vehicle where Angela and Shanagh Grady were persons of interest. The second set related to the development of an informant prior to the Strabane attack."

"Yes. I remember now. I'll look."

"I'll do the same," she said.

We finished breakfast in unpleasant silence.

* * *

I barely had time to return to my quarters when my phone rang.

Recognizing the number, I ignore it, allowing voice mail to take over. The caller was insistent, however, and called. After the third cycle I answered the phone.

"Good morning, Solicitor." Shanagh's voice sounded deeper than usual, but still cut me like a vile knife.

"I have nothing to say to you," I mumbled.

"Oh, you have plenty to say, but your broken heart can't find the words, can it?"

"I swear, Shanagh Grady, I'm going to find you, and when I do, I'm going to kill you," I growled.

"Such vitriol from a man who professes to be so loving and kind! Perhaps I should ring up the Peelers and report a threat against my life. Ah, but you're chums with so many of the lads in the Police Service, I doubt it would do a bit of good. Maybe I'll send your threats to one of the local stations so they can play it on the telly, right after that pathetic appeal for help you've been running. It will let the public know what Solicitor Costa is like when the lights and cameras aren't rolling."

"I'm sure the public has no desire to hear anything about you, other than news of your capture or death."

"Did she die in your arms like my Angela did, Solicitor? Did her eyes search yours for hope as her life faded, only to die disappointed in you? Any glorious last words?"

I answered with silence. Shanagh continued.

"Sad, but I expect she was gone by the time you even knew what was happening. I would have so liked to extend her suffering for your benefit, but circumstances dictated otherwise. Have you researched your namesake, Solicitor?"

"Mack was working on it," I muttered, "but, for obvious reasons, wasn't able to finish."

"Oh, I expect she finished, but didn't tell you, likely to spare your delicate heart from more disappointment. Let me help with that. Your great grandfather was Alfonse Costaglioli, born in Cassino, Italy."

"What of it, Shanagh?"

"He had two sons. One was named Leonardo who left for the United States sometime around 1930."

"Yes, my grandfather. His name got shortened to Costa somewhere in the process. Get to the point."

"Leonardo took his father, Alfonse, to the States with him. The older son, name Giovanni Costaglioli stayed in Cassino. He already had a family and career in Italy, and another child on the way when Leonardo left. Giovanni! Your namesake, Solicitor."

"It's a fairly common name, Shanagh…"

"Leonardo met his eventual wife shortly after settling in Boston, and in 1934, gave birth to their one and only child: Marco Costa, your father. Marco married Caiomhe O'Brien, a pretty woman from Cork, and the rest is history, isn't it, Solicitor?"

"I should feel flattered, I suppose, that you took your precious time to discover my family tree."

"I didn't spend any time on it, sweet Giovanni, I already knew all this long before we met. Do you know that your mother wanted to name you Sean, but your father held out for Giovanni?"

My stomach churned. "How do you know all this?"

"I have my ways. Do you know what Giovanni did during the war? You'd be proud of him, Solicitor."

My voice was hesitant and faltering. "I don't know."

"He fought with the resistance, most notably at the battle of Monte Cassino. He was responsible for slipping arms and munitions past the Axis, and he did it brilliantly. It was the perfect audition for the man that helped him obtain what he needed, and who would be his employer for the next thirty years: Connla Grady. Yes, Solicitor, your great uncle worked for Connla, taking care of most of his business interests in the Mediterranean."

I was too shaken to offer a response. Shanagh continued before I had the chance to utter a single, hesitant syllable.

"Your great uncle and Connla amassed quite a fortune. Giovanni put his family first, Solicitor, so when he learned that Marco's wife, your mother, had given birth, he arranged for a generous endowment for the young man. Connla helped him meticulously launder the money, hiding it in such a way that it would pass to you as if it had come from your father. It was a brilliant scheme, enough so to withstand several investigations by the FBI."

She paused, and again, I had no words.

"What's the matter, Johnny? Cat's got your tongue, does it? Your whole pathetic life is a lie!" Her voice cut through me. "Everything you are, everything you have, came from Connla Grady. So you see, as I said before, I've never lied to you. You really are working for me, boy-o, and now it's time for you to return what is rightfully mine."

She was playing me, viciously, and it was working. Gathering my fortitude, I managed to speak. "You'll get nothing, Shanagh Grady. Even if what you're telling me is true, I won't give you a penny. If Connla is, in fact, responsible for my wealth, I'll follow his lead. He left his treasure to Angela, not to you. You weren't good enough, Shanagh!"

"Good enough?" she screamed. "Look at what I've done, Solicitor! I'm one hundred times the leader Connla was! Good enough!"

What followed was a stream of profanity and unrecognizable screaming. And suddenly, I understood.

* * *

Mack had entered the room sometime during my conversation with Shanagh. "How much of that did you hear?"

"Enough," she said.

Her face betrayed the truth, and my heart sank to my stomach. "How long have you known, Mack?"

"It isn't important. What's important is what…"

I didn't let her finish. "My whole damned life is a lie, Mack. Everything."

"No it isn't," she said, sitting next to me. "You didn't ask to inherit that money, John. You didn't ask for any of this."

"I all but crucified Angela and Karen, and here I am, the real beneficiary of blood money. Both of them died because of me, Mack." A hollow feeling was spreading through my body. I tried to fight it, but couldn't. "You almost died because of me. I can't believe I put you in this situation."

"I really don't think you're being fair to yourself, John."

We sat in silence as my mind flailed hopelessly. Dammit, I wanted a drink, but I needed to keep my wits. Finally, hours later, clarity arrived.

"I know what I'm going to do, Mack," I said, staring in to space.

"What?"

"My money — I can't live with it, but I can't allow Shanagh to get her hands on it. Give it away, Mack. Reputable charities, scholarships, universities — I don't care. Just get rid of it."

"You can't be serious!"

"I'm totally serious. Leave me enough to cover all the crap I've managed to destroy over here, and to get a couple of plane tickets home.

Other than that, I want it gone."

She stared at me in silent disbelief.

"As long as Shanagh or any part of Connla's organization is around, none of us will be safe. It's poison, Mack, and I want to be rid of it. I can do it with or without your help. I'd rather do it with."

There was a long pause before she spoke. "Well, if you're sure it's what you want."

"I am."

"It will take some time. It isn't like you're going to walk into a branch bank and close a checking account with a few hundred dollars in it."

"The sooner we start, the better."

"Okay," she said, resting her hand gently on my shoulder. "But I should warn you, I'm going to continue to work on finding Shanagh, and hopefully talking you out of this nonsense."

"Fair play," I replied, covering her hand with mine.

* * *

"Mister C! I can't accept this," Laura McConnell protested. "You can't give me your bar!"

"I can, and I have. Every square inch of it is yours Laura, as well as a hefty stipend to make sure the business stays solvent and you're well taken care of for years."

"I don't understand."

"There's nothing to understand, Laura. I'm making some changes in my life, and it's time for me to get out of the restaurant and bar business. Hell, you were doing all the work, anyway. It only seems right that you get rewarded for your efforts."

"Mister C," she said, crying, "I don't even begin to know what to say. *Thank you* seems insufficient."

"It's brilliantly sufficient, Laura. You're welcome."

"Please tell me you're going to come 'round to the bar every now and again. We all miss you, and it won't be the same."

"I'll be around from time to time, I'm sure."

"We'll always keep a table for you."

CHAPTER THIRTY-TWO

"As long as I live," Finnegan said, sipping a Guinness with his dinner, "I don't think I'll ever figure you out. I'm not entirely sure you're sane…"

"That makes two of us," Mack said.

I took a deep drink of Guinness. "I'm not sure, either, but it feels right."

"It won't feel so good," he said, "when you're trying to figure out whether to buy groceries or pay the water bill."

"I'll work something out. In the meantime, where do we stand?"

"With what?" Mack said. "Draining your accounts?"

"That'll do, for starters," I said.

She sighed, "It isn't as easy or as quick as you want it to be."

"Mack!"

"All right — twenty percent. Maybe. Trades have to settle, and then there are the interest payments, and so forth. On the bright side, I've settled most of the costs related to your trip so far."

"Yes," Finnegan interjected. "One destroyed rental car, another severely damaged, damage to the parking lot at the harbor, a replacement for Dianne O'Leary's car, a destroyed lorry, a destroyed shed, damage to some digging equipment at the quarry, a new solarium for my cousin, repairs to his wall, and nine hundred quid to replace the pan that was damaged by the bullet… You have had *quite* the time here in Northern Ireland, my friend. Miss MacDonald, you should probably set aside a few million pounds, just in case…"

"Nine hundred pounds for a damned frying pan? Who the hell pays nine hundred pounds for a frying pan?"

"My cousin, apparently."

"Is the damn thing made of gold?"

"Plated, and the ions are supposedly aligned with the cosmos, or something naff like that. How the hell should I know? I didn't buy it."

"Apparently I did," I groaned.

"On the bright side," Mack said, "Queens University is absolutely delighted with you right now. I also donated to a cat shelter back home, in case you're still planning on getting one when you finally return."

"Perhaps, Miss MacDonald, you should donate to an organization that rescues homeless jackasses. I really hope you know what you're doing, Costa," Finnegan said, rising. "I've got to get back to work."

Before he could leave, Kelly Hamilton came into the room and whispered something in his ear. The smile vanished from his face as she spoke. "It seems we may need more than a few million pounds," he said, returning to his chair. "Tell them, Miss Hamilton."

"Dianne O'Leary sent us more documentation yesterday, and we were able to confirm much of it over the past twelve hours or so. Kristos Antonopoulos is pulling the strings, behind the scenes, of course, of at least a dozen holding companies we didn't know about, including at least five that are involved in shipping. She was able to match some discrepancies within her books with the arrival of freighters operating under these holding companies. All told, we are talking about many tons of unknown and unscanned freight. There are no matching customs declarations, no records, nothing."

"It gets worse," Finnegan said.

"The dates, times, and places of the shipments correspond with a series of military base thefts throughout the Adriatic region. Of particular interest are the explosives…"

"High-end, military stuff," Jim said, running his fingers through his hair.

"There's no doubt that Geryon was involved," Kelly added. "In each case, there were no breaches of the security system, and all the computer inventories matched perfectly. It was only during a monthly paper audit that the loss was discovered."

"How much explosives are we talking about?"

"Enough to create dozens and dozens of explosions worse than Strabane. It could ignite chaos all over the country."

"And if the explosives were used in one, large explosion?"

"Conservatively, it could destroy an entire city block in downtown Belfast."

* * *

"Mack," I said, massaging my temples, "when does the next round of data from our broadcast arrive?"

"Should be arriving this evening, why?"

"Maybe in your analysis you can correlate the tips to reports of crates or heavy boxes being moved. Focus on Belfast."

"I can do that," she said, smiling. "What are you thinking?"

"I don't think Shanagh is looking to restart The Troubles. I think she's looking for something far worse."

She frowned. "What's that?"

"A legacy, Mack. In her mind, she needs to prove herself to Connla, even though he's gone. Even Strabane wasn't enough."

"But destroying a major section of Belfast…"

"…would leave a legacy. Warped as it is, I think she's trying to prove herself. Nothing she does will ever be good enough, though, because her memories of Connla are those of failure, shortcoming, and being passed over in favor of others. That's why she can't get my money — and there can be no hope of her ever getting it; that's why we need to stop Kristos Antonopoulos and any other wealthy people in her network; and that's why we need to stop her *now, and permanently.* Even if she fails here, there will be another and another."

"You might be onto something, John…"

"Rightly or wrongly, she feels some odd connection to me, through the obligation she believes I hold to Connla." I took a deep breath, and said what I was thinking. "When the latest round of data comes in and you're done with your analysis, I want your best guess, and then I want you out of here. This could end badly, and enough people that I care about have been hurt or killed. Take as much of my money as you need, and disappear. Go somewhere you've always wanted to go, meet someone young and exciting, fall in love, start a family; be happy, Mack."

Her eyes narrowed as any hints of a smile faded from her face. "What are you going to do?"

"Whatever is necessary to stop Shanagh here and now. I made a promise to your father, Jillian, and I've done a terrible job at keeping it."

"Enough with the damned promise already! In case you haven't figured it out, I'm my own woman, John. I appreciate your concern, and I'd like to think that somewhere, my father does, too. But you've kept your word, and then some. I'm healthy and, of equal importance, I'm happy. I'm doing what I want, where I want, and with whom I want. Right here. Right now. Someday, things might change, but not today. So deal with it, Sir Fussbudget!" She planted a kiss squarely on my forehead. "You're stuck with me."

"I can't change your mind?"

"She shook her head."

"Even though there's a good chance for both of us to die?"

"Even though…"

* * *

I focused on the monumental job of shedding assets while Mack analyzed the latest round of data collected from the tip hotline. Not lost on me, though, was the troubling loss of our archive documents. I searched through my boxes and bags several times, but found nothing. A check of my computers also came up empty.

A call from Dianne O'Leary was a pleasant interlude in an otherwise monotonous evening.

"I stumbled on something I think you should know," she said, her voice betraying excitement.

"Yes?"

"You asked me about any properties in Dublin that Kristos might have owned without my knowledge. Unfortunately, I still haven't been able to locate any, but he does have several properties in Belfast. Are those of any interest to you?"

"Certainly, Dianne! What did you find out?"

"The buildings are owned by a property management company that is based here in Belfast. However, the company's majority owner is a corporation from Greece. In turn, the Greek corporation is owned by another corporation, the majority shareholder of which is none other than Kristos' Greek girlfriend."

"Clever! But more clever of you to find it!"

"Two look to be warehouses, while the other two are office buildings. I'll send you the pertinent details, but I wanted to share the news in person."

"Every little bit helps. How are you holding up?"

"I guess about as well as can be expected. I'm scared, of course. My solicitor seems to think we can avoid prison time, but the fines are going to be heavy. Almost starting over, so it seems. But if it rids me of the whole bloody situation, it is well worth it."

"I know the feeling," I said.

"I'm going to have to dust off my credentials and apply for a job."

"You'll do well, and feel free to use me as a reference."

"Oh, that's sweet of you! Thanks a million."

* * *

As the hour grew later, fatigue set in. I settled in with a tall glass of Irish whiskey and the last of Angela's letters. Drawing the strength to open the envelope was a far more difficult task than I anticipated. There was an odd sense of finality, and an unwillingness in my heart to accept it.

The final letter was dated early in the morning, prior to our trip to Athlone. It was the day when we recovered Connla's immense hoard of diamonds, but it was also the day Angela died in my arms. Written in Angela's familiar, steady hand, it was easily the longest of the letters.

My dearest Johnny,

You don't look comfortable sleeping on that miserable cot. I begged Finnegan to allow us to share the upstairs room, but he refused. I understand, but it made for a torturous night.

Jim tells me there is a very good chance that today will be dangerous. I pray that he is wrong, but in case things go badly, there are things I want to tell you.

My memories are rushing back, both good and bad. You do not know the entire story, nor do you know everything about me. I don't have the time or paper to share everything, but Finnegan knows and we will tell you when the time is right. There are details I remember that put the living at risk, and I refuse to be a party to any more death or suffering, even if my intentions are noble.

Much of my life has been a lie, that you know. But even some of the lies are, themselves, lies. The truth is different than you know or expect. I ask your patience and indulgence as all is unveiled. Then you may decide if your kindness was warranted.

My mother is a wicked woman, Johnny. The things she has done to me, her own flesh and blood, are rushing back into my memory; the mental games, the drugs, the pain, the lies, and her willingness to use me as a pawn in her wicked game. Were it not for your kindness and love, I would not be able to bear them. She is a tortured woman, haunted by things that you and I cannot imagine. I understand that, now that I'm able to think clearly.

There is a part of me that hates her; there is a part that wants her to suffer and die. I can not and will not allow that part to consume me, because it is in such thoughts that mindless vengeance is born. These are the thoughts that consume my mother.

You once offered forgiveness where none was deserved. I will try to learn from that example. Every time I overcome the urge to hate her, forgiveness becomes easier. I pray that we have the opportunity to help her.

I just kissed you while you were sleeping, my love. Ours is an unlikely intertwining of fate.

All my love,

Angela

CHAPTER THIRTY-THREE

"I wondered how long it would take you to get to the final letter," Finnegan said, inviting me into his quarters. "Whiskey?"

"No thank you."

"Mind if I do?"

"Not at all. On second thought…"

"Good choice," he said, pouring a glass.

"Start with this," he said, tossing me one of the archive files.

"*You* stole the files?"

"I just borrowed them for a bit. The file in your hand is the full reference set for 96-0096."

"I remember the case. The theory was it was Shanagh's rehearsal for Strabane. Angela served as the lookout."

"More or less," he said, taking a drink. "Sean Grady tried to alert us that he was being leveraged into building timing circuits that could be used as a detonator."

I read the file, and bits of the truth emerged. "Horrible," I muttered.

"Yes. Shanagh held the life and freedom of his beloved daughter in the balance. Sean had no choice but to comply, lest Shanagh kill Angela, or turn her over to the Constabulary."

"You knew? And you couldn't stop what was happening?"

"Hayes was watching everything we did. I had to withhold files from the record, just like he did, in hopes of keeping Sean and Angela alive until an opportunity arose."

He handed me a file. I read it in disbelief.

"Shanagh and Gwen Carruthers were filling Angela's head with lies and her body with drugs, all at a time she was emotionally vulnerable. In spite of that, she still tried to do the right thing. She wasn't acting as a lookout. She was trying to flag down a police officer. Sadly, none came by. I had no choice but to suppress this document. Hayes would have gotten it to Shanagh, and we know how that would have ended."

He finished his glass, refilling it without pause. He handed me another file.

"This is 97-0048 as it exists in the computers. Now, here is the entire archive," he said, handing me a second folder. "I also suppressed it for the safety of everyone involved. This damned file is the genesis of countless lies and suffering."

My hand quivered on the seal of the folder. He continued.

"Early in 1997, I received a tip that something big was in the planning stages. We used to get a fair number of such tips, and many of them were intentionally designed to waste our time or divert us, so we followed up through the normal channels. I knew something was wrong when Hayes jumped all over it. I wasn't in a place where I could stop him, either. He had too many friends within the corrupt underbelly of the Royal Ulster Constabulary. I would have ended up getting in an accident, or being in the wrong place, like my brother did."

"Did Hayes create that file?"

"No. I did. I continued to work the informant in my spare time. You see, he was smart enough to deal only with me. Hayes thought that the information ran dry, so he kicked off a sham investigation. He hired my brother, largely as a reminder to me to stay in line, and as far as Hayes knew, I did. My brother didn't understand the rules of the game. He was just trying to be a good cop. He turned up Connla's organization and, I believe, Hayes' link to it, although I'll never be able to prove that. The bomb silenced him before anything could come of it."

"Sean was your informant again, wasn't he?"

He sighed. "That he was, John. That he was. Sean Grady was a good man with the horrible misfortune of having Connla for a father and taking Shanagh Flanagan as his wife. But he wasn't our only informant," Jim said, refilling my glass. "Turn the page…"

I did, and as the words crashed onto my mind, my body grew numb, shaking visibly. "Angela?" I stammered.

"She tried to stop the Strabane attack, but she was in too deep to get herself out. Try as she might, she couldn't overcome her mother."

"You knew all this… why the hell didn't you tell me? Angela went to prison for this! She died for this, Finnegan! Damn you!"

"We didn't know then all that we know now, and frankly, we had no damned choice," he said, his voice thundering. "I could have made my case against her in 1999, John. She would have spent the rest of her life in prison. Given the turmoil at the time, I don't know if she would have survived. So I badgered the Grady family, played the bad cop, and got myself censured — effectively stalling the case. When Karen Boyle whisked her off to America, I thought maybe it was over and she'd be safe."

"You intentionally stalled the case?"

"I took a calculated risk based on what I knew of Sean Grady. As time passed, I started to second-guess myself, wondering if she played me. When the damned photograph from Strabane surfaced, and seemed to show that she was directly involved, it cemented it for me: she'd made a fool of me."

"Understandable, given the facts as you knew them."

"I hated her," he said, rubbing his beard, "and I hated what she was doing to you. When Declan Clarke showed up in America, a bloody risky move, to be sure, I realized that my hatred might be misplaced."

"I don't understand, Jim."

"We all assumed that Declan Clarke was sent to kill Angela, but *you* were his prime target."

"You're sure of that?"

"Absolutely, and it made no sense. Your sole purpose in life became Angela's acquittal, and you had the ability to make it happen. The status quo had served Shanagh's purpose for over a decade, so what had changed?"

I started to say something, but he interrupted.

"Her memories, John. Shanagh desperately needed her to get Connla's treasure, but everything else that Angela knew needed to stay buried, preferably forever."

"And with Angela convicted and in prison, she could be kept under the watchful eye of Gwen Carruthers until she was no longer useful."

"Correct. You were the spanner in the works, so to speak. When charm and deception failed, they tried more direct means. You proved much harder to kill or dissuade than she anticipated, so she turned to violence and manipulation. When you showed up at the prison with the photo album, it triggered the event that Shanagh feared the most."

"The return of Angela's memories…"

He rose, staring into space. "So it would seem, and as Shanagh feared, Angela followed your example, not the poison she had been force-fed. Of course, it could all be a bloody lie."

"What could?"

"The repressed memories rushing back. Who can ever truly know what is in the mind of another?"

"I guess not," I sighed, "but it certainly seemed sincere."

"When I talked to her that morning — the morning of the day she died — I came to the same conclusion. Unfortunately, we'll never know, and you're left with the heartache, my friend. I'm sorry."

"But you sent an innocent woman to prison. She almost took her own life," I whispered. "Why couldn't you stop it? She needed help, not punishment, Jim."

"I don't necessarily disagree, but our theories are largely conjecture, and the law operates on facts. The facts point to her involvement."

"Spoken like a true cop, Finnegan."

"Truth is, I thought if Angela was in prison, we could keep her safe while we dismantled Shanagh's network. After all, Shanagh was incarcerated, too, so it seemed like it was just a matter of time before we could get everything sorted. We miscalculated the depth of Shanagh's organizations, specifically the resources of Kristos Antonopoulos. She outsmarted us, and Angela paid the ultimate price for it. You loved her so — I was truly hoping for a better outcome, for your sake as much as anything."

I raised my glass, tearfully. "You know, Jim, in many ways, Angela saved my life."

"You're ready for another, I think," he said, pointing to my empty glass.

"Indeed."

* * *

By the time I was sober enough to walk back to my quarters, it was time to get up. I took a cold shower and went in search of strong coffee.

"Where the hell have you been?" Mack asked, taking the seat opposite mine at my office table.

"Oh, here and there. Mostly having my world turned upside down."

"It looks like you turned a bottle upside down, judging from those bloodshot eyes," she said, wrinkling her nose.

"That too," I said. What do you have?"

"Oh, not much. Just proof of my genius…"

"The bullet didn't let any of your modesty leak out, either, I see."

"Behold. I cross-referenced the tips using the criteria you suggested, including abnormal power utilization." The familiar map appeared on the screen, but this time only a handful of dots covered it, all in proximity of each other. "All of these are quality tips, too."

"And all of them are right here in good old Belfast."

"And so they are. Now… Here's the same tips filtered one

more time." The map changed, and only two dots were visible on the screen.

"And this is?"

"The same tips, cross-referenced to the properties that Dianne O'Leary discovered."

"Two buildings. Dammit. They're both right here, Mack!" I pointed to one of the dots on the screen. "This one is only half a block over. If I'm right about Shanagh, we're right in the blast radius."

"True," she said, "but this one," tapping the other dot, "is the only one where we've gotten a facial recognition hit on Declan Clarke."

"When?" I said.

"Right after sunrise this morning. A camera caught him rounding the corner of an alleyway. A crew went through a day or so ago and repositioned the cameras to eliminate a couple of blind spots. I don't think he realized it. He's grown a beard, but his face is unmistakable."

His image appeared on the screen, and I gritted my teeth. "I hope everyone's being careful. Not only is he dangerous as hell, there's all those explosives to worry about."

"They know, and Kelly's got a plan. You should see her, too! "

"Oh?"

"She's going out as a prostitute — you'd probably like her."

* * *

Coffee and relentless pacing filled my morning until word arrived from Finnegan: Declan Clarke was dead.

"He decided to fight," Jim said, ruefully. "We weren't left with many alternatives."

"Any word on Shanagh?"

"Sadly, no." He said. "We caught up to him on his way back to this building," pointing to the map. "He took off, leading us away from the structure, so if she was inside, it isn't likely she heard or saw anything."

"I think we'd know if she did."

"We've got crews standing by to move in, but we can't create a panic in downtown Belfast. A couple of good lads from the bomb squad managed to slip in through an alleyway entrance. No word yet. It's a big building, though, and with only two people it is likely to take a while."

"The explosives are in the other building," I said, confidently tapping on the map. "I'd bet money on it."

"How can you be so certain?"

"Shanagh knows where we are; she *has* to. Hayes knew, so she knows. And how to make her legacy even better that leaving a crater in downtown Belfast? Do it right under the noses of the Police Service and the team formed specifically to take down her organization and capture her."

"If that's the case, we should consider evacuating," Jim said.

"No! If I'm right, the only thing keeping any of us alive right now is that she hasn't exacted her final revenge on me. If she gets wind that we're evacuating, she's very likely to put a match to the entire bit. Hayes is gone, but we don't know who else might be lurking in the weeds, passing her information."

"Then what do you propose?"

"We wait. Then when she beckons, I'll answer. But not right away."

"You're going to stall her?"

"Yes, until later in the day, when there are fewer people downtown — and I know exactly the way to do it."

"I hope to God you know what you're doing, Costa," Finnegan said.

* * *

As I waited for the inevitable ring of my phone, I sat alone in my quarters staring at the sealed box that contained Angela's ashes and final wishes. I had stared at the simple, cardboard box before, but was never able to bring myself to do anything with it. I chastised myself for it, but couldn't will myself into action. My friends told me that when the time was right, I would prevail. They were right.

A calm rushed over me as I took the box and placed it on the table. Carefully, I cut open the first layer of tape and removed the brown paper wrapping. The inner seal followed, and I pried open the strong, double-cardboard box.

Three containers awaited. One was smaller, clear, and held dried rose petals. The second, taller cylinder was wrapped in plastic. The third was a rectangular box, similar to what would be found in a jewelry store.

An envelope bearing my name in Angela's handwriting caught my attention. I slid my letter opener along the seal and removed the page within. The writing on the front was generic, addressed to anyone who might read it, and expressed her simple, basic wishes. The back, however, was addressed to me.

To my Johnny,

I hope you find it in your heart to carry out these wishes.

Find a peaceful park, one with tall trees, gentle shade, and a peaceful view. See us walking there, arm in arm, with the troubles of the world behind us. Send some ashes to the wind, and wish me safe home.

Find the place where dear Maggie died. Offer a prayer for her.

Scatter some ashes at the base of the tree, and wish us both peace.

As a girl, I would watch the Lagan River slip quietly toward the sea, jealous of its freedom, envious of its resolve. Scatter my ashes and rose petals on its waters. Let it carry me out to sea, and wish me freedom.

Wear the locket close to your heart.

As you were always in mine, let me remain in yours.

Angela

CHAPTER THIRTY-FOUR

It was mid-morning when the inevitable call arrived. Even thought it was expected, it still knotted my stomach.

"Good morning, Solicitor."

"Good morning, Shanagh."

She coughed. "Have you considered the situation thoroughly?"

"I have."

"And do you understand your obligation?"

"Fully, Shanagh. I've given it extensive thought, and have a newfound understanding of things. What am I to do?"

"I will send an address to your phone. Be there in one hour, alone, Solicitor. Failure to comply will not be tolerated."

"Shanagh, I have one request, if I may…"

"What is it, Solicitor?"

"I have my remaining obligation to Angela. You instructed me to deal with it on a prior call, but I was unable to do so. I would like to fulfill that duty today, then I am yours."

"You've had many weeks to honor Angela's last wishes. You do her memory an injustice. You disappoint me, Solicitor."

"Not as much as I have disappointed myself. Her wishes require about an hour of preparation and some travel if I'm to do them properly. If I start now, I should be back in Belfast by seven. Is that acceptable?"

"No tricks!"

"No tricks. Do you want me to bring dinner?"

The question caught her off guard. After a brief pause, she answered, hesitantly. "That would be lovely, Solicitor."

* * *

"I hope I didn't overdo the ass-kissing," I said, collecting my things.

"Hard to say," said Jim, "although I'm not sure it really matters. She isn't going to trust you either way."

"It made me want to puke," said Mack, making an unflattering face. "Do you have everything you need?"

"I think so. Wish me luck."

Mack hugged me, tightly.

* * *

It had been four years since I made the drive from Belfast to

Strabane, and it brought back a flood of memories. Four years ago, my trip was supposed to free Angela Grady. Now it was to say my final goodbye.

I knew exactly the park she had in mind. The image on the scatter urn depicted it at sunset, but I didn't have the luxury to recreate the scene exactly as pictured. I pulled my car into the simple, gravel parking lot and followed the narrow trail.

The park was nearly abandoned, save for two older women sharing a bench and enjoying the view, oblivious to my presence. I followed the trail around a curve and gently downhill until reaching the spot that matched the image on the urn. With my back to the wind, I opened the urn and cut open the inner seal.

"Safe home, dear Angela," I said, gently tossing some of the ashes into the air with a small scoop. Most fell to the ground quickly, but the breeze carried some lightly into the distance. I watched until they faded from view, then made my way back to my vehicle. The women were no longer at the bench, but I saw them walking slowly along the side of the road, heading back toward town. I collected my thoughts and climbed into my vehicle.

* * *

The gentle, cool breeze made for a nice drive through the winding back roads that would take me near the small town Drumquin. The church parking lot was empty, as it was the last time I visited the spot of Maggie Albin's death. Maggie, Angela's best friend at school, was murdered by Fergus Clarke because she unwittingly stumbled on incontrovertible evidence that Angela could not have been in Strabane at the time of the explosion. The proof, tucked carefully in the pages of her notebook, seemed to seal Angela's innocence.

The road, the stone wall, and the tree that collected Maggie Albin's out-of-control car and claimed her life were unchanged. I ran my hand gently over the tree's bark, which now fully obscured the injuries it sustained when struck by the car. Frank Albin's fatherly pain was still a poignant memory for me, as I recalled the sad day he recounted the details of his daughter's murder.

Prayer was an uncomfortable notion for me, but I tried my best to complete Angela's wishes. I knelt and offered a simple prayer of peace. A scoop of ashes spread around the base of the tree completed the ritual. As I rose, I noticed, on the side of the tree, something out of place. An earring, a shiny green shamrock, had somehow found its way onto the tree, lodged in the bark. Less than a centimeter in size, I could have easily missed it, save for its bright, green hue. Little more than costume jewelry, I surmised it to belong to a child or young woman who lost it on a walk. I looked briefly for its matching partner, but found nothing.

A footstep behind me startled me. I turned around to see a man walking toward me.

"A fine day, it is," he said, smiling.

"It is. Say — I found this earring stuck to the bark of this tree. I expect someone lost it. You wouldn't happen to know who it might belong to?"

"Hard to know," he said, examining the earring. "Not too many come along here that would wear such a thing. But you know the legend, don't you?"

I frowned. "No, not really."

"Finding such a thing brings good luck. Keep it, and see if it works." He smiled, and continued on his way.

"I could use a bit of extra luck right now," I said, slipping the earring into my pocket.

* * *

The final wish turned out to be the most challenging of all, and I was glad I had built a hefty cushion into my time line. Finding a suitable spot proved to be difficult. After some searching, however, I found what I was looking for.

A walking path traced the bank of the Lagan River. Near an overpass, and nestled behind some trees, a small platform extended out over the water. A flimsy barricade blocked the entrance, informing me that I shouldn't be there. I didn't care; I bypassed it and walked out.

I unsealed the urn for a final time, but this time also opened the container of dried rose petals. My mind told me to hurry, but my heart hesitated, overcome by the finality of everything. Tears welled in my eyes as I watched the water slip by.

My hand trembled as I gripped the urn. Taking a deep breath, I steadied myself and sent the remaining ashes into the water. I followed with the rose petals. I watched them spread out and drift away. "Be free, my love," I whispered, as I took one parting glance at the waters of the Lagan.

As I walked to my car, the sun worked its way out from behind the clouds. I glanced across the river, suddenly aware that several people were watching me from the matching walking path on the far shore. All but one continued on their way as soon as they realized I'd seen them. The last remained, leaning against a tree observing me, until I turned a corner and disappeared from view.

CHAPTER THIRTY-FIVE

"Are you sure you're ready for this?" Mack said.

"I think so. I just need to pick up some food and go to the address."

"For what it's worth, we have some good news."

"I could use some of that right now."

"The Italian authorities nabbed Kristos and his girlfriend as they tried to make their way into Venice. I'm sure the U.K. is going to be interested in extraditing him, but the Italian and Greek authorities are going to want their pound of flesh as well."

"That's wonderful news, Mack! Make sure Finnegan increases the protection for Dianne. Shanagh likely kept her around at Kristos' behest. If she finds that he's out of the picture, she'll be able to complete her purge of the entire family."

"Already done, John."

And the other thing?"

"I set the final phase in motion yesterday. I really hope this is what you want, because there's no way to stop it now."

"So I'm on the path to the poor house?"

"Inexorably."

"Are we going to be able to minimize the loss of life if I can't figure out a way to stop Shanagh?"

"We're doing what we can, but it's a large area and we're running out of time. Getting people out and keeping them out isn't as easy as it sounds. We've seen to it that a few businesses have experienced connectivity issues sporadically through the afternoon. Another has had some power issues and started letting employees leave early. The more time you can buy us, the better."

"I'll do my best, Mack."

"Finnegan has arranged for some emergency road repairs at strategic locations, and we can stage a traffic collision or two. This could still be horrific, though."

"I know it. I wish you'd reconsider and get yourself to safety."

"We're pretty well protected here, John. I'm more worried about you."

"Aw, Mack, you really *do* care."

"I do. Hot mess and all…"

* * *

Armed with little more than my wits and two foam containers of take away food, I made my way to the address listed in Shanagh's message. The lower floor had at one time housed a business, but now looked empty. The upper stories looked equally vacant in spite of several signs advertising available space. Although the building presented a modest storefront, it was long with numerous side entrances along a narrow alleyway.

My phone chirped.

`Third door on the left. Lock it behind you. No tricks, Solicitor. I'm watching.`

Undoubtedly she was. The building was adorned with numerous security cameras watching every entrance and approach.

I made my way down the narrow alley that ran along the side of the building. The third door was unremarkable, apart from the fading outline of a former tenant's name. I reached for the handle, turned it, and stepped inside. I turned the lock, testing the door to make sure it was secure.

I waited on the small landing area, undoubtedly under Shanagh's watchful eye. A security camera unfailingly monitored the entire area.

`Up the stairs, then walk to the end of the hallway. Take the last doorway on the left.`

I followed her instructions, my footsteps echoing as I passed a row of empty offices. The last doorway was, in reality, access to another set of stairs. I passed through, waiting for my next message.

`Up you come, Solicitor. Fourth floor.`

Again, I complied, making my way up the deserted staircase. I was hardly alone, though; cameras watched my every step.

The door to the fourth floor was strikingly different than its counterpart on the lower stories. Metal and reinforced, it looked recently installed. There was no handle on my side. Nevertheless, the door swung open as I arrived on the landing.

Two tall, serious men eyed me with uncertainty. "Empty your pockets. Put everything you have on the table," one of the men ordered, nodding to his left. The second man frisked me, heavily.

"Call me, will you, love?" I said to him, smirking.

He grunted some profanity, shoving me away. I laughed.

"What'cha bring us for dinner," the first man said in a heavy Derry accent, as he removed the battery and SIM card from my phone. He turned his attention to the take away containers.

"Not a damned thing, I answered. Take it up with the boss. I'm dining with her tonight."

"Better leave it alone," the second man grunted.

"What if it's poisoned?"

"Oh shut up, the lot of you," I growled. "Here," I said, grabbing one of the plastic forks. "I'll take a bite from each."

It seemed to, for the moment, assuage them.

"Wait here," one of them said. "I'll see if she's ready for you."

I glanced around the room, trying to assess my adversary's strength and locate possible exits. Both tasks proved futile. Partitions blocked my view of the larger, open floor space, and all of the doors in the row of offices stretching out along the left hand wall were closed.

The thug emerged from one of the doors and walked back to

where I was waiting.

"Gather up your things, but leave the SIM card. She'll see you now."

CHAPTER THIRTY-SIX

It took only a glance for me to know that Shanagh Grady was ill. She looked tired, haggard, and ten years older than the last time I'd seen her in person. It made her no less fearsome, though, as her gaze cut through me. She stretched out her hand, motioning me to sit.

"What's for dinner, Solicitor?" she asked.

Surprised be the civility of her tone and opening statement, I opened the two containers. "This one is a burger, topped with an egg; the other is chicken."

"Which is mine?"

"Your choice," I said, still slightly off balance.

She took the burger. "Eat, Solicitor," she said. "You'll have to settle for water. I'm afraid our supply of your beloved Guinness is out at the moment."

I smiled, nibbling at my food. It was mostly to be sociable and avoid her ire — I had no appetite.

Shanagh, on the other hand, ate with gusto. It was easy to see why. Glancing around the room revealed a dwindling supply of military-style provisions and bottled water.

"Eat!" She said, mouth full. "We'll have plenty of time to talk, I promise."

I took a few more bites before my stomach would tolerate no more. "I'm sorry, Shanagh. I've had a draining day, and I really can't eat any more."

She paused, studying me. "So you have. Do you mind?" she said, extending her hand toward my container.

I shook my head. "Please."

"Tell me," she said, cutting a piece of chicken, "what did Angela ask you to do?"

As much as I didn't want to relive the exhausting and heartbreaking events of the day, I realized that every minute gave Finnegan and the Police Service more opportunities to save lives. I took a deep breath and related my painful journey.

Shanagh listened to each word, expressionless as she finished the last of the food. "A shamrock earring, you say?"

"Yes. The man there told me it was good luck."

"Angela always loved those things," she said. "Maybe it will bring you some luck, Solicitor. Perhaps you'll even survive the day."

"That is my sincere desire."

"Peace is overrated," she said, casting me a cold glance, "and largely imaginary. And freedom? Who among us is really free, other than the dead? I learned both those harsh lessons at an early age."

"In Mullingar?" I said, frowning from honest confusion.

"Where do you think I was born?"

"All the documentation I've ever seen lists Mullingar as your place of birth. I apologize if my information is wrong."

"I was born right here in Belfast, Solicitor Costa. When the riots broke out in 1969, our neighborhood was hard hit. I was only nine years old at the time. My parents took me to the Republic for my safety. The documents were created by Connla to protect me and my family. You think of him as a monster, but to us, he was a trusted friend. I was the youngest of three, by ten years — a surprise blessing, my mother would say. My brothers stayed behind to try to protect what little we had. Were it not for Connla getting money to them, they might not have survived at all."

She rose, coughing roughly and steadying herself with the table.

"Did you ever read about Operation Demetrius?"

"I did. It was the start of the Internment."

"That it was," she said, retrieving a water bottle from the shelf and returning to her chair. "In August, 1971, the damned British started rounding people up and throwing them in prison without so much as a trial! And not a damned Ulsterman in the bunch, only people thought to be republicans. Never mind that the UVF was out there killing our families and our children! My oldest brother was taken into custody as part of Operation Demetrius. They beat my younger brother with batons, and when he tried to get away, they arrested him, too. All they wanted to do was have a job and a home to return to at the end of the day! When the British were done, they were homeless, though neither was ever found to have committed a crime."

I saw the rage building in her eyes as she continued.

"Do you know what they did to them in captivity?"

"No, I don't," I whispered.

"They took the younger one and tied a rope around him, then they dragged him behind a truck to see how loud they could make him scream. The older one was beaten, blindfolded, and dropped from a helicopter. He was only a few feet off the ground, but they told him he was a thousand feet in the air. When he hit the ground, he soiled himself, Solicitor. So they stripped him and shot a fire hose at him, laughing at him the whole time. Dirty Catholic pig, they called him. No wonder he put a gun to his head after getting out."

She pounded her fist into the table.

"And there I was, all of eleven, and utterly helpless. Voicing my thoughts on the matter got me whipped, and told to mind my tongue. So I seethed, helplessly, while my brothers suffered. Then, a year later, Connla's wife was murdered in Belfast. When he came back from the funeral, I saw a kindred rage boiling in his eyes."

"He was the vehicle through which you could get your revenge," I said.

She glanced up at me with a chilling expression. "Precisely. He taught me what to do, and I was damned good at it. I could slip in and out of places without drawing suspicion. *Stupid little Irish bitch*, the British soldiers would call me, among other things. Connla would speak of his ideal solider, his Siobhan, as he called her, and I knew he was speaking of me. Have you ever killed anyone?"

"No, I haven't"

"I was fifteen, Solicitor. I pleasured a British soldier while my compatriots stole ammunition. When the pig was done with me, he fell asleep. I slit his throat and watched the bastard die. It felt good, and at that moment, I knew I was Connla's Siobhan."

"Siobhan O'Connor," I muttered.

She nodded, her face drifting into a distant, disconcerting smile. "I admired that man."

"Was that about the time when this picture was taken?" I handed her a copy of the picture we found in Mullingar.

Her eyes widened. "Where did you get this?"

"Tucked away in a pub in Mullingar. The way you're looking at him… You loved him, didn't you."

A tear ran down her cheek, and for the briefest of moments, Shanagh Grady was human. "Truly, I did, and it would have been grand." The smile drifted from her face.

"What happened, Shanagh?" I knew I was tempting a fatal torrent of rage, but the risk seemed worth it.

"I made a mistake, Solicitor. We were planning to ambush some British soldiers. I accidentally gave away our position. My bloody foot slipped on some rocks, and the noise betrayed us. Our best explosives expert died in the firefight that followed; two others were captured. Connla was furious. It could have happened to anyone, but he would hear nothing of it. I could never be his Siobhan, he told me. I begged him for another chance, but he told me I wasn't good enough. I told him I'd do anything to earn another chance."

"Even sleep with him? Is Connla Angela's father?"

She looked up at me, like a teacher glaring at an impudent child. "I would have been honored to bear his children, Solicitor! Sadly, that opportunity never arose. He fell in love with that awful old hag! How could he, after what we'd had?"

"Alicia O'Leary?"

"Yes," she said, visibly angered by the mention of the name. "The thought of that whore makes me sick! Connla even gave their child my name: Siobhan O'Connor."

I chose my words carefully. "The name you weren't good enough to carry?"

"I was more than good enough," she said, the fire returning to her eyes. "I was carrying his son's child out of wedlock. We *had* to get married, and that kept me in the family."

"And close enough to the action to prove your worth."

"Yes, but he was blind to it. The worthless whore seduced him, softened his mind. When Angela almost died from a UVF bomb, I thought things would change, that we'd be united once again by a shared cause."

"It didn't happen, though, did it?"

"No," she growled.

"You felt betrayed didn't you? Betrayed by the one you loved." My words were taking us into dangerous territory.

"Just one in a long series of disappointments and betrayals," she said, staring into space.

"Like Sean?"

"He was never half the man his father was. Disappointing."

"Especially since you had a child with him. He was more than a disappointment, though…"

"What do you mean?"

"He betrayed Connla. In 1974, he provided information to the Royal Ulster Constabulary, to none other than James Augustine Finnegan, investigating one of his first cases."

"Bastard!"

"I wonder if Connla knew…"

Her eyes grew wide. I continued.

"And you slept with this man to get close to Connla. No wonder he deemed you too careless to take over… One mistake after another…"

"Damn you and your lies, John Costa!"

"You even tried to mold your daughter into Siobhan O'Connor. In spite of all the drugs and in spite of all the mental and physical abuse, you still failed."

"She never betrayed me; even with you poisoning her mind, she never betrayed me."

"And yet another mistake. She betrayed you, too. In 1997, Angela, along with her father, tried to stop the Strabane attack. Don't believe me? Check out this document." I pulled a folded, wrinkled copy out of my pocket and tossed it across the table at her.

Her hand shook as she read it.

"No wonder Connla thought that you weren't good enough."

"I was absolutely goddamned good enough!" she screamed. She retrieved a device resembling a gun's trigger from a nearby drawer. "Good enough!"

The two thugs came in the room to check on us, their eyes growing wide at the sight of the device in her hand.

"Miss O'Connor," one of them said, "we were supposed to be on the chopper when you armed that thing!"

"What? Afraid to die for what you believe in?" she screamed, followed by deep coughing.

"The hell with you!" he said. "I'm getting out of here!"

With unexpected speed, Shanagh retrieved a pistol hidden beneath the table and shot the man, dead. The other guard briefly considered moving for the trigger device, but thought better of it.

I sat back in my chair, folding my arms behind my head, desperately pretending to be relaxed. "Too bad he didn't live to see how wrong he was," I said, just loud enough to command everyone's attention.

Shanagh turned slowly, pointing the gun directly at my head. Summoning every ounce of fortitude at my disposal, I continued.

"In spite of being betrayed, you still managed to pull off the single, biggest bombing during the Troubles. You managed to keep Connla's organization afloat, even without the benefit of his treasure, all while under the watchful eye of the Police Service. And the revenge you collected! Far beyond anything Connla could have achieved."

"You're placating me, Solicitor," she said, glaring. "I hate being placated!"

The pen, tucked unobtrusively in my pocket, vibrated once, so faintly that I almost missed it.

"Hardly," I said. "I talked to Karen Boyle before you hung her from that bridge. After all that you had done to her and her family, she was already dead. Only the formality of the time and place remained in question. Her sister, Dianne O'Leary, is like that now. She knows her time is coming. And she has no interest in the name Siobhan O'Connor, by the way. It is rightfully yours."

Shanagh started to speak, but I continued, unabated.

"Mack knew it, too. When she escaped from Paddy Bannion, her death wasn't in doubt — just where and when. It wore on her, too. So that brings things around to me," I said, sighing as I rose from my chair. "I'm here because you've won. I'm done fighting. Let's finish things, right here, right now."

"And you have decided to surrender what is rightfully mine?"

"Every last penny of it."

"And you brought with you what I need to access it?"

"Between what is in my pocket and what is on my phone, you will have it all. Your man disabled the phone, though. I'll need to unlock it and give you the code."

She frowned. "No tricks."

"Without Mack, I lack the savvy for subterfuge. Anything clever I did against you was always her doing. The SIM card is out on the table," I said, pointing to the door."

"Go get it," she growled to the man.

"Keep an eye on him," I said, lowering my voice and moving ever so slightly closer to her. He's already shown a willingness to betray you."

My words were chosen carefully. I watched and waited while they sunk in. Shanagh's attention was inexorably drawn to the man as he reached the table and collected the missing card. At that moment, I lunged for her arm. The gun fired once, but hit nothing. The struggle was short lived. Shanagh was weak, and quickly lost her grip on the firearm.

The man shouted, pulled his gun, and ran toward us. Then, abruptly, he stopped, his eye growing wide. He turned, sprinting out the heavy door and onto the stairs.

"You and your damned tricks!" she screamed, waving the trigger in the air. "Drop the gun, or I let go of the trigger. This whole block and everyone in it will die!"

"As you wish," I said, tossing the gun far out of the room. "If you let go of that trigger, nobody will ever know that you beat me. The Police Service will concoct a story about a natural gas explosion, and the press will run with it. Or perhaps they'll blame somebody in the Middle East. One thing is certain: you'll never be mentioned. People will go back to talking about Connla Grady, with never a mention of Siobhan

O'Connor."

"You speak with a glib tongue, Solicitor," she said, reaching for her cell phone. "Give me what I want, and you might stand a chance of living."

"How so?"

"When my helicopter arrives, you run. If you make it, fair play to you…"

"Sounds like a deal I can't refuse." I pulled my wallet out of my pocket. I removed all of the cash within, and placed it on the table.

"What the hell is this?" she growled.

"All that's left of my fortune. I gave the rest away, every last penny donated to good, worthy causes. I take back what I said earlier. Connla *was* right about you. You're *not* good enough!"

She glared at me, smirked, and released the trigger.

CHAPTER THIRTY-SEVEN

Nothing happened. Shanagh looked at me in disbelief, then started frantically pressing the button.

"It's over," I said, effortlessly removing the trigger from her shaking hands. I threw it on the ground and stomped until all its lights were extinguished.

"Thanks, Mack," I said. My pocket vibrated gently in response.

Shanagh looked at me, perplexed.

"Oh, about that? We borrowed a page from your little book of tricks. Instead of recording video and audio, this pen now streams it, along with ultra-precise location information. Mack disabled your dead-man switch remotely. And she's quite healthy, thank you; Declan's shot missed. And in case you're wondering, Declan's dead."

I felt the strength drain out of her as she collapsed into the nearest chair. Searching the room, but watching her closely, I found some rope, and secured Shanagh's hands behind her back. She offered no resistance.

"What happens now?" she said, her voice fading to a cough.

"I'm going to get you to a doctor," I said, pressing the back of my hand against her forehead. "You're burning up."

"And then?"

"I'm going to get you some help."

"Why?" she said, lifting her head. "Were the situation reversed, I would end things."

"Because someone asked me to. Shanagh, have you ever wondered what would have happened if Connla would have forgiven your mistake?"

"No. It didn't happen that way, so what's the point? Nobody ever forgave me for anything. Not my parents for speaking out of line, not Connla for my mistake, nobody."

"You never forgave yourself, did you?"

"Probably not," she said, slumping again.

"There was one who did. Ironically, it was the one person you hurt the most: your daughter. Angela wrote me letters from prison, but never sent any of them. The last one was written the morning she died. In it, she forgave you for what you did to her. She begged me to do everything in my power to get you some help. After all you've done, God knows I would have slept well had a sniper's bullet killed you today. It was only for the sake of Angela's memory that I did what I did."

She stared at me, tears welling in her eyes. "Solicitor, what are you wearing around your neck?"

I showed her the locket.

"Where did you get that?"

"Angela left it to me as part of her final wishes."

"My mother gave that to me when I was a girl. It was the only bit of love or affection I remember from her. If you ever have any doubts that Angela loved you, this should chase them away forever."

I heard pounding on the heavy door to the stairwell. "That will be the police and medics, Shanagh. They're going to take over from here."

She nodded. "One thing before they do, Solicitor."

"Yes?"

"Your money — did you really get rid of it?"

"Every penny, just like I said. It's poison, Shanagh, and I want nothing more to do with it."

She paused, staring tearfully into space. "I think you might be right, John."

I nodded, and opened the door to a stream of police and medics.

* * *

"I must confess," Jim Finnegan said, bear-hugging me, "I would never want to be against you in court. I've never seen anything like that in my life, even from our best negotiators."

"Thank you," I said. "See? I *am* good at something other than worrying! Inside, I'm still shaking like a leaf, but don't tell anybody."

"Your secret is safe with me. One thing I don't understand."

"And that is?"

"How did you know that she only had two thugs there with her? There could have been two dozen of them on that floor."

"I didn't at first, but when they took me back to meet Shanagh, I got a glimpse of the rest of the fourth floor. The shelves were bare and the computers were off, like they'd already packed up most of their belongings. From the way Shanagh attacked the dinner I brought, I knew their supplies were dwindling, too. They couldn't feed more than a few mouths."

"Clever. You still took a hell of a chance, though. I would've tried to lure her out into an area where we could take a shot."

"I think she would've expected that. Besides, I had faith that Mack could disable the switch."

"Child's play," she said, rolling her eyes.

"You saved my life, Mack. Thank you."

"You're welcome, but I have to do it one more time in order for us to be even."

"I'll keep that in mind," I said, winking. "Jim, do you think I can stay in my quarters a few more days? I can't begin to afford a hotel room here. Right, Mack?"

"I did exactly what you asked me to do, John. I set up an escrow account to cover taxes, insurance, and basic repairs on your house for ten years. Other than that, you've got just enough to cover a ticket home, a cab ride, and a few small incidental expenses. Coach, by the way. You're flying coach…"

'Could be worse," I said.

"You're more than welcome to stay at my cousin's place until you're ready to leave," Jim said.

"Oh, no!" I said, waving my hands in protest. "I'd be afraid to touch anything! If his frying pan was worth nine hundred quid, I can't begin to imagine what the bed sheets cost. Staying here will be just fine."

"I'm sure that'll be fine," Jim said, looking at Mack and shaking his head. "Get some rest, John. We'll meet for breakfast tomorrow."

* * *

I dreaded the dreams that might arrive, but none did, and I enjoyed my first restful sleep in quite some time.

On my trip to the cafeteria, I was treated like a minor celebrity. Police officers stopped to congratulate me; many shook my hand, and a few even wanted to take selfies with me. I smiled, quietly willing myself through it.

Finally, I arrived at breakfast.

"Why the troubled look?" Finnegan said. "Don't like the life of a legend within the Police Service?"

"It isn't that," I said, laughing gently. "We broke some laws along the way… I don't have any money to pay fines… Do I, Mack?"

A strange voice answered me before anyone could say anything. "Nothing to worry about, Solicitor Costa."

I looked around, confused.

"I'd like to introduce Assistant Chief Constable Mary Walsh," Jim said, smiling.

I rose and clasped her outstretched hand. "Nice to meet you."

"Everything Jim and his team did was cleared through my office. We owe you and Miss MacDonald a tremendous debt of gratitude."

"You're welcome," I said. "I'm just glad this whole unpleasantness didn't cost my friend his job."

"His job was never in jeopardy. In fact, I expect a promotion is long overdue for consideration. We're having a dinner in your honor on Friday. Please tell us you'll be there."

"Of course," I said, still mildly disoriented.

* * *

"So," I said, scowling at Jim while sipping my coffee, "you were never really suspended?"

"Not really. This was all the Assistant Chief Constable's idea, and bloody brilliant it was!"

"And the forgeries of Ms. Walsh's signature…"

"Completely genuine."

"And the whole bit at the archives with Mack's uniform and credentials?"

"Directly issued by the Assistant Chief Constable herself and revoked later that evening. She used a rather obscure proviso dating back to the Troubles to do it, so we don't know how it would hold up to a challenge in court. Fortunately, we're never going to have to worry about that."

"Mack! You were an officer of the law in Northern Ireland for all of three hours," I said, pretending to salute.

"So it would seem," she said, pretending to adjust a necktie.

"We'd love to make it official," Finnegan said. "That position is still open, in case you're interested, especially since your previous employer has recently undergone self-induced bankruptcy."

"You know my feelings on the matter," I said. "If it's something you want to do, you should go for it."

She smiled. "I'll give it some serious thought, I promise! But for right now, I hear a scone calling me."

* * *

The knocking on my door finally broke me away from what I was working on.

"Are you coming to dinner with us?" Mack said. "Finnegan's buying."

"Well, if he's buying, of course I am!" I glanced at the clock, shocked at the results. "I'm sorry. I guess I lost track of time."

"Napping?"

"No. Working on something."

"Working? On what?"

"This," I said, handing her the small shamrock earring.

"I don't think it's really you, John," she said, holding it up to my ear. "They sell these in souvenir shops all over Ireland, you know."

"I know, Mack. I just think it's odd where I found it... It was stuck in the bark of the tree where Maggie Albin died, precisely where Angela's last wishes directed me to scatter her ashes."

The smile left her face as she handed me the earring. "I hope you're not trying to turn this into some sort of cosmic sign..."

"Not cosmic. Quite mundane, really. Remember how I've been having the same dream over and over?"

"Yes. It's just your brain sorting through memories, trying to figure out what filing cabinet each one belongs in. Nothing more."

"The last time I had the dream, it woke me up. I wrote down what I remembered. I've been too busy to give it much thought, but today I had some time to do some searching." I pointed to my screen, my browser showing at least a dozen active tabs.

"Well, look at you, Searchy McGoogles! There's hope for you yet."

"When Declan shot you, I thought you were dead for sure. The medic told me that I didn't know much about gunshot wounds, and he was right. I've been researching them, and their treatment, extensively."

She frowned. "Where are you going with this, anyway? Because I have the feeling that nothing but pain is going to come out of it…"

"I get it now, Mack. I understand the dream."

"Enlighten me…"

"I was having the dream because my mind couldn't come to grips with everything that happened."

"Of course," she interrupted. "None of us can really come to grips with losing a loved one."

"No. Not like that. My memories weren't making sense, and now I know why. I remember glancing over and seeing the medics wheeling her toward the ambulance. There were IV bags hanging, and tubes everywhere."

"Yes. It makes sense."

"And one of the medics was leaning over, talking."

"Probably telling her to hold on…"

"But she died in my arms, Mack, or at least that's what everyone is telling me. If that's the case, why have multiple IVs ready?"

"Isn't it standard procedure?"

"In an abdominal gunshot wound, protocol is to transport as quickly as possible, and get the patient into surgery. They might establish an IV en route, but only if the patient has a pulse. Doesn't any of this strike you as being odd?"

She paused, a frown forming on her face. "I'm not sure… Oh, hell, now you've got me doing it! We don't even know if your memories are accurate. Trauma can do strange things that way."

"Like making me insert a turkey baster in the dream?"

"Exactly! Now will you *please* come to dinner?"

"It took me a while to remember why I wrote the words *turkey* and *syringe* on my notepad, but it finally came to me. I saw something I couldn't identify, so my mind put in something it understood. In this case, a turkey baster. What if it was this that I saw, Mack?"

I clicked on one of the tabs, and a video appeared, demonstrating a new tool for treating gunshot wounds. The device, resembling a large syringe with a wide, baster-like nozzle, was designed to be inserted into the bullet's entrance point. From there, the plunger dispensed dozens of small sponges into the wound, specifically to absorb blood and help stop bleeding.

She looked at the screen, then back at me. "Impressive searching," she muttered, raising one eyebrow in appreciation.

"I wouldn't do any of this if it wasn't for what happened on my last stop with Angela's ashes. When I tossed those rose petals into the water, I could feel her energy. She was there with me, Mack. I *know* it. And after all, this is Ireland, the land of miracles and where dreams come true. Why not mine?"

"She *was* there with you, John," she said. A tear ran down her cheek as she kissed my forehead. "Right here," she said, tapping my heart, "where she'll always be."

I sighed, and rose from my chair, hugging Mack tightly. "I guess you're right," I whispered.

"You probably need some grief counseling, John. I'll stay with you if you want to skip dinner tonight."

"Nah. I don't need grief counseling, Mack. I need dinner. And Guinness. Lots of Guinness."

CHAPTER THIRTY-EIGHT

The drive from Belfast to Dublin was unusually quiet. A few conversations started, but quickly faded back to silence.

We arrived at the airport well in advance of our scheduled flight. I pulled my luggage out of the back of Finnegan's car.

"I appreciate you driving us, Jim. The airfare out of Dublin is significantly cheaper. I have enough left over to get lunch and a souvenir or two!"

"Are you sure I can't convince you to stay," he said. "I'm sure we could find suitable employment for you somewhere on our lovely island."

"No, Jim. I appreciate the hospitality that everyone has shown, and I love it here, I really do, but I need some time to get my head together, and that's best done at home."

"Well, I didn't expect you to change your mind, John, but I'd never have forgiven myself for not giving it one last try. And you, Miss MacDonald? I can't talk you into a high-paying job that you'd absolutely love?"

Mack laughed. "No, not right now, but if that ever changes, you'll be the first to know."

"Fair play," he said, grabbing several pieces of luggage.

* * *

The Dublin airport was bustling, but everyone was friendly. I settled down at one of the many restaurants to enjoy one final pint before our gate would be ready for us. In the distance, I saw a young man, one of the waiters, chatting with a woman. After a brief conversation, the woman handed him a mandolin case. He removed the instrument, looked at it, and played a few notes. I laughed as the tune reached my ear: Miss McLeod's reel, my favorite.

I didn't get to hear more than a few familiar bars before Jim announced that our gate was open. I finished my Guinness, and made my way there. The line was short, so we said our goodbyes quickly.

"Kelly sends her regards. She's busy mopping up the rest of Shanagh's network, and then she's going to turn her attention to Kristos. Keep in touch, will you, John?"

"Of course, Jim," I said, clasping his outstretched hand.

"You, too, Miss MacDonald," he said, hugging Mack.

"Will be my pleasure, Chief Inspector Finnegan. That has a nice ring to it, doesn't it?"

"Aye, that it does," he said. "Keep your phone on, Costa, in case we need your help again."

"Shouldn't Ireland's problems be left to the Irish?" I said, smiling.

"Normally, I'd agree with you, but in your case, I think you'll be more than welcome."

We embraced one final time.

"Now get on that damned airplane, you two, before I start crying. It isn't suitable for a Chief Inspector to shed a tear."

* * *

"I'm sorry, Mister Costa," the gate attendant said as she tried to scan our tickets, "these tickets aren't coming up on our system. It looks like a valid confirmation number, but I can't get them to scan properly."

"These are what I was sent," I said, shrugging my shoulders.

A woman from the ticket counter came over and pulled us out of the line. "Let me see if I can help," she said, walking us over to her terminal.

She tapped vigorously on its keyboard, her expression unchanged. "I'm sorry… I'm not seeing those tickets…" she said, her attention still on the screen. "I see you and a Jillian MacDonald in here, is that correct?"

"Yes," I said, showing her my passport. Mack followed suit.

"Oh! I see what the issue is," she said, smiling broadly as relief spread through my system. "You've been upgraded. I'll print you new boarding passes."

"That's nice," I said, "but I didn't request an upgrade."

She handed me the tickets.

"These are first class! I can't afford first class tickets," I said, handing them back to her.

"There were no charges to your card," she said, looking at the screen. "In fact, we refunded the entire amount of the original tickets when the new ones were purchased."

"This has to be some sort of mistake," I said.

"No," she said, looking at the screen. "Everything was verified and approved. There's even a memo attached to the order: *Compliments of Mrs. O'Brien.*"

Bewildered, I took the tickets without additional protestation.

* * *

"Mack," I said, settling into my seat, "who do you think is responsible for this? Not that I mind — this is a whole lot better than coach. I'd like to at least thank them."

"I really don't know," she said. "But I'm sure you'll figure it out."

We were still allowed to use our devices, so I started texting people. From Jim Finnegan on down, nobody would admit to purchasing the upgrade. Laura McConnell responded with a video call.

"Hello Mr. C!" she said, beaming ear to ear.

"Laura! Thank you for the upgrade to my tickets home."

The smile left her face. "Upgrade? Wish I'd thought of it, but I wasn't entirely sure when you were flying home. I do have a confession to make, though: I did tell you one small fib. Check it out! Here's your new and improved corner in the pub."

The view spun around to show a round table surrounded by chairs. Her smile returned. "First of our weekly Irish traditional music session starts in a couple of hours. Wish you could be here!"

"I'll take a rain check for tonight, but count on me next week, Laura. Thank you! What a wonderful surprise!"

"Have a good flight, Mr. C! See you soon."

The screen went blank, and I turned my attention to the next suspect: "You, Mack! You bought the tickets!"

"No," she said, wrinkling her nose, "I didn't. I work for an employer that can barely afford the cab fare home from the airport. Where am I going to get that kind of money?"

"You didn't hack their system did you," I whispered.

"No," she whispered back. "You never let me break any laws."

Stymied, I changed the topic as the plane thundered down the runway. "Dammit," I said, staring into space.

"What is it?"

"It just dawned on me: I'm going to have to get a job! I've got to buy food, buy gas... What the hell was I thinking?"

"We've all been asking you that…"

"I guess I can re-open my law practice." My stomach churned at the sound of my own words.

"Is that really what you want to do, John?"

"No."

"Then don't."

"That's easy to say, but I'm going to have bills to pay. I've never been without a safety net before."

"You'll survive. I have confidence. Tell me: if you could do anything, what would it be?"

"Truth?"

"Truth," she said, her full attention focused on my answer.

"What we just got done doing — solving mysteries, and such. With you."

She smiled. "Me, too. So why don't we? We could call

ourselves the Jillian MacDonald Agency. Your name would be there, too. Somewhere in really small print — you know, like the kind they use to engrave the entire Bible on the surface of a pin. I've got the brains and the computer skills, you've got the contacts and the neurotic worrying problem. We can't miss."

I chuckled. "Funny, Mack. It takes money, even to start."

"I've got a little bit saved up, John," she said. "It isn't much, but you're welcome to it."

"What if it didn't work? I'd never be able to pay you back."

"Oh, you can," she said, an odd smile crossing her face.

"Mack… what is it that you're not telling me?"

"Nothing… Much…"

"Mack!"

"Just a simple matter of semantics, really…"

"Mack!!"

"Oh, all right! Not long after we first met, you gave me some money to invest for you. Remember?"

"Of course I do. You doubled it, and quickly, too. That was when I let you take over most of my investments. But all that's gone. You sold it."

"I did precisely what you told me to do, and sold off everything that came from your inheritance. But there is the matter of the money from your law practice and the job you took after leaving your practice. That money didn't come from Giovanni Costaglioli."

"Giovanni's money paid for my law school. The money is tainted."

"No it isn't. You went to law school on a full scholarship, and your father paid for your expenses with his own money. I researched it, John. Giovanni's money wasn't available to either of you at that time. And it certainly had nothing to do with your later job."

"What are you telling me, Mack?"

"You had so much money from the inheritance, you weren't even spending the interest. I took all of your law earnings and, later, your salary from your job and invested it for you. I've been caring for it all this time."

"And you didn't get rid of it?"

"It wasn't from the inheritance, so no, I didn't. Someone had to protect you from yourself!"

I laughed. "So… how much are we talking about here?"

"Well, you can't buy the entire airline any more, but I'm pretty sure you could buy this plane… and a smaller one to have as a spare… and have some left over…"

"Mack!" I said, pretending to be furious, "has anyone told you how amazing you are?"

"And don't you forget it! I'm going to get some rest," she said, reclining her seat. "This whole sordid mess has worn me out." She pulled a mask over her eyes.

"Sounds like a plan. I'm going to read for a bit, and then I'm going to do the same thing."

* * *

"Excuse me," the fight attendant whispered. "I have your champagne. I can bring it back when your friend is awake, if you'd prefer."

"Thank you," I whispered, "but I didn't order this."

"I know," she said. "It's by special arrangement. There's a card with it."

"Okay," I said, taking the card. "We only need one glass though. My friend doesn't really care for bubbly."

The envelope was simple and plain, with my name printed on it. Taking a sip from my glass, I slid the card out and opened it.

`Safe home, Johnny Costa`

In the corner of the otherwise plain card was a green shamrock. My mind swirled until I realized I had seen the design before: on stationery at one of the airport gift shops. I laughed at my foolishness as I finished my drink. Then I dimmed my light, and reclined my seat. Covering my eyes with a mask, I allowed the steady hum of the engines to take me off to sleep.

And in my dream, Angela waited, every bit as magical as the first time I'd seen her. She extended her hand, inviting me onto the floor.

And we danced.

Made in the USA
Coppell, TX
03 November 2020